Praise for *The Hen House*

"Sharon Sala has created a one-of-a-kind, unforgettable character in Letty Murphy. Her rags-to-riches story is a mythic journey filled with moments of devastating emotional truth and soaring triumph. Readers will cheer for Letty and the denizens of THE HEN HOUSE long after the book is closed."
—**Susan Wiggs**, *New York Times* bestselling author.

"Sharon Sala once again proves she is a master storyteller. THE HEN HOUSE reveals the very heart and spirit of Letty as she leads the reader into adventures that grip the emotions and the heart."
—**Debbie Macomber**, *New York Times* bestselling author

"Sharon Sala works her familiar magic and creates a story line that grabs your attention, along with a cast of unlikely characters who work their way right into your heart."
—**Jasmine Cresswell**, *USA Today* bestselling author.

"Earthy, poignant, funny, sad and triumphant, Sharon Sala has written another engrossing story. Creating characters who come alive on the page, and backgrounds that make the reader want to live in them, are only parts of Sharon Sala's magic."
—**Stella Cameron**, *New York Times,USA Today and Washington Post* bestselling author.

Praise for *Whippoorwill*

"Masterfully crafted players... and a story with a lasting sense of hopefulness."
—***Romantic Times BOOKclub***

"Whippoorwill is hopping with weddings, namings, and burials. All that's missing is the minister—but there's this small problem...Wear a corset because your sides will hurt from laughing! This is Sharon Sala at top form. You're going to love this touching and memorable book."
—**Debbie Macomber**, bestselling author, *New York Times, Publishers Weekly* and *USA Today.*

"Whippoorwill is a funny, heart-warming story, set in a raw, untamed land and rich with indelible characters that will stay with you long after the last page is turned. I didn't want it to be over."
—**Deborah Smith**, *New York Times* bestselling author.

Praise for *The AmenTrail*

"The delightful Sharon Sala brings back her most memorable characters, Letty and Eulis, in a rousing adventure that is by turns dramatic, funny, touching and ultimately uplifting. Readers are in for a treat!"
—**Susan Wiggs**, *New York Times* bestselling author.

"The Amen Trail is filled with characters that grab you by the funny bone and shake you till you laugh! No one does love and laughter in Sharon Sala's style. You'll definitely want to take a journey down The Amen Trail."
—**Joan Johnston**, Bestselling, award-winning author.

THE HEN HOUSE

Also Available from Loveland Press
and
Sharon Sala

Whippoorwill

(ISBN 0-9662696-6-7 6x9 paper)

The Amen Trail

(0-9744851-1-X 6x9 paper)
(0-9662696-9-1 hard bound)

The Hen House

by

Sharon Sala

Loveland Press
Book Publishers

ISBN 978-0-9744851-2-6

First Edition 2007

Printed in the United States of America

The Hen House is published by:

Loveland Press, LLC
P.O. Box 7001
Loveland, CO 80537-0001
970-593-9557
www.LovelandPress.com

Production Credits:

Edited by: Teresa Hoy
Cover Photography: Craig Nelsen
Front and back cover photos taken at the historic Stanley Hotel in Estes Park, Colorado.
Design, Layout and Production: Sandi Nelsen

DEDICATION

Finally, it's done. The last book in the trilogy that began so long ago.

Like Letty, so much has happened in my own life since the first book, Whippoorwill, was written, sometimes it seems as if it happened to another person.

I've changed. I've loved. I've lost. I've grieved.

And always, I've had the knowing my family was there, ready and willing to offer what I needed at the time to survive.

I've been blessed in ways too numerous to count, but the most precious blessing I've ever been given was being a part of my wonderful family.

To Mother, who is always there for me no matter what, and to Kathy, Galen, and Daniel—to Chris, Kristie, Chelsea, Logan and Leslie—to Crissy, Andy, Destiny, Devyn, and Courtney—to the Shero family and to the Smiths —and the Sala family to which I once belonged—and to Bobby, who left me behind to pick up the pieces of my heart—I can only say that were it not for you all, my life would have been a lesser, sadder existence than the feast you've let it be.

Thank you. Bless you. Love you.

PROLOGUE

Letty Murphy had come to Denver City a single woman, although she'd gone through more hell in her twenty-nine years than she would have ever thought possible. She'd nearly starved as a child and had sold herself to a man for money before she'd managed to grow breasts. She'd fallen in like with a gambler who'd up and gotten himself killed, then bedded a preacher from back East who'd died in her bed.

In a fit of panic, she'd cleaned up Eulis Potter, the town drunk, and passed him off as the dead preacher, thereby saving herself from what she feared would have been a hanging. She'd seen just about every low-class behavior humanity could inflict upon itself and survived it all.

But that was before she and Eulis had traveled to Denver City, survived a buffalo stampede, a smallpox epidemic, an attack from a half-starved wolf, discovered gold, and gotten married.

It wasn't just Letty's last name that had changed, even though she had money—more money than a person could spend in several lifetimes. It was her situation that had changed, even though she had yet to come to terms with the power and respectability that money could buy. There was still that part of her childhood self that listened each night for a whippoorwill's call, while struggling with the memories of being a fifty-cent whore.

1

RICH MAN—POOR MAN

It was the dead skunk Harley Tatum's dogs were dragging down the main street of Denver City that was causing everyone to wrinkle their noses in disgust. But it wasn't the biggest stink in town by a long shot. The news that Eulis and Letty Potter had struck a gold bonanza struck a nerve.

The news had gone through the tent city faster than the smallpox that had killed so many last winter, evoking just about as many emotions. Tempers flared. Envy set in like a splinter under a fingernail, burning and festering until something was bound to pop.

Every no-good in the territory converged on Denver City to see if they could wrangle a contrivance that would divest Eulis and Letty of their newly found wealth. Others tried to corner Eulis and Letty when they'd come in from the mine in hopes of getting a grubstake or a handout, or —as a last resort—the possibility of a job.

Eulis had grown tight-lipped and stern, fearing he would not be able to protect the mine, although he'd made sure that it was registered in Letty's name, since she was the one who'd actually found the gold.

And, they'd gone out of their way to do the same with the land they'd claimed on a bluff overlooking Denver City and the house they were having built on the property.

They'd been working the mine for more than three months now, but Eulis was nervous about the conversations he kept overhearing from his own employees and from the whispers he heard when he went into town. It appeared the hired hands were not above trying to steal a little of the gold for themselves. Eulis heard talk from a friend here and there that the men claimed the Potters had so much gold that surely they wouldn't miss the occasional smuggled nugget.

Eulis had kept his fears to himself, unaware that, not only had Letty also heard the gossip, but she was bound and determined to be the one to put an end to the talk and the fear of God in every man who worked for them.

* * *

Spring had finally come to the Rockies, although the high peaks were still snow-capped. Rivers were gushing with overflow—running wild from the snow-melt above the valley. Tiny purple flowers, hardly more than two or three inches high, were popping up through the winter mulch of dead grass and leaves. Color had come to the mountains in the form of bright red cardinals, sassy blue jays, and the soft buckskin color of spotted fawns. Trees, other than the prevalent evergreens, were budding. Plum thickets were awash in pale blossoms more white than pink, promising a bumper crop of fruit in the coming months.

And it was into this scene that Letty emerged, ignoring the scandalous glances of the few decent women by wearing men's pants and accouterments and riding astride, as a man would have. Her hat was wide-brimmed and black. Her hair was long and wavy, but tied back at the nape of her neck with a piece of blue ribbon—her only concession to femininity.

She wore a permanent expression of 'don't piss me off' and had become quite a marksman with a gun. She didn't have time to priss and preen. Eulis had hired some men to work their mine. She felt it not only her right, but her obligation, to set them on the right path.

* * *

A new supply of track for the ore carts and lumber to shore up the tunnel had come in on the last freight shipment. Milton Feasley, the owner of the dry goods store, had sent word to Eulis the day before that his order had arrived. Eulis had gone into town early this morning to meet the men before they left for the mine and get them to help bring out the load.

Letty was tossing out dishwater when she saw movement from the corner of her eye. As she turned, she saw Eulis and the men coming down from the ridge and into the wide, verdant valley leading to their old home and the mine beside it.

Even as she was looking forward to living in a fine home, there was a part of her that was still sentimental about the tiny, one-room cabin where she'd found herself and found love.

She often watched the workers from time to time and felt as if they were constantly considering a way to steal. She knew, if given a chance, there were at least three of them who would give it a try and one who would most likely kill to have what they had. The bad part of it was, moral turpitude was sadly lacking in most of the available workers. The diligent were already engaged in working their own claims or trying to set up as shopkeepers. Letty and Eulis had to make do with what they had.

Still, she'd made a pact with herself last night as she'd watched Eulis sleeping so soundly beside her. She never thought she would have a life like this and with a man who treated her like a proper lady. There was no way she was going to chance having it taken away from her by some good-for-nothing lout. As soon as the workers arrived tomorrow, she intended to make a few things plain. Then, if they wanted out when she was finished, there would be no hard feelings or retribution taken.

Originally, the entrance to the mine had been inside the old cabin, but as soon as they'd started working the mine and hauling ore into Denver City to the smelter, they'd dug a new opening away from the cabin, giving them some privacy and eliminating the aggravation of bringing the ore out through the home.

When morning came, Letty busied herself with chores as Eulis left for town, and now he and the men were coming back with the shipment. It was time to put her plan into motion.

She dried her hands and got Eulis's rifle. She was already outside when the men finally arrived at the mine. The men dismounted and began unloading the shipment as Eulis started toward the cabin. But when he saw Letty leading her horse out of the shed behind the house and that she was packing his gun, he knew she was up to something.

His eyes narrowed a warning as he watched her mount up, but she ignored it and him. It took the men a little longer to realize that something was afoot. They were talking and jesting among themselves as they moved about the area, then one by one, they noticed the Missus was mounted and also armed. The sight was enough to set the hair on the backs of their necks to rising. In their opinions, a woman with a loaded gun was more dangerous than a rabid dog.

When Letty had their full attention, she shifted the rifle from one arm to the other then laid it across her lap, making sure they saw her hand was damn close to the trigger.

"Gentlemen... and I use that term lightly... it has come to my attention that some of you have been talking loosely about my husband and myself. There is supposition flying about on the streets of Denver City that gold could be had from this mine if a man was smart enough to steal."

There was a collective gasp, then icy silence. The men wouldn't look at each other, nor would they look at Letty. Instead, they chose to study the footprints they'd left about in the yard, as well as those leading into the mine.

"So, here's the deal," Letty said. "If any among you are thinking about just such a thing, then I'm giving you fair warning. Leave now and it will not be held against you. Stay and do your worst, and you will suffer the consequences."

A squirrel suddenly scolded from a stand of trees a few feet away, as if debating the truth of what she'd just said, but she ignored it, just as she was ignoring the frowns on the men's faces.

"Hear me now. I swear to you, in front of God and the man who is my husband, that if any one of you steals so much as a nugget or tries to harm a hair on his head, I will shoot you dead, nail your balls to a tree, and scatter what's left of you to the wolves."

They flinched. Some paled a bit at the threat of an armed woman, while the others heard the truth of her words. Eulis would swear later, at that moment, he felt a physical shift in their behavior. As for himself, he was torn between the urge to grin and an overwhelming pride.

Damn, but he'd sure picked himself a winner. His Letty was something else and that was a fact.

Letty leaned forward just the least little bit and then smiled. It wasn't a friendly smile and all twelve men knew it.

"Is there anything about what I just said that you don't understand?" she asked.

Twelve men answered in unison.

"No, ma'am."

"Are any of you planning to give me any trouble?"

"No, ma'am."

"Well then... that's that. Do have yourselves a good day."

She shifted her gaze to Eulis. "I would appreciate a word with you before I go."

Eulis arched an eyebrow. She wasn't in the habit of asking permission from him to do anything. Still, this was her show and he wasn't going to ruin it for her. He took off his hat as he followed her a short distance away.

"Reckon you laid it on a mite thick?" he asked,

Letty turned in the saddle and stared back at the men.

"No. Those red-headed Scotsmen will be good workers. The three men who call themselves the Dorsey brothers would steal a person blind, and that tall, skinny man with the dirty blond hair is a killer."

Eulis looked askance. "Do you know him?"

"No. Just his type," Letty said.

"Reckon I should fire him?" Eulis asked.

Letty thought about it for a moment, then shook her head.

"No. Probably better to have him under your nose than out hiding behind some tree, waiting for a chance to back shoot you."

"I know," Eulis said. "But we've got to have workers, and we ain't exactly in a place bursting at the seams with an overflow of men who are willing to mine someone else's gold."

"Just be careful," Letty said.

Eulis grinned and then winked at her.

"I'm always careful, girl. You mind yourself, too."

Letty nodded. "I'm going to ride up to the new home site and see how the work is coming along. I'll see you later."

Eulis watched her ride out across the valley and then up into the trees. When he returned to the men, they were suddenly acting as if they'd taken vows of diligence. Before long, they'd fallen into a kind of rhythm that boded well for the mine. Eulis took it as a good sign.

Meanwhile, Letty's trip to town had taken a sudden turn for the worse. She had just ridden up to what was going to become their front yard when her horse did a fancy little sidestep, reared up on its back legs, and promptly dumped her into the dirt.

She'd already discovered that the men who'd been working on the property were not on the premises, which meant they'd gotten themselves another grubstake and were out trying to strike it rich. The way she figured it, their big fancy house might never get finished, what with all the fools suffering from gold fever.

Cursing the horse and all manner of males, she was dusting herself off and reaching for her hat when she became aware of a rustling in the undergrowth. Mindful that there were grizzlies fresh out of hibernation, as well as all manner of two-legged varmints, she ran for the horse to get her rifle.

The horse shied once as she made a lunge for the dangling reins and would have bolted if she hadn't caught them. Yanking hard on the bridle, she pulled the horse to a halt, grabbed her rifle out of the scabbard, and aimed it toward the sound. Within a matter of seconds, a bone-thin, half-grown pup of questionable heritage came slinking out on its belly.

Letty didn't know whether to be relieved or disgusted. The pup stunk to high heaven—all the worse for wear because of a previous bout with a skunk. It was a brown and white short-hair, obviously part hound, with huge feet, floppy ears, and the beginnings of mange. She could count every rib. The humane thing would have been to put a bullet in its head right then and there, but it would have been easier to shoot a man than a helpless animal who meant her no harm. She tried threats instead and began waving her arms and shouting.

"Get, you mangy critter! Go on! Get away before I put a bullet between your eyes!"

The pup whined as it continued to belly crawl until it had crawled all the way to her feet. At that point, it gave a big groan and rolled over on its back. Submission was all it had to offer and gave it gladly.

Letty rolled her eyes and then stomped her foot.

"Go on now, I said! Get! Get!"

The pup added another soft whine to the belly he'd bared.

"Oh, for the love of—"

Something rattled in the grass behind her. Before she could turn, the pup had sprung to its feet and lunged past her, barking and snarling like a dog gone mad.

She saw the rattlesnake at the same moment her horse reared up and bolted. Before Letty could aim her gun, the pup had the snake in its mouth, shaking it like a rag doll. Just when she feared the pup was going to get bitten, it turned the snake loose.

It went flying, like a thick, brown piece of rope, coiling and uncoiling as it sailed through the air.

Letty blasted the head from the body in mid-air. The silence that came afterward was deafening.

Her heart was pounding so hard she couldn't hear herself breathe. Every hair on the pup's back was standing up like the quills on a porcupine.

She lifted a shaky hand to her forehead, swiped away the hair that had come loose from the ribbon, and jammed her hat back on her head.

"Well now," she muttered, still eyeing the half-starved pup.

Hearing her voice, the pup turned and looked up at her, as if waiting for a sign.

Letty sighed.

The pup took the sound as some inner signal. Within seconds, the hair on his back smoothed out like the feathers on a duck.

"Well now," she said again.

The pup wagged its tail once, like a soldier wagging a white flag of defeat, then sat down without taking its eyes from her face.

Letty eyed the dead snake, cursed the horse she was going to have to retrieve, and then squatted down until she was eye level with the pup and offered her hand. To her delight, the pup reached out a paw, as if it understood what was meant, and together, they exchanged a handshake.

It was a silent but irrevocable understanding. Without another word, Letty stood up, shifted her rifle to her other hand, and started walking toward what was left of the snake.

No longer cowering, the pup followed at a hasty trot, confident that no more begging was needed. Letty frowned, then glanced up, eyeing the direction in which her horse had gone.

"I don't intend to walk all the way back to the valley, so let's go get that blasted horse."

It took the better part of an hour, but she finally caught her mount, led it back to the new home site, dropped the snake into the saddle bags, and tossed them across the horse's back. The horse did another neat little side-step and rolled its eyes as it looked back at Letty.

"It's dead, so get over it," she said, grabbing the saddle horn and mounting in one smooth motion.

She looked down at the pup, took a piece of deer jerky from inside her pocket, and dropped it on the ground. The pup ate it quickly, then looked up at her for more.

"If you're a mind to follow me home, I reckon I can furnish a bit more to go with that."

The pup seemed willing, and when she rode away, it followed.

By the time she got back to the cabin, the men were deep inside the mine.

She took the snake out of the saddle bags, turned the horse out into the corral, and then headed for the cabin. She paused at what passed for their smokehouse long enough to cut off a large hunk of fatback from a crock inside the door, then turned around and handed it to the pup.

It took the meat neatly from her fingers with all the delicacy of a gentleman, then held it in its mouth until she gave the pup permission to eat.

"Go ahead," she said. "You've earned it."

The pup laid down and began chewing on the meat. Letty leaned the empty rifle against the door of the smoke house, knowing Eulis would have to reload it for her that night. She sat down on a stump and waited until the pup was finished.

As soon as the pup had swallowed the last bite, Letty stood.

The pup followed suit, waiting for a signal as to what to do next.

"Okay now," she said. "Let's skin out that snake."

By the time Eulis came home for supper, the pup had been doused with axle grease for mange and fleas and was chewing on the leg bone of an elk they'd butchered over the winter. A fine stream of smoke was coming out of the chimney, and the skin of the rattlesnake was nailed to the side of the house.

Eulis watched the men mount up and ride off, then headed for the cabin. It wasn't until he came around the side of the house that he saw the pup lying on the doorstep between him and Letty.

The pup growled softly beneath its breath.

Eulis frowned. "Ease up, fella. I live here."

The pup got up and sniffed Eulis's feet, then picked up his bone and moved off to the side of the doorway.

"Thank you for the vote of confidence," Eulis drawled. But when he looked up, he saw what Letty had nailed to the wall.

His flesh crawled as he eyed the snake skin, stunned by the size and the knowledge that, once again when he was too far away to help, Letty had been forced to save herself. He was torn between pride in her ability to bounce and a feeling of inadequacy. It seemed Letty was always two steps ahead of him.

He looked down at the pup, taking note of the prominent ribs and the careful application of axle grease, and frowned.

"Exactly what part did you play in all of this?" he asked.

But the pup had nothing more to say.

Eulis shook his head as he opened the door. The scent of cooking meat and baking bread met him as he entered.

"Something sure smells good," he said, as he hung his hat on a wall peg and kissed the side of Letty's cheek.

"I made some johnnycake," Letty said.

Eulis lifted the lid on the pot cooking over the open fire in the fireplace.

"Umm-Unn, snake. My favorite."

Letty's face was flushed from the heat of the fire, but she turned a little redder when she caught the teasing tone of his voice.

"So, I guess you saw the skin on the wall."

Eulis arched an eyebrow. "Well, yes, ma'am, I did. A blind man couldn't of missed it. Are you all right?"

Letty grinned. One of her favorite things about Eulis was his ability to overstate the obvious.

"I'm fine, of course. It was just a snake. Oh... you need to reload the rifle for me, too."

"If you're gonna go about shootin' it off all the time, you oughta be learnin' how to reload."

"I guess," Letty said, and kept stirring the stew.

Eulis knew that was the end of the conversation about the gun and set about waiting for her to talk about the pup, but she didn't.

"So... I understand how the snake come to be nailed on the wall, but I ain't quite figured out how that greasy, half-grown hound figures into the situation."

"He showed up about the same time as the snake."

Eulis had known Letty far too long to believe that was all.

"And... what? You just invited 'im to supper?"

Letty knew when she was being made fun of, but when it was Eulis, she never seemed to care.

"Of course not," she said. "He earned it and then some."

Eulis could tell they were getting to the meat of the subject as Letty continued.

"I rode into the yard at the new house. The workers were gone. The outside of the house is finished and the roof is on, but the windows still aren't in. I didn't get a chance to go in because the darned pup was thrashing about in the brush and scared my horse. I fell off and–"

"You fell off?" Eulis grabbed her by the arm, his eyes wide with concern. "Are you all right, girl? Did you hurt yourself somewheres?"

Letty eased his fears with a smile and a touch of her hand against his cheek.

"I'm fine. As for the horse, I was already disgusted for having been thrown from it when the pup came crawling out of the bushes on its belly. It was mangy and starving. I tried to run it off. Instead, it repaid my bad attitude by saving my hide from that snake. So...it's here. I've named him T-Bone."

Eulis laughed out loud.

"That's a fine piece of meat, but I can't say as I've ever heard it used as a name for a dog."

Letty fixed Eulis with a pointed stare.

"He's a fine dog... or he will be when I get him healed and fattened a bit. Do you want to meet him?"

"I reckon I already did," Eulis said, then pointed to the pot over the fire. "How long before the snake is done? I'm so hungry I feel like that dog looks."

Letty rolled her eyes.

"It's all done. I was waiting on you."

"Let me just wash up a bit first," Eulis said and went back out the door.

There was a bucket of water, a wash basin, as well as some lye soap and a rag on the bench outside the door. He poured water in the basin, splashed his face, wet down his hair, then picked up the soap, scrubbing fiercely until the day's dirt from the mine was gone from his face and hands.

He tossed the water onto a bush Letty was trying to grow and then began to dry off. The pup looked up from chewing on the elk bone long enough to emit a low growl.

Eulis hung up the rag and then looked down at the pup.

"Listen here, T-Bone. There won't be no more of that. I was here before you and you best not forget it."

The pup cocked his head to one side, as if studying the wisdom of what Eulis had just said, then got up and sauntered over to Eulis's feet, flopped down and rolled over.

Eulis shook his head and then grinned.

"One minute you're tryin' to eat me for supper and the next you want a belly scratch? You're somethin' all right."

He leaned down, found a spot that was free of axle grease, and gave the pup a quick scratch. As he did, he saw knots on the pup's ribs and realized that, at one time or another, those ribs had been broken.

"You know something, T-Bone? Danged if I ain't been right where you are. However, all is not lost. You got yourself a really good woman. Take good care of her and I promise she'll take good care of you."

Eulis wiped the ends of his fingers on his pants, just in case he'd gotten some axle grease on them, and then went back inside to get his share of snake.

2

rich man, poor man, BEGGAR MAN

A couple of days passed with no more problems from the men. It was just after sunrise when Letty stepped outside to toss the dishwater and saw the stranger walking across the valley. Seconds later, T-Bone saw him, too, and bounded up from his bed beneath the trees, barking as he ran.

"T-Bone!" Letty yelled.

The pup stopped immediately, looked back at her and then trotted back to where she was and sat down at her feet.

"Good boy," she said softly and laid a hand on his head, giving him an absent pat as she watched the stranger's arrival.

The trail across the valley didn't go anywhere except to their cabin, so whoever he was, he was obviously coming to see them.

Letty glanced back at the doorway.

"Stranger comin'," she called.

Eulis was inside shaving when he heard Letty call out. He wiped the last of the shaving cream from his face and stepped outside.

"What did you say?" he asked.

She pointed across the valley.

"Stranger coming."

Eulis strode across the yard, his steps slow and measured. When he got to Letty, he put his hand on her shoulder, never taking for granted his right to do so, and thought how pretty she was in the early morning light.

The tension in Letty's body eased. As long as she had this man by her side, she could face the world.

"He looks right poorly," Eulis commented.

Letty nodded. The man was little more than a mirror image of the way the pup had looked upon his arrival. His clothes were in rags and his body was bone thin. Even though he was still a distance away, Letty could see the hollows beneath his eyes and the sunken places in his cheeks.

"Is he packin'?" Letty asked.

Eulis squinted. "I can't tell from here."

"Better get the rifle, just in case," Letty said.

Eulis stopped her.

"Just wait."

Letty didn't listen but walked straight to the cabin, grabbed the rifle leaning against the wall inside the door, and walked back to where Eulis was standing.

"You don't trust anyone, do you, girl?" Eulis asked.

"That's not true," Letty muttered. "I trust you."

The pup whined.

She looked down at the dog and grinned.

"And maybe T-Bone."

At that point, they stopped talking and waited. The oddity of it was the closer the stranger came, the more familiar he seemed to Eulis. It wasn't so much that he recognized his facial features. It was more about the way his shoulders tilted just a tiny bit to the right, and how his fingers on his right hand curled slightly inward, like he was about to grab onto something important.

His hat was wide-brimmed and black, although it appeared more white than black because of the dust covering the surface. His boots were as dusty and run-down at the heels, and he was sporting at least a week's worth of whiskers.

All of a sudden, Eulis flinched.

Letty felt it, but before she could ask what was wrong, the stranger had arrived.

"Ma'am," he said, taking off his hat as he acknowledged Letty's presence.

Letty nodded back without speaking.

The stranger's gaze immediately moved to Eulis.

"Reckon you'd be Eulis Potter?"

Eulis nodded.

"They told me down in town you might be hiring."

Eulis exhaled slowly, as if he'd been holding his breath.

"I'm hiring miners."

"I can do that," the stranger said.

Letty saw Eulis's eyes narrow. She knew something was up but couldn't tell if it was good or bad. She shifted her rifle to a more comfortable position and settled her finger on the trigger—just in case.

The stranger saw her and held up his hands in a gesture of surrender.

"I mean no harm," he said softly.

"Got a horse?" Eulis asked.

"Shot out from under me."

"How did you come to Denver City?"

"I walked."

"When did you last eat?" Eulis asked.

The stranger's face turned red, as if he'd just been insulted. He hesitated answering, and then it seemed hunger won out over pride.

"Maybe a day or two back."

Eulis glanced at Letty.

Letty still didn't know what Eulis was doing, but she recognized his intent and offered a meal.

"There's biscuits and fatback left over from breakfast. I'll heat up some coffee."

Letty saw the man swallow and knew it was pride going down with the spit.

"I'd be real thankful for the food," he said.

"Eulis, maybe you could show him where to wash up," Letty said and started toward the cabin, then stopped and handed Eulis the rifle. She sensed the unfolding drama but trusted Eulis enough to deal with whatever needed to be done.

She was heating up the red-eye gravy when Eulis and the stranger came inside.

"Have a seat," Eulis said and pointed to the chair he usually sat in.

The man had dropped his hat near the doorway. His hair was wet and slicked back from his face, and Letty could see that he'd tried to remove most of the dust from his clothes. But when she slid the plate of food in front of him and then set down the cup of steaming coffee and a spoon, she saw his hands were shaking.

He looked up at her then, his eyes swimming with tears.

"I thank you kindly, ma'am," he said softly.

She nodded. "Sorry we don't have any regular cutlery for you to eat with. We ordered some from back East, but it will take a spell to get here."

"Ma'am, it's been so long since I've eaten with anything but my fingers, I'm not sure I remember my manners." Then he added. "This sure looks good."

Letty nodded and turned away so he would feel comfortable enough to start eating. She glanced at Eulis, who arched an eyebrow, but shook his head slightly. She was going to have to wait for answers to her questions.

No one spoke as the stranger ate, although Letty filled his coffee cup more than once.

T-Bone had followed the men as far as the doorway and was now lying across the threshold with his head inside the cabin and his backside out on the stoop. Letty couldn't figure out if the pup was intent on keeping an eye on the stranger or on the biscuits he was eating.

It wasn't until the man had sopped up the last bite of red-eye gravy with the last bite of biscuit, then chewed and swallowed that he bothered to look up. At that point, he had the grace to be embarrassed.

"That was just about the best food I've ever eaten," he said. "I can't thank you enough."

"You had to be hungry to say that," Letty said. "I'm just a passable cook, and Eulis here will be the first to tell you so."

Eulis grinned.

"Now, Letty I don't say nothin' bad about you. Ever."

At this point, he leaned forward, fixing the stranger with a cool, studied look. "I might be willing to put you to work."

Letty saw relief wash over the stranger's face.

"But not in the mine," Eulis added.

Letty frowned and so did the stranger, but it was obvious he wasn't going to be picky.

"That's fine. Whatever you need me to do I'll be—"

"I know who you are," Eulis said.

The man went still. An expression came and went on his face that set the hair to rising on the back of Letty's neck. She glanced toward the doorway, wondering how long it would take her to get to the rifle before the man could get up from his chair.

"But you don't remember me, do you?"

The man frowned as he shook his head.

"About six years ago, you rode into a little town out in the Kansas territory called Lizard Flats. Three cowboys were hassling a drunk out in the street in front of the White Dove Saloon, taking turns shooting at his feet to make him dance."

Letty froze. She remembered the incident all too well, and to her shame, also remembered no one had bothered to try and stop it.

Still frowning, the man glanced at Letty, then at Eulis. "Yeah, so what?"

Eulis leaned across the table and then offered his hand.

"That drunk was me. I never did sober up enough to thank you then, but I'm doin' it now. I don't need to know how you come to this point in your life, but I know when I owe a man a favor."

The man stared at Eulis for the longest time, as if trying to place that overweight drunk with the wild hair and beard, to the man sitting before him. Finally, he nodded.

"You should know that trouble has a way of finding me."

Eulis shrugged.

"Ain't no one in this house about to point the finger of blame. Now, down to business. I reckon you heard Letty here discovered herself one hell of a gold mine or else you wouldn't be here."

"I heard."

"Here's the deal," Eulis said. "I need a guard. You'd be on the site day and night. This here cabin would be where you stay, and we'd keep you grub-staked with food and ammunition, as well as a good horse. A man needs a good horse. Never know when you might need to go somewhere."

The man's mouth dropped. Again Letty saw unshed tears in his eyes. He looked at Letty, then at Eulis, then down at the coffee cup he still held in his hands. Letty saw him take a deep breath before raising his head.

"I'd be staying here with you folks?"

"No," Eulis said. "We're building us a house near town. I reckon if we don't move onto the site soon we'll never get it finished."

"You trust me to do this?"

"I reckon I do," Eulis said.

"What's to keep me from stealing some of your gold and riding off with it?"

"I reckon the same thing that made you stop them men who was shootin' at my feet."

"Maybe I just had a headache that day. Maybe I just didn't want to hear the noise," he said.

"No sir," Eulis said.

The stranger glanced at Letty. "I appreciate what you're saying. God knows I do. But I need to remind you to think about your wife. I haven't been around decent folk in so long that I don't know how to act."

Letty snorted lightly.

"Me, either," she said and got up to refill his coffee again.

Eulis grinned.

"Umm, my wife here has had a few obstacles in her life as well."

Letty's snort was a little bit louder.

"I worked at the White Dove...and I wasn't scrubbing floors." When she smiled at Eulis, she was unaware her affection for him shone all over her face. Then she turned around and offered the man her hand. "Leticia Potter. But you can call me, Letty."

There was a moment of hesitation, and then the man pushed his chair back and stood.

"My name is Robert Lee Slade. Some people call me Robert Lee." He hesitated for a moment, then reluctantly added. "And some call me the Cherokee Kid."

It was to Letty's credit she didn't falter when she shook his hand. She'd seen a man who called himself the Cherokee Kid draw down on a gambler who was cheating and shoot him through the heart, then sit back down and ask for a new deck of cards. But he was a far cry from looking like the man standing before her. Maybe one day they'd learn how he'd come to these hard times, and maybe they wouldn't.

For now, it seemed his arrival could be the answer to their problems, and his presence would also put an end to her worries about Eulis's well-being.

"Pleased to meet you," Letty said, and then smoothed her hands down the front of her shirt before adding. "I feel it's only right to tell you the same thing I told the other men who work for us."

"And that was?" Robert Lee asked.

"If you so much as harm a hair on my Eulis's head, I will hunt you down like a dog, nail your balls to a tree, and scatter what's left of you to the wolves."

For the first time since his arrival, Robert Lee looked—really looked—at the woman who'd just fixed his food. And in that moment, there was a tiny part of him that envied Eulis Potter for the woman who'd claimed his heart.

"Fair enough," he said.

"All right then," Letty said and glanced toward the door. "You can move now, T-Bone."

The pup stood, eyed the stranger one more time, then turned and trotted away, leaving the doorway empty.

* * *

A week had passed since Robert Lee's arrival into their lives. His coming had lifted the weight of Eulis's responsibilities so dramatically he was now actually sleeping through the night. Before, he hadn't had one calm moment since the day Letty had found that gold, although he'd hidden the worst of his fears from Letty, or so he'd thought.

But Letty had known. She'd been lying beside him every night since their marriage. She'd felt the tension in his body and the way he'd tossed and turned. The burden of being rich was more than either of them could have imagined, even though their lifestyle had yet to reflect the gold and currency piling up in the Denver City bank in their name.

However, Robert Lee's arrival afforded them the perfect opportunity for change. Having given up their cabin, they were residing in Denver City's only hotel, on the second floor, last room on the left at the end of the hall.

Their new house was now sporting windows, but the furniture they'd ordered months ago had yet to arrive, and they weren't particularly interested in sleeping on the floor and cooking over a campfire again.

Eulis had settled in real easy. After the life he'd had, he didn't need much to be happy—just Letty and a bed in which to sleep suited him just fine.

Letty, on the other hand, was having issues. There was a young woman and a baby in the room next to them. It was Letty's opinion the woman cried more than the baby. The room across the hall was occupied by a woman named Delia who had more male visitors than T-Bone had hairs. Not that Letty was judging her. Lord knew she'd been in the same boat for years. It was just a bit noisy from time to time.

As for T-Bone, he'd barely gotten used to the cabin before Letty had moved him into town. She didn't know that he'd come from Denver City, and that every bad thing that could happen to a dog had happened to him here. If it hadn't been for his devotion to Letty, he would have abandoned the hotel days ago. Letty knew T-Bone wasn't happy, but for the time being, there wasn't anything she could do about it. Until their furniture arrived, they were stuck there.

After the year that Eulis and Letty had survived, living back in town seemed stifling. There had been too many nights sleeping out on the prairie under the stars, too many quiet mornings wakened by only the sound of a jaybird's fuss, or a squirrel's noisy chatter, to readjust easily. Gunshots and loud voices had a tendency to set a person's teeth on edge, making them jumpy all the rest of the day. Then, on the ninth day of their stay in the hotel, Letty had what could only be described as a fit.

* * *

The woman next door had been crying since before daybreak. Eulis had given Letty a nervous look, apologized for having to leave for the mine so early, and left before Letty could argue. They were going to be blasting today, and he didn't want her anywhere around it. Letty was tired of waiting for tables and chairs that might never arrive and had contacted the carpenters who'd built their home to start building some furniture. Yesterday they'd begun building a bed and a wardrobe and when they were done, would begin working on a dining table and some chairs. Their tools were few, so the furniture would be plain, but it suited Letty's taste just fine. She wanted out of the hotel and into her own home in the worst way.

With no food to cook and no cabin to clean, she was left with few options. Denver City was growing, but it still wasn't a place where a woman could while away a day—unless she was occupied in whiling it away with men —for fifty cents a poke. Letty was forever thankful for the change her life had taken, even if it had nearly killed her to get there.

So, while she was brushing her hair, she dallied with the notion of going to the general store to look at the bolts of fabric with an eye to making some curtains for her new house. As she was brushing out the last of the tangles, the woman next door let out a particularly loud wail.

Letty rolled her eyes, puffed out her cheeks, and then laid down her hairbrush. If Eulis had been there, he would have recognized the look on her face. He'd seen it plenty of times back in Lizard Flats when she'd been tired of waiting for the hot water he was supposed to bring up for her bath.

She got up from the chair and headed for the door, muttering under her breath and stomping off the distance in long, angry strides. Once in the hallway, it became apparent the wailing had increased.

"For the Good Lord's sake," Letty muttered and hit the door three times with her fist.

The wailing stopped—instantly.

Letty whacked the door again.

Silence continued.

"Hello!" Letty called, hitting the door again with her fist.

"You might as well open up because I'm not leaving until we talk."

There was another brief moment of silence, then Letty heard footsteps moving toward the door. A few seconds later, the doorknob turned, then the door swung inward.

Letty stifled a gasp. She'd seen plenty of depravity in her time, but never had she seen a woman in such horrible shape.

"Oh good Lord," Letty murmured.

The woman glanced nervously around the hallway.

"You need to go away," she whispered.

"I don't think so," Letty said.

Blood dripped from the woman's right nostril onto the front of her dress. From the shape of her clothing, it was Letty's opinion that it was only the latest in a series of similar stains. She would have glared at Letty, but one eye was swollen shut and the other was bloodshot and purple from bruising.

"What do you want?" the woman asked.

Letty pointed to the room next door, then introduced herself.

"I'm Letty Potter. Me and my husband are staying next door."

The woman sniffed, then wiped her nose with the back of her hand. The baby on the bed behind her whined weakly. Letty saw it then and thought to herself it sounded like a sick kitten.

Letty had a fleeting thought about turning around, going back into her room and minding her own business, but her eyes couldn't move away. Her body couldn't move—there was no minding her own business. Suddenly this poor thing before her was most definitely her business. Dismayed to the point of speechlessness, she had to clear her throat before she could find the breath to speak.

"Reckon I might come in?" she asked.

The woman looked nervous and glanced up and down the hallway again.

"I'm alone," Letty said.

Finally, she shrugged and stepped aside.

Letty was met with the stench of soiled diapers and sour milk. She saw the diapers in a pile on the floor and a pitcher half-full of curdled milk. But it was the bleeding cuts, swollen flesh, and bruises on the woman's face and body that worried her most.

"What's your name?" Letty asked.

The woman shook her head.

"What? You don't have one or you don't want to talk?"

The woman turned away.

Letty's eyes narrowed angrily.

"Look, lady, your name is beside the point. I've been in this hotel for nine days now, and I've had to listen to you and this baby cry for every one of those nine days. Now, I know why. Is the bastard who's beating you your husband or just your man?"

The woman drew herself up as if she'd just been insulted.

"I'm not like that woman across the hall. I'm a wife... two years married."

Letty's upper lip curled. It wasn't the first time she'd heard comments from so-called 'decent' women regarding other women who found themselves in dire straits.

"I'll tell you something about that woman across the hall," Letty snapped. "She's got better sense than to stay with some bastard who beats her on a regular basis."

"I never—"

Letty held up her hand. "It doesn't matter."

The baby squeaked.

Letty turned around. "May I?" she asked, pointing to the baby.

"I guess," the woman said and then started to cry again, only this time the tears were silent.

Letty touched the baby's forehead. It was cool—almost clammy. When she picked the child up, she could barely feel the weight in her arms.

"Is it a boy?"

"Girl," the woman said. "George...he's my man... wanted a boy."

"What's wrong with her?" she asked.

"She can't feed," the woman said. "George says girls are a lot of trouble."

Letty laid the baby back down and then put her hand on her hips.

"So are you saying he's mad at you because the baby was a girl instead of a boy?"

"George says—"

Letty snorted.

"I couldn't care less what George says," she muttered, then fixed the woman with a calculated stare. "What's your name?"

The woman snuffled around a sob.

"Alice. My name is Alice."

"Where are you from?"

"Boston."

"Do you have family back there?"

Alice's features crumpled.

"No."

"Friends?"

"I reckon," Alice said.

"Why don't you go home?"

Alice lifted a hand to her mouth, as if Letty had suggested something foul.

"And leave my husband?"

Letty rolled her eyes again.

"Unless you're interested in being buried out here beside that baby...yes."

Alice picked up the baby, then clutched it to her chest.

"George says it's my fault that the baby is sick, but I couldn't help it. My milk dried up. I've been trying to get her to drink this goat's milk, but she keeps spitting it up."

"God in heaven, woman...the milk is sour. Can't you smell it?"

Alice swayed on her feet, then finally shook her head.

"Everything stinks in here. I didn't know it was the milk."

Letty sighed.

"Wrap the baby in her blanket and get yourself together. We're going to find the doctor."

Alice blinked slowly.

"There's a doctor in this town?"

"Yes. His name is Angus Warren."

"I asked George if there was a doctor here. He told me no."

"That's what you get for trusting a man who beats the hell out of you on a regular basis," Letty said.

Alice reeled from the truth in Letty's words.

"You don't understand," Alice whined. "George—"

"If I had ever been stupid enough to marry a man like your George, he would not have lived past the first day he laid a hand on me."

"You would kill your own husband?" Alice asked.

"Hell, yes," Letty said.

The woman's face was so swollen and distorted she could hardly blink, and yet she managed to show her disdain for Letty's words.

"How could you?" she asked.

Letty stood up.

"It's called self-defense." Then she grabbed the woman and turned her toward the door and the mirror hanging on the wall.

"Have you looked at yourself lately?"

Alice flinched, then laid her baby back on the bed.

"I should have been able to give George a son, and it's my fault that my milk is gone. As a woman, I'm a failure."

"Okay, if you're all set on being some kind of a martyr, then have at it, lady. But just because you're stupid, doesn't mean you have the right to let your baby die."

Alice pressed a hand against her mouth.

"I don't want my baby to die."

Letty stomped to the door and yanked it open.

"Then get off your ass, pick up the kid, and come with me."

Alice hesitated.

"It's now or never," Letty said.

Alice grabbed the baby, wrapped her up in a blanket, and stumbled out the door behind Letty.

"George will kill me if he sees us," Alice muttered.

"No, he won't, because I won't let him," Letty said.

Alice shuffled behind Letty as they moved toward the back stairs. The baby whimpered once. Letty prayed it wasn't the baby's dying breath.

By the time they got out on the streets, Alice was staggering.

"Give me the baby before you drop her," Letty said and then took the child before Alice could argue. "Lean on me," she added when Alice staggered again. So she did.

Men saw them coming down the sidewalk and stepped aside, unable to hide their shock. A woman and two little boys were coming out of the general store. When she saw Alice's face, she let out a weak cry of disbelief, then turned her children's faces to her waist, unwilling for them to see such a sight. Another man, Henry Smith, who knew Letty by sight as the woman who'd struck it big, got off his horse and stepped up on the sidewalk as they passed by.

"Miz Potter?" he said.

"Mornin' Henry."

"Jesus, ma'am. What's happened here?"

"Henry, if you're not too busy, would you do me a favor?" she asked.

"Yes, ma'am. Anything."

"Eulis is up at the mine. I'm thinking there's a good possibility I might be needing him soon."

"You want me to go get him?" Henry asked.

"Yes, please," Letty said, and then kept on walking.

Henry Smith mounted his horse and headed out of town at a lope.

Alice was leaning against Letty harder now. Letty could hear her labored breathing and figured at the least, she had some broken ribs—maybe internal injuries as well. She didn't give much hope for either one of them seeing next month, but she couldn't live with herself without giving this a try.

"Just hang on a little bit longer," she said. "We're almost there."

3

rich man, poor man, beggar man, THIEF

George Mellin had been hiding in the underbrush on the north side of Cherry Creek for the better part of two hours, watching Robert and Mary Whiteside working their claim. His latest had played out weeks ago, and his grubstake with it.

He'd heard all about the big Potter strike and knew they were hiring, but he didn't want to work someone else's claim. Selfishly, he had no thought for his wife or baby's wants and needs. He had gold fever and he had it bad—bad enough to do something desperate—even illegal.

Yesterday, he'd followed the Whitesides into the general store, subversively eyeing the nuggets Robert shook out onto the pay scale for the goods they'd purchased. When he saw Mary pick out a pair of new boots and pay for them with no thought for the cost, he'd been struck with envy.

He had already hit up everyone he knew for another grubstake, but with no success. His gut was burning. His head was throbbing with every beat of his heart. He needed a way out of the situation he was in and decided to just take what he needed.

These days, his wife, Alice, did nothing but whine, and that brat she'd whelped was no good to him. What was a man to do with another female to feed? A man needed sons. He was nothing without sons to continue his lineage.

And so he sat, watching the Whitesides work while greed and envy continued to choke out the last of his good sense. Several times during the past hours, he'd seen one or both of the Whitesides stop and exclaim at a nugget they pulled out of the pan. The more he watched, the more angry he became. It wasn't fair. He deserved a strike as much as the next man, but he kept coming up empty. He was beginning to believe he was cursed, and the burden of his family was the curse. Oblivious to the fact that his life in all its ugliness was about to be revealed, he moved from a sitting to a squatting position. As soon as the couple moved back to their camp, he would slip away, then come back after dark.

Within fifteen minutes, he'd made his escape and headed back into town.

* * *

Letty felt the baby wheezing. She was scared to death it would die in her arms before she ever got to the doctor's house. Alice was glassy-eyed and stumbling, which was no surprise. She'd been beaten so badly over such a long period of time she had moved to a place inside her head where the pain couldn't go.

The doctor's house was up at the end of the street. When Letty saw his horse and buggy tied at the side of the house, she breathed a sigh of relief. At least Dr. Warren was home. When she'd stomped out of her hotel room to berate her next door neighbor for making such a racket, she had never dreamed she would wind up involved in such a rescue.

To make things worse, there was always the danger Alice's husband would show up and try to reclaim his family. Letty hadn't ever killed anyone before, but she was pretty sure she'd have no trouble pulling the trigger on Alice's George.

"Okay, okay," Letty murmured. "We're almost there."

Alice moaned.

The baby made a mousey little squeak.

Letty wanted to cry. Instead, as soon as they were inside the doctor's front yard, she began to yell.

"Doc! Hey, Doc! Help us! We need help!"

The front door opened almost instantly. Letty recognized, Mildred, the doctor's wife. Her expression went from questioning to horrified in seconds.

"Oh dear Lord," she muttered, then yelled back over her shoulder. "Angus! Angus! Come quick!"

She ran out the door and the down the steps, catching Alice just before she pitched forward.

The doctor was only seconds behind and quickly lifted Alice into his arms and carried her into the house. "What's happened here?" he asked, as Letty followed behind, still carrying the baby. "Was there an accident?"

He laid Alice down on the examining table, then motioned to his wife.

"Unbutton her dress. We need to see the extent of her injuries."

"The baby...what about the baby?" Letty asked.

Dr. Warren turned, took one look at the child, and paled.

"Give it to me," he said softly, then nodded to Mildred. "Make a pad out of that blanket and lay it on the table, quickly."

His wife folded the blanket to fit the table, then laid a small piece of linen over it. Angus laid the baby down and removed the blanket in which she'd been wrapped.

Her skin was so fragile, Letty could see the tiny blue veins beneath, and her limbs were hardly more than matchsticks. The baby was so lethargic it could do little more than squeak.

"Dear God," Mildred said, as she looked from mother to baby and back again. "What's happened here?"

Letty sighed. "I'm not sure. I just got myself involved by accident. This lady and her family are staying in the hotel room next to me and my husband. We've been there nine days now, and I can count on my hands the number of hours of silence. Most of the time one or both of them have been wailing. Today, I knocked on the door." Letty's eyes filled with tears. "I'm sorry I waited so long."

"Mildred! Warm up some milk. Fill one of the nursing bottles and bring it here as quickly as you can."

Mildred flew out of the room to do his bidding, leaving Letty alone with Alice.

Angus Warren pointed to Alice's dress.

"Would you please unfasten her dress for me."

Letty nodded.

There were a few moments of silence as Letty undid buttons. Dr. Warren stood beside her, his expression unreadable.

"She's been beaten, hasn't she?" he asked.

Letty nodded.

"Her husband?"

"Said his name was George," Letty added.

"Damned gold fever makes fools out of all manner of men."

"Wasn't no fool that beat Alice half to death. It was a devil."

Dr. Angus sighed.

"They happen, too, sometimes."

Letty bit her tongue to keep from saying anything more.

"Look here," Dr. Angus said, as he moved the fabric aside on Alice's dress. "Broken ribs. One is close to protruding through the flesh. I'll have to set these before they puncture a lung."

"Is she going to make it?" Letty asked.

"Maybe," Dr. Angus said.

Letty glanced over to the tiny baby lying so still on the adjoining table.

"What about her?" Letty asked.

Dr. Angus just frowned and shook his head.

"Jesus," Letty muttered.

At that point, Mildred came back into the room carrying the milk. She lifted the baby into her arms and sat down in a nearby rocking chair.

Just as she was about to put the nipple to the baby's mouth, she froze. Letty heard her breath catch, and her voice began to shake.

"She's gone, Angus."

The doctor spun around.

"Let me see," he said and laid a finger against the baby's neck, feeling for a pulse.

"Damn it," he said softly. "Damn it to hell."

"Cursing won't help either one of them," Mildred scolded.

"I wasn't cursing for them. I was cursing for me," he mumbled.

Letty felt as if she was smothering. Only minutes ago, she'd held that tiny life, and now it was gone. The pain in her chest was spreading up her throat. Her vision blurred.

"She's dead?" Letty asked.

Mildred nodded, then set the bottle aside and clasped the tiny baby to her ample breasts and began to rock.

"Mildred, don't," Angus said. "I need you to help me. Maybe we can save the mother."

Mildred's chin was quivering as she got up from the chair. She carried the baby back to the table and laid it down.

Letty felt as if she was caught in a nightmare, unable to wake up. On one table, the tiny body of one victim had already escaped the hell into which she'd been born, while on the other, the mother wasn't far behind. "I've got to go," Letty muttered and stumbled out the door.

She paused on the porch and took a deep breath, but it didn't help.

Desperate to get away from the pain, she strode off the porch and headed back up the street. Her hands were doubled up into fists, and her head was down as if she would head-butt anyone who got in her way. When she stomped off the sidewalk and into the street, she was outrunning the dust stirred up by her feet. She didn't know she was crying—huge, hiccuping sobs that shook her to the bone, or that people were whispering and staring as she moved through town. Everyone knew Letty Potter as a tough, no-nonsense woman. They couldn't imagine what had happened to cause this kind of reaction.

Letty didn't know she was gathering so much attention. All she wanted to do was get to her room. She was almost running when she entered the hotel and was heading for the stairs when she heard what sounded like a roar of rage from the second floor. The sound startled her enough she hesitated. As she did, a man came storming down the hallway above and took the stairs down to the lobby two at a time, then headed for the clerk behind the desk.

"Where is she? Where's my wife?" he yelled and grabbed the young clerk around the neck.

"I don't know," he said. "I just got back from eating my noon meal."

Letty froze. She'd never met this man, but she had a sinking feeling she knew who he was. And, there was only one way to find out.

"Hey," she said.

The man turned the clerk loose so quickly he staggered backward and fell.

"You talkin' to me?" the man growled.

Letty stared at the man—all six feet plus of him—and could only imagine how Alice had felt.

"By any chance, is your name George?" she asked.

George Mellin looked taken aback, and then he recognized her as the woman who was in the room next door.

"You're that Potter woman, ain't you?"

"I asked you first," Letty muttered.

George blinked. He wasn't in the habit of being back-talked by anyone, especially some female, no matter how rich she was.

"You don't talk to me like that," George said softly.

Letty glared. "Or what? You gonna beat me, too?"

The clerk behind the counter had scrambled to his feet and made a run for the door. He wasn't sure what was about to happen, but it didn't look like any good was going to come from it. He headed for the sheriff's office as hard as he could go.

"You think because you're rich that you're better than ever'body, don't you, bitch?"

Letty shuddered. She'd been beaten up a few times in her early days as a prostitute, before she'd settled in at the White Dove Saloon. There, she'd at least had three meals a day and a roof over her head, as well as protection from the ones who liked to hurt a woman first before they had their own pleasure.

George doubled his fists and took a step toward her.

Letty was so focused on the man in front of her she didn't know the clerk had disappeared. She waited for George to take that second step, fearing it, and at the same time, wanting some recourse for that dead baby on the table back in the doctor's office.

She could hear the rasping sounds of his heavy breathing and smelled the stench of his unwashed body. Her stomach rolled. She felt suddenly light-headed, as if she'd had too much to drink. She heard the sound of men drinking and laughing from the bar in the adjoining room. From where she was standing, she could see the man who drove freight wagons to and from Denver City finishing off a big steak. The bullwhip he used on his team of mules was hanging on the back of his chair only a few feet from where she was standing.

Without giving herself time to think, she stepped through the doorway, snatched the bullwhip from the back of the chair, and uncoiled it as she walked. It snapped once, getting the attention of everyone in the bar, including the freight driver, who thought he was being robbed.

"Hey, mister! That's—"

"That ain't no mister," someone said. "That there's Letty Potter."

It was the first snap of the whip that got George's attention. He pointed at Letty as she walked back into the hotel lobby.

"You put that down before I—"

Letty swung it over her head once, then aimed it at George's face.

The leather tassels at the end of the whip tore at the flesh on his cheek as neatly as if he'd been bitten.

"Godalmighty!" he yelled, grabbing the side of his jaw.

Letty was already swinging the bullwhip again when George lit for the door. She was right behind him, running as she went.

George stumbled just as he was about to jump from the sidewalk. The bullwhip snaked around his ankles as Letty jerked.

He went down like a felled ox. Dirt went up his nose and in his mouth. He tasted blood at the same time he felt a wave of intense pain.

He'd bitten into his tongue so hard that the end had come off. At that point, he rolled over on his back and unwound himself from the bullwhip, spitting blood as he went.

"You're crazy!" he bawled. "Somebody stop her. She's crazy!"

People in the buildings heard the ruckus and began spilling out onto the sidewalks and into the streets. They didn't know George, but it didn't take long for them to recognize Letty. Everyone knew the woman in men's pants who'd struck gold.

Letty was past rational thinking as she drew back the bullwhip, cracking it time after time onto George's back, and his legs, and his face.

George Mellin was lying in the middle of the street, rolled up as small as he could get with his arms over his head, screaming and begging for someone to make her stop.

Someone yelled at her. She didn't know it was the sheriff, and at the time, couldn't have cared. Every time she drew back the whip, she taunted him with a dare.

"What's the matter, George? You like to hit women. Why don't you get up out of the dirt and take a swing at me like you did your wife?"

Suddenly, the onlookers got a sense of Letty's justice.

She swung the whip in the air. It cracked against the back of George's neck like the echo of a rifle shot down in a canyon.

"Come on, you sorry sack of shit! Your wife is broken in so many pieces she can't stand up any more, and you starved your baby to death. She's dead, George. Do you hear me? She's dead."

Letty didn't hear the collective gasp from the crowd or see the disgust spreading across the onlookers' faces.

"Take a swing at me, you sorry bastard. I'm not like Alice. I'll fight you back."

She popped the whip again. It ripped the back of George's jacket, through the shirt, and all the way to the flesh on his back.

George bucked like he'd been shot as he rolled, trying desperatcly to get out of her way. Every time he tried to get to his feet, she yanked them out from under him again. Just when he was convinced he was going to die, he heard the sounds of running horses and then a man shouting Letty's name.

* * *

Eulis had been deep in the mine shaft when Henry Smith reached the mine. Robert Lee was on duty. His first instinct had been to reach for his gun when the man had ridden up, then Henry had shouted.

"Get Eulis! Letty's got trouble."

Robert Lee turned on his heels and ran into the mine, shouting Eulis's name.

Eulis was loading ore into the mine cars when he heard Robert Lee.

"Here! I'm here!" he called back and leaned his pick against the wall. "Mose, take over here for a minute until I see what's up."

He lifted a lantern from a peg in the wall and started walking back toward the entrance. Even though he'd heard concern in Robert Lee's voice, he had not connected it with the possibility that Letty was in trouble.

He rounded a bend in the shaft about a hundred yards from the entrance and ran into Robert Lee.

"Whoa, there," Eulis said. "What's so all fired important?"

"Henry Smith just came riding in from town. He said Letty's in trouble."

Eulis felt the ground go out from under him.

"Letty?"

"Henry said she's in trouble," Robert Lee repeated.

Eulis pushed past Robert Lee and started running. He heard the footsteps behind him but didn't stop to wait. Moments later, he burst out into the open. Henry had saddled Eulis's horse and was waiting by the mine, holding the horse's reins.

"What happened to her?" Eulis cried, as he swung up in the saddle.

"I don't know what all happened, but when I saw her, she was carrying a baby and helping a woman down the street. I reckon they were on the way to the Doc's house."

Immediately, Eulis thought of the baby and the woman who'd been crying in the room next to theirs.

"Oh lord," he muttered.

"I'm coming with you," Robert Lee said, mounting his horse.

Henry took off his hat and shoved a hand through his hair, as if uncertain of what else to say.

"Hey, Eulis...about that woman who Letty was helping...."

"What about her?" Eulis asked.

"She looked near beat to death."

Eulis paled.

"You said she was on her way to Doc's house?"

"Looked like it," Henry said.

Eulis spurred his horse and took off across the valley at a gallop with Robert Lee right behind.

There had been a warm, steady wind blowing all day, whipping through the new growth of ankle-high prairie grass and rustling through the trees, but Eulis didn't hear it. He didn't hear anything but the hard, steady gallop of his horse's hooves and the bone-jarring sound of his own heartbeat thundering in his ears.

Each leg of the trip he often made to town was marked by a large boulder in the shape of a man's bowler hat—and the lightning struck tree that had been split into three pieces, yet still grew—then the twin pines at the crest, before the road began to slant downward toward the city below. It was three miles from Denver City to the Potter mine, and it was the fastest trip he'd ever made.

As he rode into town, he saw a huge crowd gathered at the far end of the street. From the corner of his eye, he saw the sheriff come running out of his office as he went riding past. Then, only a few yards from the edge of the crowd, he saw her.

It was his Letty. But he'd never seen her this way. Her face was streaked with tears and dust—her features contorted with rage. It was the bullwhip in her hand and the bloody man on the ground at her feet that sent him flying off his horse. He went running through the crowd, shouting her name. Robert Lee had dismounted and was right behind with his hand on his gun.

* * *

One minute Letty was pulling back her arm for another blow, and the next thing she knew, the whip was yanked from her hand. She reacted like an animal, spinning around in a crouched position, readying herself for a fight.

Then she saw Eulis. His lips were moving, but she couldn't hear what he was saying. There was nothing in her head but the hammer of blood pounding through her veins and the memory of a baby's last cry.

Eulis could tell something awful had happened. He tossed the bullwhip into the dirt and then wrapped her in his arms.

"Letty, darlin', it's me, it's me. Let it go, girl, let it go. Whatever he did, let it go."

Letty froze. The voice in her ear was familiar, as was the feel of the arms holding her close.

"Can you hear me, honey? It's okay now. It's okay."

Letty shuddered. Eulis. Was he truly here?

"Eulis?"

Her voice was so soft, at first, Eulis imagined she'd spoken, and then he felt her trembling and looked down at her face.

"It's me, Letty. It's me."

She swayed where she stood, and if he hadn't been holding her, she would have dropped.

"What happened here?" the sheriff yelled, as he ran onto the scene. Then he saw the bloody and beaten man on the ground and turned on Letty. "Did you do this?" he growled.

Robert Lee stepped between Letty and the sheriff without saying a word.

The sheriff had heard about Potter hiring a gunslinger at the mine and took a quick step back.

"Now see here," he said. "I've got to do my duty. Step back, mister. Step back now or I reckon I might have to arrest you for obstruction of justice."

Robert Lee grinned, but he didn't move.

Letty turned to face the sheriff and gathered what was left of her wits.

"It's all right, Robert Lee," she said, and then pointed at the man on the ground. "Is he dead?"

George was rolled into a bloody ball, whimpering like a dog.

Robert Lee glanced down.

"No, ma'am."

"Damn," Letty muttered and kicked the bullwhip. "I should have used a gun."

Robert Lee stifled a grin. The sheriff was speechless. It was Eulis who asked the first question.

"Letty...what happened?"

"He beat his wife up real bad. I got her and the baby to Doc Angus's house, but she's all broken up inside." Then her voice shook, but her gaze never wavered. "The baby's dead. He let it starve to death."

The onlookers began to murmur among themselves as shock spread through the crowd. Suddenly, Letty Potter's behavior began to make sense.

"See here, Miz Potter, you can't take the law into your own hands like this," the sheriff said.

"He came at me. I stopped him."

The hotel clerk stepped out of the crowd.

"It's true, sheriff. He knocked me down first, then he was challenging Mrs. Potter as I ran out the door to get you."

The sheriff mumbled something beneath his breath, then spit in the dirt.

"All right then," he said and motioned toward some men in the crowd. "Here you two. Help me carry him to the jail. I'll have the Doc come take a look at him."

Letty felt as if all the bones in her body were melting. As she turned, she stumbled over the bullwhip, then stopped and picked it up, rolled it neatly back into a loop, and looked around at the crowd for the freighter.

"Thanks for the loan of your whip," she said, thrusting it into his hands.

"Yes, ma'am," the freight driver said and walked away.

Eulis put his arm around Letty. She leaned against him for a moment, then pulled herself together when she realized there was a crowd of people watching her every move.

She glanced at Eulis first, and then at Robert Lee and sighed.

"I don't think I'm made out to be a lady. I made quite a spectacle out of myself, didn't I?"

Eulis patted her on the shoulder, and then put his arm around her waist.

"Now girl, they're just admiring your spunk. Besides, when have you ever cared what people thought about you?"

Letty stifled a grin.

"Never, I guess."

"Okay then," Eulis said.

Robert Lee cleared his throat as he holstered his gun.

"If you'll pardon my language, Miz Letty, you're one hell of a woman. You did yourself proud." Then he looked a bit taken aback and cleared his throat once more. "I'll just go get our horses," he told Eulis and disappeared into the crowd.

Eulis put a hand beneath Letty's elbow and began walking her back to the hotel.

"Are you mad at me," she asked.

Eulis shook his head.

"No, ma'am. Ain't no way I'll ever be mad at you. I was, however, scared half out of my mind thinkin' you was hurt."

Letty looked startled. She'd been so caught up in her own fury she hadn't thought of how her message might have sounded.

"I'm sorry, Eulis."

Eulis patted her shoulder.

"No apology needed. I'm just glad you're okay."

4

rich man, poor man, beggar man, thief, DOCTOR

Four little girls were playing in the alley between the general store and the assayer's office as Letty passed by. Two were turning a long piece of rope while the other two were taking turns jumping in. They were chanting a little rhyme as they played, and when one of them stumbled and stopped the rope, the others would squeal out in childish glee.

Letty stopped on the sidewalk to listen.

"Rich man, poor man, beggar man, thief, doctor, lawyer, merchant, chief. One of them will make you tarry. Which one of these men will you marry?"

They would repeat it over and over until someone tripped. Whatever man they stopped at was supposedly the man they would marry.

Letty shook her head in wonder at their innocence. By the time she was their age, she'd been orphaned and well on her way to permanent employment at the White Dove Saloon.

It made her sad, thinking about what a rude awakening they were going to get when they grew up. Likely as not, they'd all wind up married to some hard-scrabble farmer or cowboy, or end up in the same boat Letty had been in. Life in this country wasn't easy for anyone, but for a woman, it was quite often brutal and brief.

Case in point, Alice Mellin. Letty had just come from Dr. Warren's house. Alice was going to live but would most likely never be able to have children again. The poor woman was distraught by the news. Letty felt sorry for her, but there was nothing more she could do.

Angus Warren had tended to George's wounds in the sheriff's office, then watched in silent satisfaction as the man was put behind bars. As a doctor, he'd taken an oath to do no harm, but for the first time in his life, he could have willingly put an end to George's life without losing a second of sleep.

Letty was of the same opinion, but she would have much rather seen him drawn and quartered for what he'd done to his wife and child.

There was a small cloud of dust surrounding the girls as they played, stirred up by their stomping feet and the thump of the jump rope against the hard, dry ground. The little girls' stockings and shoes were covered in dirt, as were the hems of their dresses, but they didn't care. They were too caught up in the fantasy of fate having a hand in choosing their mate. Their rhythmic chant matched the turn of the rope as they jumped in and out of the wide, dusty arc. When one of them finally tripped, the other three squealed out loud.

"Beggar man. Beggar man. You're gonna marry a beggar man!" they cried.

T-Bone had been trotting ahead, but when he realized Letty was no longer behind him, he had run back and sat down at her feet. Letty shook her head, looked down at T-Bone, and then clicked her tongue against the roof of her mouth.

"Come on, T-Bone. Let's get out of here before the fussing starts."

The pup was oblivious to everything but the gentle tone of her voice and touch. When she moved, he moved with her.

Letty walked away from the alley, ignoring the whispers and stares from the people she passed. It hadn't taken long for word to get around about what she'd done now. She'd already been judged and found wanting for wearing pants like a man and riding astride instead of side-saddle.

Today, she'd just added to her notoriety by taking a bullwhip to a man. While the citizens of Denver City were disgusted by what George Mellin had done to his wife and child, most of them were of the opinion that Letty Potter had overstepped her bounds and should not have involved herself in the situation.

Letty would have liked their acceptance, but she'd lived on the wrong side of society for so long she no longer cared. Eulis was the only person whose opinion mattered, and so far, he had kept his disappointments to himself.

She thought back to the earlier events of the day. When Henry Smith had stopped her on the street. Her first instinct had been to send for Eulis. She hadn't known how much she'd been counting on his arrival until he'd come running through the crowd and snatched the whip from her hand.

And then there was Robert Lee. When the sheriff started threatening her, Robert Lee had immediately put himself between her and the law. It had all happened so fast she hadn't realized the impact of what he'd done until it was over, at which point, he'd quietly made himself scarce. It gave her an odd feeling to know he'd stood up for her like that.

She paused at the corner, waiting for a stagecoach to pass before starting across the street to the hotel. Eulis had sent Robert Lee back to the mine while she'd gone to the doctor's house. He promised to meet Letty in their room, and as she stepped off the sidewalk, she felt an overwhelming urge to run. Instead, she crossed the dusty street with her head held high and her steps long and steady, unconscious of the stern jut of her jaw. When a man on horseback rode too close to her, T-Bone barked and nipped at the horse's heels. By the time the cowboy had his horse under control, Letty was entering the lobby of the hotel.

The young clerk was already back at work. He looked up, then smiled when he saw Letty.

"You did something real brave today, ma'am," he said, and then blushed.

"A little foolhardy, too," Letty said.

The clerk shook his head.

"No, ma'am. It was amazing, and so are you."

Uncomfortable with the unexpected praise, Letty hurried up the stairs and down the hall with T-Bone at her heels. She was almost running when she reached their room. The door was ajar. The pup ran in, headed for his bed in the opposite corner, and was already in it and settled as Letty entered.

Eulis was standing at the window. His pants were hanging a little loose and there was a small tear just below his right knee. His gray shirt was a collar-less homespun with long sleeves he'd rolled up to his elbows. His face was lean and expressionless, delineating his rough-cut features more than usual. He could have used a shave and a haircut, but to Letty, he looked just fine.

Then it occurred to her he'd been watching her from the window as she'd crossed the street. What had he been thinking? Was he upset with what she'd done?

"Eulis?"

He took a deep breath and turned.

"Come here, girl. I need a hug."

Letty relaxed, then hurried across the room and walked into his arms. When they closed around her, she shuddered.

"Oh Eulis...that poor woman...and that baby...that poor, poor baby. We laid in our bed and listened to her dying."

"We had no way of knowing," Eulis said.

"I should have done something sooner. If I had, maybe—"

"No. Stop thinking like that. The only person at fault is the man who did it." He held her close as he rubbed the middle of her back, gentling her as much as himself. "You did a real dangerous thing today, but I have to say, I've never been prouder to know you, girl."

Letty struggled with tears, then finally let them fall.

"It's okay," Eulis kept saying, as he did all he could to ease her pain. "Shoot. I could'a told that George Mellin he'd done the wrong thing when he ticked you off. After all, I know how your temper used to spew just because your bath water wasn't ready."

Letty laughed, which was exactly what Eulis intended. He led her to the side of the bed, then pulled her down beside him.

Letty grabbed his hand and held it. As she did, a notion she'd been harboring in the back of her mind took rise.

"Eulis...I've been thinking...."

He groaned. "Now, that can't be good."

She punched him lightly on the arm, then crawled the rest of the way up on the bed, hugging her pillow like a child.

"I'm serious," she said. "I want out of here. There's too many people down here trying to mind our business for us."

Eulis frowned. "But honey, there ain't no other place to go. We don't have any furniture, and Robert Lee has settled in real good in the cabin."

"I don't care," she said. "We slept in and under our wagon all the way across the prairie then up the mountains to Denver City. I'd sooner sleep back under the stars with you, or on a blanket on the floor, than spend another night under this roof."

Eulis grinned.

"Then I reckon that's what we'll do," he said.

"Good. I'll pack up our stuff. You go get our wagon. T-Bone and I will be waiting when you get back."

Eulis wrapped his arms around her and gave her a slow, gentle kiss, then grabbed his hat off the bedpost and headed out the door.

The pup raised its head and looked at Letty.

She grinned.

"We're getting out of here, T-Bone. Tonight, we'll be sleeping in our own home."

The pup didn't know what she'd said, but the tone of her voice made him happy. His tail was still wagging when she started out of the room, dragging the trunk with their belongings.

She paused outside in the hall, glanced at the room next door then increased her stride, anxious to be rid of this place and all its memories.

* * *

Angus Warren was a big man with a thick head of hair, although in deference to Mildred's preference, he maintained a clean shave. He'd seen a lot of bad things in his life since he'd hung out his shingle, but none of them worse than the shape Alice Mellin was in. He ached for her grief and was doing what he could to help her make arrangements for the baby's funeral. He'd learned the baby's name was Mary—Mary Elizabeth Mellin. He'd had Alice spell it out for him so he could give it to the man who was building the coffin. He could make a grave marker, too, and carve her name into the wood.

Angus was so angry he knew he was going to have to get down on his knees and pray for forgiveness for what he wanted to do to George Mellin. It was difficult being a doctor in a land where the gun ruled and fair was an adjective for weather, rather than a metaphor for life.

He paused in the act of mixing a tincture for his latest patient, a little girl named Charity Talmadge, who'd been brought in with a bad case of eye infection. Her eyes were swollen and raw, and the infection was so bad, as it dried, it stuck her eyes shut. According to her parents, Charity had been unable to see for the past three days.

Charity was four, but she had the fortitude of a woman of forty as she sat with her jaw clenched and her hands doubled into fists as Angus and Mildred had tried to soften the crust on her eyes with wet cloths. Every now and then she would whimper, but it was the only sign she had given that she was in pain.

It had taken both him and Mildred over an hour to get the crusted infection cleaned from her eyes so they would open and another thirty minutes to convince her father, Homer Talmadge, that unless and until they practiced better bodily hygiene, she might get well, but she wouldn't stay that way.

Finally, he'd escaped into his office to compound a medicine for Charity's eyes. The sound of the mortar and pestle with which he worked was a comforting sound. To Angus, it signified healing. He glanced at Alice, who was asleep on a cot in the next room. If only he could concoct a salve that could heal a broken heart.

A knock on the door distracted his thoughts. He looked up as Mildred came into the room.

"Angus...are you finished?"

"Almost," he said.

Mildred glanced over her shoulder, then whispered, "Please hurry. I don't think I can bear the smell of that family any longer."

Angus grimaced.

"Sorry," he said and quickly finished the preparations, then followed her back into the examining room.

"Mrs. Talmadge, watch how I apply this to your daughter's eyes. You will need to do this three times a day until the salve is all gone. If Charity has a recurrence of the infection, bring her back in immediately."

Vera Talmadge glanced nervously at her husband, then ducked her head.

"Reckon this'll cure her right up. We cain't afford no doctorin' bills."

Angus glared at both Vera and her husband. "I have yet to charge you a penny, so don't use that excuse on me again. Your daughter's disease and suffering is a direct result of living in filth. I'm assuming you have access to water."

His sarcasm was unusual, but he'd seen his share of children's suffering today and was in no mood to mince words.

"Well, yes sir, we live right next to Cherry Creek and—"

"Then use that water for something besides drinking and panning. Bathe, woman. Clean this child's body and clean her eyes. Apply the salve as I've shown you or as sure as I'm standing here before you, she'll go blind. Then one day you'll be saddled with a grown woman, who will not only be unable to take care of herself, but will most likely never marry. You'll be stuck with her for the rest of your lives."

Homer Talmadge's mouth gaped. He stared at his little girl as if she'd just grown horns.

Mildred hid a giggle. It was obvious that Angus had struck a nerve.

"We'll see to her bathin'," Vera promised.

Angus handed her the tin in which he'd put the salve. "Don't forget to doctor her. Three times a day."

"Yes, sir," Vera said, then took Charity into her arms and started out the door.

Homer Talmadge followed without comment.

Mildred rolled her eyes as she fanned the air with her apron.

"Such a stench," she muttered.

"Poor child," Angus said.

Mildred looked at Angus, then grinned.

"They may not bathe themselves, but I warrant they'll bathe the child. It was real obvious that they don't want to be stuck with an old maid."

Angus grunted as he went back into his office to clean up, while Mildred went to check on Alice.

At the same time, Eulis and Letty were pulling into the yard of their new home, while T-Bone did a quick reconnoiter in the woods, barking happily to be out of town.

George Mellin was lying on his cot in the jail, bemoaning his condition and his fate, which had yet to be decided by a judge who would not arrive for at least another month. He was a miserable two hundred and seventy-five pound man, trying to figure out where he'd gone wrong.

Alice Mellin chose to remain in the shadow land of opiate sleep and had turned her face to the wall.

Paddy O'Brien, down at the livery stable, was measuring and sawing up green lumber for baby Mary's final bed, while a young man of sixteen had volunteered to dig the grave in return for a meal.

Within an hour, the sun would set and a good portion of the citizens of Denver City would go to bed. What had happened today would be nothing but gossip to be told and forgotten.

As night drew near, the sky darkened and the stars disappeared. By midnight, it had begun to rain.

* * *

The roof on the new Potter home was solid. If it had been going to leak, they would have known it by now. When it had begun to rain, they'd moved their bedrolls from beneath the wagon to inside the house and had settled in the middle of the big room, thankful to be dry.

T-Bone had, as usual, chosen a corner of the room in which to sleep.

Letty lay on her side with her face to the windows. The dampness in the air was chilling, as was the constant clash of rolling thunder and lightning flashing through the sky. As storms go, it was magnificent, but not one to be caught out in.

Eulis had thrown his arm across Letty's waist as he slept and was snoring lightly near the back of her head, but she didn't mind. Despite their discomfort and lack of amenities, this felt right. It was their first night in their new home. The first, she hoped, of many.

The rhythm of the raindrops falling on the roof above their heads finally lulled her into a deep, dreamless sleep, while down in Denver City, Cherry Creek, fed from numerous mountain streams above the town, continued to rise.

* * *

Robert and Mary Whiteside had cooked salt pork and johnnycake for their evening meal. Mary had washed up their tin plates and spoons near the spot where they'd been panning only hours before. Then she'd taken her hair down, undone the long braid she wore like a crown upon her head, and washed it clean in the water of Cherry Creek.

Robert sat nearby, teasing her about wearing gold dust in her hair. They'd laughed easily then. They had found some good color today and their bellies were full. A few more months of this life and they would have enough to buy some land—maybe in California, where they had heard the weather was mild all year long.

By the time the thunderstorm hit, they'd been asleep for hours. The thunder woke Robert, who got up to take a pee and check their campsite. It was sprinkling a bit as he made the rounds of the camp, but when the rain began to fall in earnest, he made a run back into the tent and crawled into his bedroll. Even though winter was gone from the mountains, a rainy night at this elevation was always cold. Mary roused as he pulled the covers up around his chin.

"Everything all right?" she asked.

"I reckon so," Robert said. "Go back to sleep."

Confident that Robert knew what he was talking about, Mary settled easily and was soon back asleep, but Robert wasn't as convinced he'd been right. Through flashes of lightning, he'd seen the rushing water in Cherry Creek, and lying there inside the tent, he could hear the continuing roar of wind and water.

He thought about the bags of gold dust and nuggets they'd buried beneath his bedroll and thought about the tools he'd stacked beneath some trees north of where they were sleeping. If that water kept rising, they might need to move to higher ground, in which case, that meant digging up their gold.

Mary was already snoring. He hated to wake her up, but he also didn't want to make the mistake of waiting to move until it was too late. They'd worked too hard and too long to take a chance on losing it now.

A hard gust of wind pushed at the tent fabric. Robert thought he could hear the squeak of protest from the tent stakes. At forty-nine years old and sporting a bad knee, he wasn't as fast as he once was, so he stayed beneath the relative safety of the tent, unwilling to go out into the storm unless it was absolutely necessary.

The storm rose in intensity, and as it did, the thunder was so loud it sounded as if it were right on top of them. The lightning that flashed afterward was so close it lit up the inside of the tent. When it did, Robert saw something that made the hair rise on the back of his neck.

Water was coming into the tent, and from the creek side of their camp. He grabbed his wife roughly and shook her awake.

"Mary! Get up! Get up! Water is comin' into the tent."

Mary Whiteside rolled to her knees before her eyes had time to open and began throwing their meager belongings into the bedrolls and rolling them up. When she reached for Robert's bedroll, she remembered the gold.

"Robert! Get a shovel and dig up the gold or we'll lose it sure as shootin'."

Robert bounded out of the tent and made his way in the darkness, stumbling twice and falling once before he found the cache with their tools. He felt around in the darkness for the shovel, and when he felt the spoon-shaped metal beneath his fingers, breathed a quick sigh of relief. Now, all he had to do was find his way back to the tent.

At that moment, another flash of lightning illuminated the sky long enough for him to get his bearings. He saw

Mary running out of the tent toward higher ground. She was screaming his name.

"I'm here! I'm here!" Robert called. "Keep going. I'll be right behind you."

Rainfall was so heavy Robert found it difficult to breathe without inhaling water. Covering his face with his arm, he made for the tent, then fell over it in the dark. By the time he got to his feet, the tent had fallen in, and he wasted precious moments pulling it aside so he could dig. He hadn't expected it to be difficult. There were only a few inches of dirt over the box, but he'd become disoriented. Every time he lifted a shovel full of dirt from the ground, the hole filled up with water so fast he couldn't tell where he'd been digging.

Panic began to set in as he toyed with the idea of having to abandon the dig to save himself. The water of Cherry Creek was completely out of its banks now, and more than once, he'd been staggered by the swift, unexpected power of the flow.

Just when he thought it was over, Mary appeared at his elbow.

"Leave it!" she screamed, grabbing his arm.

"Our gold! Our gold! I can't leave our gold!" he yelled and turned to thrust the shovel back into the dirt, only to have the water sweep it out of his hands.

Lightning struck a tree near where they'd built their campfire only hours earlier. The sudden smell of sulphur was strong, despite the pouring rain.

Robert gasped and started to dive for the shovel when Mary yanked him around and slapped him hard on the side of the face.

"Run, you fool! Run with me now before it's too late!"

Robert grabbed her by the hand and, together, they managed to stagger out of the rising water.

"This way!" Mary cried.

Robert held on to her, fearing that if he didn't, he would lose her the same way he'd lost their gold.

They ran and ran, climbing up as they went until they'd reached ground high enough to escape the rushing flow of Cherry Creek, then they collapsed beneath an outcropping of rock. Huddled together, with their sodden bedrolls at their feet, they held hands and prayed.

Hours passed, and so did the storm, although the rain continued to fall. They were forced to move twice more before morning. When daylight finally came, it was gray and gloomy and a mirror of unseen terrors they'd escaped.

Their campsite was gone—buried beneath a good six feet of roiling water. God only knew how their box of gold fared. And there was another horror they had yet to face. When the water went down, more than likely, their claims would be worthless. Whatever pockets of gold Cherry Creek had been hiding were long gone, buried in silt and mud, miles and miles downstream.

The Whitesides could take comfort in being alive, but little else. It would be several hours before they ventured out long enough to realize they were not the only miners to suffer the same crushing blow. Every man, woman, and boy that had laid claim along Cherry Creek had been wiped out.

Faced with the devastation of their losses, they still had to deal with the rain that continued to fall.

5

rich man, poor man, beggar man, thief, doctor, LAWYER

It had been raining off and on for days, and even when the rain would cease, the sun refused to shine. Cherry Creek was still out of its banks, and every building south of main street had been evacuated.

Dr. Warren and his wife had been forced to leave their home and set up a makeshift office inside a tent north of the livery stable, with a second one he and Mildred were using as a place to sleep. But their forced evacuation had, once again, left Alice Mellin homeless. Her broken ribs were healing. Dr. Warren had told her to come back in a week, and he'd remove the stitches from her other cuts. He didn't know about Alice's predicament when she'd walked away, and she was too ashamed to tell him.

The grave that had been dug for her baby was full of mud and water, and the coffin with little Mary's body was in the loft of the livery stable, waiting for the flood to subside before she could be buried.

Unknown to the owner of the livery stable, Alice had spent the night in the loft, sleeping next to the little box that held her baby's body. She was feverish and hungry and about as desperate as a woman could be.

She'd tried to go back to her room in the hotel, only to find out her meager belongings had been confiscated for money owed on their bill. With George in jail and no place to live, Alice was afraid. She had tried to find work, but the hotel already had a cook, and there were only two other places in Denver City that served food. One was run by a China man, who did his own cooking, and the other was the saloon where, on occasion, the bartender could be talked into serving some bread and meat. None of it was fancy, and none of it required the hands of an extra employee.

She didn't mind scrubbing and mending and thought about taking in laundry. But that required money and a place to live, which once again, she was sadly lacking. There was only one other thing she knew how to do that might earn her some money, but she was going to have to heal up some first. She thought about how she'd turned up her nose at the woman in the hotel who'd had a room across the hall. She'd been selling herself to men for money. Alice was beginning to understand why.

And, she wasn't the only person suffering from being displaced.

The flood had caught a lot of people besides the Whitesides unprepared. Some of the people searching for their own bit of gilded heaven had gone the same route as Letty and Eulis, by tunneling into the surrounding peaks of the Rocky Mountains. Those were unaffected by the Cherry Creek flood or the recurring downpours. But a good portion of the prospectors—men, women, and even some with children—had been panning, which meant they'd been residing in tents on their claims near the creek. Now, they were all afoot, without shelter to be had, and the small bags of dust and nuggets they had with them were being swiftly depleted.

Despite Dr. Warren's temporary location, he was doing a booming business. People had sores and foot rot from walking around in wet shoes all day, and children were coming down with coughing spells that turned into pneumonia.

Denver City had been a place of chaos since the first gold strike had been announced, but this latest event had caused a different kind of chaos. Last winter's smallpox epidemic had been a tragedy. The flood was causing a different kind of disaster, but in a way, winding up with the same results. People were dead. A few more would end up the same way, and those who survived would never be the same.

* * *

Letty's new house smelled of freshly sawed wood and dampness. But the fire she'd built in the parlor fireplace was taking the chill out of the air, as well as providing her with a place to cook their food. Eulis had intended it to be a focal point of the room—a grand edifice that would impress their guests and give them comfort through the long winters. The opening was six feet wide with natural rock facing the mantle and wall all the way to the ceiling. The hearth extended more than six feet into the room, providing a safe boundary for any escaping sparks or embers. It had not been intended for cooking, but Letty was a practical woman. Her new cook stove was en route somewhere between Denver City and Boston. She would make do with what she had and be thankful.

She'd put a pot of stew on to cook less than an hour ago. It would be a few more hours before it would be done. She would have loved to ride out to the mine and check on Eulis and the men, maybe take Robert Lee some fresh supplies, but if she rode off and left the food unattended, most likely the fire would go out or the food would burn. So, she was stuck in a house full of empty rooms with memories yet to be born.

Frustrated, she walked out onto the front porch. T-Bone was lying near the front steps. He looked up and wagged his tail when he saw her.

"Hey, puppy," Letty said and sat down on the steps, absently scratching behind the pup's ear as she looked into the valley.

The tents of Denver City looked like so many toadstools, and the people moving about on the streets were hardly larger than ants. Still, she could see enough to know people were in a bad way. She hadn't been back to town since they'd left the hotel, although Eulis came and went with some regularity. Because of the rains, they'd temporarily stopped hauling to the smelter. After they'd spent most of a day digging the last ore wagon out of the mud, Eulis had stopped hauling all together. They'd taken the downtime to shore up some braces inside the mine and replace a few others.

Weather had little affect on their work, but it had brought Letty's plans to a halt. Cooking one meal a day was hardly what she called work, and she'd been taking care of herself for so long being idle didn't set all well with her.

She got up and went back into the house to stir the stew, added a couple of sticks of wood to the fire, then went back outside. T-Bone whined as she resumed her seat on the porch, but she didn't respond. Ever since she'd held that dying baby in her arms, she'd had a feeling she'd left something undone.

And while she was struggling with new emotions and a whole new way of life, Robert Lee was also changing. He'd gained some weight and followed Eulis's lead by shaving nearly every day. He'd gotten a hair cut and some new clothes with his first pay. For the first time in years, he felt good about life.

And there was also the fact he had fallen in love with Letty.

He'd admired her from the first day they'd met, when she'd calmly announced the fate of men who tried to cross her husband. But after she'd taken a bullwhip to the man who'd beaten his wife, he'd been in awe. In his eyes, she could do no wrong. She was what God meant a woman to be—beautiful, strong, and faithful. No one knew how he felt, and he would have died before admitting it. He knew she was devoted to Eulis, and he admired the man tremendously. Anyone who'd gone from the drunk he remembered in Lizard Flats to this stoic, hard-working man demanded respect. Still, it was Letty who held his heart.

* * *

It was a little past noon when it began to drizzle again. Letty's stew was finally cooked, and she'd taken it off the fire and set it aside. It wouldn't take long to warm it up when Eulis got home. She wanted to make some bread to go with it, but she was out of flour and cornmeal. Despite the weather, she decided to saddle up her horse and ride down into Denver City. She might get some of that fabric she'd been admiring at the general store. She didn't need furniture to make curtains, and it would be something to do.

She dug an old poncho out of the trunk and pulled it over her head, then grabbed her hat on the way out the door. T-Bone was sitting in the rain beside the saddled horse, making sure she couldn't slip away without him. As soon as she stepped off the porch, the rain blew into her face. She settled her hat a little firmer on her head as she mounted. Even though she was soon soaked to the skin, it felt good to be outside and moving. The trail into town was sloped and winding, but it was solid and, in some places, sheltered by the trees. It seemed like no time before she was riding into town.

Shock came quickly.

The roar of rushing water from Cherry Creek was plainly audible and the number of displaced people was obvious. They huddled anywhere there was shelter. Their misery was reflected in the gloomy looks they cast her way.

She ducked her head and kept on riding until she got to the general store. She dismounted in ankle deep mud, and when she tried to walk, struggled to stay in her boots.

"Here ma'am, take my hand," a man said, and she did, thankful when he pulled her up and onto the narrow wooden sidewalk.

"Thank you," she said, venturing a quick look at his face. He was a stranger to her and from the cut of his clothes, probably a gambler—certainly not a miner. However, a gold camp brought in all sorts of people hoping to capitalize on the gold dust and money rolling around.

She stomped as much of the mud from her boots as she could before entering the general store, only to find it so packed with people she could hardly move about.

She nodded to some of the women she recognized, and then kept moving toward the counter to where Milton Feasley was standing.

When he saw her coming through the crowd, he beamed. At last, a paying customer.

"Howdy, Miz Potter. How can I help you today?"

Letty nodded at the store owner, and as she did, the image of Vern Goslin popped into her head. Vern had owned the general store back in Lizard Flats and was the exact opposite of Milton in every way possible. Vern had been the human equivalent of a grizzly bear and smelled worse than the buffalo skins he was so fond of wearing. Still, he'd been kind to her when nearly everyone else had judged and found her wanting. She wondered how Milton would behave if he knew what she'd been in the past, then figured from the glitter in his eyes he wouldn't care as long as she could pay.

"I'm needing some flour or cornmeal," she said. "Can't cook a proper meal for my husband without fixing him some bread."

Milton nodded. He was partial to bread, himself.

"Yes, ma'am, but it'll have to be cornmeal. I'm plumb out of flour until the next freighter comes through."

"That's fine," Letty said.

"...oughta' be ashamed."

The words drifted over the murmur of voices from the crowd gathered inside the store. She knew they were talking about her. God only knew how many times she'd been judged before and found wanting. It shouldn't have mattered. But it did.

She turned away from the counter and moved toward a table where Milton had displayed about a dozen bolts of fabric. Letty had seen them plenty of times before, and had made up her mind as to the pieces she wanted for curtains.

Milton followed her to the table.

"Will you be needing some fabric today, Miz Potter?"

"Yes." She pointed to a couple of different patterns. "I'd like ten yards each of those two."

"...showin' off cause she's rich."

Milton glanced nervously at Letty, well aware she'd heard that comment, too. He'd expected to see tears, or at the least, a show of emotion. He was wrong.

Letty lifted her chin and turned abruptly, catching the women who were talking about her before they could look away. Startled by the confrontational look on her face, the women found themselves under scrutiny, as well.

Letty stared at each one as if she'd never seen such a specimen before, eyeing them from head to toe, taking in the sodden state of their clothing as well as their raw, chafed hands and faces. They had to be miserable. They didn't have to be rude.

"Mr. Feasley, I'd be obliged if you'd go ahead and cut off those lengths for me. I'll be right over to pick them up."

"Yes, ma'am," he said quickly and took the bolts to another counter to measure off and cut.

Letty pushed her hat to the back of her head and then sauntered toward the women. The room grew quiet. The women who'd been hiding behind the anonymity of the crowd were suddenly singled out by Letty's stare. With her between them and the door, they had no where left to run and were forced to stand their ground.

"Ladies," Letty said. "Real miserable weather we've been having, isn't it?"

One of them started to speak, but another woman, somewhat older and definitely more aggressive, elbowed her, then frowned.

Letty grinned, then changed tactics.

"I'm sorry. I just assumed you could speak English. Obviously, that's my mistake. I knew there were a lot of foreigners who'd come chasing gold, but I guess I didn't realize how many."

Two of them fidgeted. Letty could tell they wanted to answer her, but the big one was obviously in charge, and she wasn't talking.

Letty peered at the woman, then took a step closer and raised her voice to just below a shout.

"Maybe you just can't hear me good. That would be my mistake, too. Lots of people are hard of hearing. There's no sin in that. I suppose I should have spoken up. I said...real miserable weather we're having, isn't it?"

Someone snickered in the back of the room. Letty heard it but never broke her stare. It was past being a matter of pride.

The big woman lifted her chin and stared down her nose at Letty, as if she were looking at a bug.

Letty looked around at the people who were staring and shrugged.

"Any of you people speak their language?"

No one spoke up, although a couple of men standing nearby grinned.

"Too bad," Letty said. "Someone needs to tell that big woman in the middle there's a dried-up booger hanging out of her nose. With her being taller than just about everyone in the room, it's a right scary thing to be looking at."

The woman gasped and reached for her nose as the crowd erupted into laughter. When she felt the offending bit of offal hanging from her nose, she turned a bright shade of red.

Letty, however, was done with the drama and turned toward Feasley, who was waiting with a sack of cornmeal and her fabric.

"Reckon I'll be needing a packet of needles and some thread, too."

"Yes, ma'am, got 'em right here. I'll send the bill to the bank as usual. Will that be all right, Miz Potter?"

"That'll be fine," she said and gathered up her purchases, dropped them into an oilskin bag, and headed out the door.

The crowd parted to let her pass and then closed up behind her.

Letty tied the bag behind her saddle, and then with monumental effort, managed to mount by herself despite standing in the mire.

She struggled with a sigh of defeat as she rode away from the store and told herself she didn't care. She was halfway out of town when she happened to glance toward one of the saloons. Through the doorway, she saw a room full of men availing themselves of the amenities offered, as well as the women who were part of the deal. Thankful she was no longer a part of that life, she started to look away, when a familiar face caught her eye.

Alice Mellin was standing near the doorway and looking in at the crowd. Her shoulders were slumped, and Letty could tell she was trembling. Her features were gaunt and the dress hanging on her body was soaked clean through. She had no coat, no jacket, no extra clothing of any kind to protect her from the chill of the rain. At that moment, a knowing shot through Letty that caused her actual pain.

Alice Mellin was on her last leg. Either she gave up her dignity and walked through those doors, or she was going to die.

At that moment, Letty pulled her horse to a stop, then turned it toward the saloon. She had the means to stop this woman's step into hell and knew she would never be able to face herself again if she looked away.

She rode up to the saloon, dismounted into the mud once again, and tied her horse to the hitching rail. As she stepped up onto the wooden sidewalk, her steps were somewhat muted by the rain.

"Alice."

At the sound of someone calling her name, Alice Mellin jumped. Whitewashed with guilt, she looked up to, once again, find herself face to face with Letty Potter.

"It's you."

Letty sighed. "Yeah, last time I looked I was still me. What about yourself?"

The pallor of Alice's skin turned even paler.

"I'm...uh...."

Letty sighed, then pointed to her horse.

"Can you ride?"

Alice looked startled. "I guess, but—"

"You interested in spending the rest of your life spreading your legs for those bastards inside?"

Alice froze, too shocked by the question to answer.

"Well? It's what you're thinking about, isn't it?"

"You don't understand," Alice finally said.

Letty laughed, but it was not a happy sound.

"Oh, I understand, all right. More than you will ever know. Now. Are you going through that door or getting on that horse with me?"

Alice looked at Letty as if she'd lost her mind.

"I don't know what you're talking about."

"Can you cook?" Letty asked.

Alice nodded.

"Are you good at it?"

"Some say I am," Alice said.

"Then come with me," Letty said softly and held out her hand.

It was the first step that was the hardest. After that, Alice moved rather quickly. It took some doing to get Alice and her sodden skirts mounted. Letty swung up behind her, settling herself behind the saddle, then took the reins.

"Just hold onto the saddle horn," she said. "We'll be home before you know it."

Alice didn't know what she was getting in to, but it was the word 'home' that settled her indecision. Even if the home wasn't hers, it was a better place to be than where she'd been heading.

6

rich man, poor man, beggar man, thief, doctor, lawyer, AND ONE SORRY ASS JUDGE

Eulis thought he'd gone beyond being surprised by anything Letty did these days. But when he got home from the mine and found a strange woman stirring stew in his parlor, he was more than a bit taken aback. That the woman looked like she'd been beaten to hell and back was of minor consequence to the reason for her presence.

"Ma'am," he said and quickly yanked off his hat, then started through the house, calling Letty's name.

Letty appeared at the top of the stairs with an armful of quilts.

"I'm up here," she said.

Eulis took the stairs two at a time, then took Letty by the elbow.

"There's a woman stirring stew down in the parlor."

"That's Alice," Letty said and spread one of the quilts on the floor.

Eulis blinked. “Oh. Then that explains her face.”

Letty nodded. “Her poor body doesn’t look any better.” Then she frowned. “I don’t think it’s proper to talk about a woman’s body to a man, so forget I just said that, okay?”

Eulis wasn’t about to comment regarding female body parts.

“What’s she doin’ in our house?” he asked.

“I hired her to cook.”

Eulis frowned.

“I like your cookin’ just fine.”

Letty kept fussing with the quilts because it was easier than explaining the real truth to herself and to Eulis.

“She didn’t have anywhere else to go,” she finally said.

“What do you mean?” Eulis asked.

Letty dropped the rest of the quilts, then lowered her voice.

“She was standing outside the door of one of the saloons in town. I couldn’t make myself ignore what that meant.”

“Oh.” Eulis laid a hand against Letty’s cheek. “You keep that secret of yours pretty good, you know.”

“What secret?” Letty asked.

“That one about your heart bein’ all soft and gentle.”

“You aren’t mad are you?”

Eulis grinned.

“No, but I have yet to see that matter when you’ve made up your mind.”

Letty grinned back.

“It will be all right. There’s plenty of room here for her, and it won’t be forever. Just until she heals up good and can find some direction in her life.”

“It don’t matter,” Eulis said. “If it makes you happy, it makes me happy, too.”

Letty stilled. The honesty in her husband’s voice humbled her. If she let herself think back to all the times in their past that she’d been downright mean to Eulis Potter, she would never be able to face him again.

“There are times when I think I don’t deserve you,” she said quietly.

Eulis smiled, and as he did, his love for her was so strong it made his well-worn face almost handsome.

"Well now, reckon that might get me a second helpin' on the stew cooking downstairs?"

Letty threw her arms around him and kissed him soundly.

"Seconds on the stew *and* the dried apple cobbler Alice said she was making."

Eulis rolled his eyes.

"I'm in heaven."

A gust of wind rattled the windows.

Letty turned toward the sound, then wrapped her arms around herself, stifling a shudder as a fresh wave of rain began to fall.

"Lord in heaven, I wish this rain would stop."

Eulis nodded, then added. "They might have to move the gold out of the bank."

Letty gasped and turned abruptly. "Where to?"

"Don't know, but if that water gets any closer to the bank, they won't have much choice."

"Well, that's not good," Letty muttered. "There has to be something we can do."

Eulis shrugged. "Last time I checked, God was still in charge of the weather. There ain't nothin' we *can* do."

"We'll see," Letty said. "Meanwhile, come help me lay down these quilts."

Eulis picked them up and followed Letty into an empty room down the hall.

"What are we doin' here?" he asked, as he spread them to her satisfaction.

"We're making a bed for Alice."

"Oh. Right."

They laid one down, then another to the side for covers.

"I wish the things we ordered would hurry up and come," Letty said, as she continued to fuss with the quilts. "Can't even make a proper bed up here."

"Honey, I don't reckon as how your Alice will be too worried about the lack of a pillow...not after you as good as saved her from a fate worse than death."

Letty sighed, then walked back to the window. The view from the second floor of their home was grand—even though they were looking at it through a downpour.

"Eulis?"

"Yeah?"

"Remember how flat the land was back in the Kansas territories?"

"I reckon I do."

"I was always afraid of it."

Eulis turned to her. Surprise was evident on his face.

"I didn't know that. In fact, I don't reckon I ever saw you afraid of anything...except that day the preacher from back East died in your bed and you passed me off as the man they'd all been waitin' to see."

She shuddered. "Lord. Don't remind me. I thought I was a goner, for sure."

"So, why did the flat land scare you, girl?"

"I don't know...maybe because it appeared there was nothing to hold on to. You know how it got when the wind blew. It just went on forever. And in the winter... when it snowed...it blew and blew without anything to stop it. I guess I was afraid I'd blow away, too."

"You got too much grit to be all flighty," Eulis said.

Letty shrugged. "Still...I like the way these mountains make me feel. Sort of like I'm being cradled in big, strong arms. You know?"

Eulis tugged at her hair, then gave her a big hug.

"I reckon I'd just as soon keep you in my arms, if it's all the same to you."

Letty smiled.

"You don't have to politic me any more. You're already getting your second helpings."

Eulis shook his head.

"Honey, with you it ain't ever politicin'... just the plain, honest to God, truth."

"So, let's go eat," Letty said.

"I thought you'd never ask," Eulis said and followed her out of the bedroom and down the stairs.

* * *

Alice didn't know what to make of Letty Potter, but she was grateful for the job and the shelter. It was shame enough that everyone knew her husband's weaknesses. To have him jailed was even worse. But it was her little baby that was breaking her heart. Their time together had been far too brief, and not being able to lay her to rest was weighing heavy on her mind. If only this terrible rain would stop—at least long enough for them to be able to put her baby in the ground—she'd feel better.

A burning ember popped as Alice bent over to stir the stew. A drop of the savory liquid sloshed over the side of the iron pot and into the fire, hissing briefly before it dried.

The cast iron pot in which she'd baked the apple cobbler was sitting at the edge of the fire to keep it warm, and her biscuits were just about done, but Alice felt faint. She hadn't done this much physical work in a long time and was still weak from her injuries. But she wasn't complaining. Far from it. She had a safe, dry place to sleep and food to eat. For now, it was all she could ask for.

"Somethin' sure smells good."

The man's compliment was unexpected. Alice ducked her head as the Potters came down the stairs.

"Yes, sir. Thank you, sir," Alice said. "But I can't take credit for the stew. Your wife already had that finished before I got here."

"Well, we're proud to have you," Eulis said.

Alice ducked her head again. "It's I who owe you. I was desperate. Your wife's offer was an answer to a prayer."

Eulis glanced at Letty and winked—a reminder to each other of their time together on the Amen Trail, when he'd been a practicing preacher and she, a devoted, but somewhat controlling, companion.

"Is the cookin' done?" Eulis asked.

Alice nodded.

"Then let's eat," he said. "My belly's been complainin' for hours."

Alice looked startled. They were behaving as if she would be having her meal with them. That couldn't be right. Surely, she'd misunderstood. Then Letty handed her a plate.

"Here," Letty said. "You did most of the work so you should get the first dip."

"But I'm just the hired—"

"Let's get something straight right now," Letty said, frowning. "There is no "just" in this house. Get yourself some stew and quit fussing. Maybe by next week we'll have us a table and some chairs, but for now, we're sitting on the floor."

Alice took the plate, then bit her lip to keep from weeping.

"The last three nights, I slept in the stable. From where I'm standing, this is a drastic improvement, and I thank you for it."

"You're welcome," Letty said. "Get yourself a biscuit to go with that stew and step aside before Eulis slobbers all over your shoulder."

Eulis blushed.

Alice grinned, then winced from the use of still-healing, facial muscles. Still, she added a biscuit to her plate and eased her bruised and battered body down until she was leaning against a wall.

T-Bone had been sleeping in another room, but obviously heard the clank of spoon to tin plate and came to check things out. Letty caught movement from the corner of her eye and frowned.

"I already fed you," she said.

The pup whined.

"And you stink," she added.

T-Bone sat down in the doorway, unaffected by her criticism.

"There's a bone in this stew here. I'll dig it out and give it to him," Eulis said.

"It'll be too hot," Letty said.

Eulis grinned. "Well then, he can sit and look at it while it cools."

Alice eyed the pair, as well as the rangy pup, and took another bite of her stew, thinking to herself as she ate that these people were unlike any she'd ever known. As for the pup, she remembered it from the alleys down in Denver City. They obviously adopted more than displaced people. She didn't know how this was going to work out, but for now, she was profoundly grateful.

* * *

George Mellin could see the rising water from the window of his cell. Every night when he lay down on the cot, he couldn't help wondering if he'd be alive in the morning, or if he'd just drown in bed. He couldn't believe his life had come to this. If he had it to do over again, he would never have married Alice or fathered their child, although the child was no longer an issue. He wondered a bit about the fact he felt no sadness for her passing but didn't dwell on it. This was a harsh land and no place for the weak. It was simply a case of survival of the fittest.

Still, it seemed he was going to have to face a judge for the disagreements he and Alice had been having. He didn't consider it anybody's business but their own, but obviously some did. The some—mostly being that bitch, Letty Potter. If she'd minded her own business, none of this would have happened. Oh, the kid would have died. Nothing could have prevented that. But at least, he and Alice would have been back to where they started, which might not have been all bad. They wouldn't have been fighting over dragging that weakling to a doctor—as if they'd had the money for such foolishness. It's what he got for marrying someone from back East. Those big cities didn't produce women used to hardships. He should have picked himself a woman who'd been born and raised in the territories. They knew how to make do with little to nothing.

Now, because of the choices he'd made, he was stuck in this cell, waiting for some stranger to make the decision as to how the rest of his life would go—and all because of Letty Potter's meddling. When he got out, he was going to pay her back in a big way.

* * *

As a young man, Joshua Dean had studied law back in Virginia and had been practicing law for the past twenty years in Atlanta—up until the last six months. But there were rumblings going on in the southern states that had not set well with him. His life had been based on interpreting the Constitution of the United States of America and the laws of the land. And, because of his background, he was struggling with the current mood of his fellow Southerners.

The suggestion from the Northern States that slavery should be outlawed had set the emotions of the South on fire. It challenged and threatened their livelihood in a way they could not ignore. There was no way the big landowners could operate their vast plantations without slave labor, and the Southerners were of the opinion that the Northern states had no business trying to regulate or change their way of life.

The Honorable Joshua Dean knew that if the rumblings actually came to fruition and the southern states seceded from the Union as they were threatening to do, he would not be able to stay true to himself and still reside in the place where he'd been born.

Joshua Dean was a man born ahead of his time—a man who did not believe in the buying and selling of other human beings. He also held to an unpopular theory that the blacks were not lesser beings, but simply a race of people with a different way of living, and just because they'd been sold into slavery should not reflect upon their capacity for learning or being treated fairly.

Because he'd been unable to make a decision as to which side to back, he'd made an unusual choice. He'd opted to remove himself from the discord before he was forced to make a stand.

Going west into the territories had been an option he'd considered, as had taking himself to Europe, possibly England, or France. But he considered the British a cold-mannered nation, and since he didn't speak French, the decision had been made for him. West it was.

He'd been in the territories for just over six months, and the news he got from home convinced him he'd done the right thing. Every day, the southern states came closer and closer to seceding, at which point, he just kept taking himself further west.

He had enough judicial pull to get himself an appointment as a judge and was actually enjoying traveling from one outpost to another, delivering justice whenever it was needed. Of course, he had to accept that, more often than not, the people who populated these places were accustomed to meting out their own brand of justice. Several times, he'd traveled days at great discomfort only to discover the locals had taken the law into their own hands and hanged an offender without due process of the law. In those instances, he'd rendered his disapproval and moved on before he became the next target of their ire.

Such was the case when he received word that a judge was needed in Denver City. He started out with a sense of fatalism. Either he got there before a crowd mentality developed, or he didn't. Considering there was an ongoing gold strike, he could only imagine what might be waiting for his disposition.

* * *

Amos Trueblood, a middle-aged man with the physique of a scarecrow, stood on the back steps of his bank building, absently tracing the part in his thin and graying hair as he watched the rush of flood waters a few hundred yards below. His long, black topcoat and black pants were stained around the hems with mud splatters. His shoes, normally shined, were filthy and rimmed with dried mud. No matter how many times a day he cleaned them, at the end of a day, they were still filthy.

In the early days when he'd first opened for business, he'd worried about many things, including being robbed. But he'd never imagined, on his worst day, he might be ruined by a flood.

He had opened the bank less than two months after the first gold strike had been made in the area. And, in loaning money to first one prospector then another, he'd acquired, by default, more than a dozen claims. While he had no intention of panning for gold, he was more than happy to acquire the land. He had a feeling that, one day, this boom town was going to make it past the gold strike to grow into an honest to God city. When it did, he would be in on the ground floor in development. However, if the flood waters didn't stop rising, he was going to have to rethink his future plans.

Last night when the rain had ceased, he'd hoped today the flood would crest, and then the waters could begin to recede. Instead, it was raining again.

He looked up at the sky, squinting against the rain drops peppering against his face. God only knew how this all would end.

* * *

Letty woke with a start and glanced toward the window as she sat up. It was still raining.

Lord have mercy.

"Eulis."

Eulis woke abruptly.

"Hmm? What? Is ever'thing okay?"

Letty slumped.

"No. It's still raining."

Eulis threw back the covers and sat up, then rubbed the sleep from his eyes as he, too, looked toward the window.

"Yep. So it appears."

"I think we just made a mistake building this house," Letty muttered.

Eulis frowned. "How so, honey?"

"We should have built ourselves an ark, instead."

Eulis grinned. He got the biblical reference quickly.

"Don't worry, we're safe and sound up here."

"I'm not worrying about us. I'm worrying about what's going to happen to the town below. If everything floods, that might mean the end of the gold strike, and if that happens, people will begin leaving. I've seen it before. We'll wind up living in this big old house without another living soul within a hundred miles except critters and Indians."

Eulis lifted an eyebrow. "Well, that's a pretty drastic statement. If I was you, I wouldn't set myself up for Denver City turning into a ghost town just yet. The rain will stop. It has to."

"But the claims along Cherry Creek are ruined."

Eulis nodded. "Yeah. I thought about that myself."

"That could put us in danger," Letty said.

"How so?" Eulis asked.

"Think about it," Letty said. "If you're starving to death and your gold claim just went downstream with the flood, then there will be some who'll look to where gold is still intact. That means people like us. Mining isn't the same as panning. I'm afraid for you."

Eulis leaned over and kissed the top of her head.

"I'll be fine," he said. "Remember, we've got Robert Lee."

"He can't be everywhere at once," Letty muttered.

"Stop fussin'," Eulis said, then sniffed deeply. "I smell coffee brewin'. Seems like our cook might be earnin' her keep."

Letty watched Eulis crawl out of their bedrolls and dress quickly, combing his hair with his fingers as he walked out of the room. He was probably going outside to relieve himself. She needed to go, too, but wasn't in the mood to get soaked. Still, until their furniture arrived with all the accessories that came with it, like slop jars and wash stands, she didn't have any other options.

Muttering to herself as she put on a clean clothes, she opted for her boots, rather than the slippers she liked to wear around the house. No need to get her slippers all wet and muddy. She dug through their trunk until she found a clean shirt to go with yesterday's pants and dressed without fuss. By the time she got downstairs, her stomach was growling from the enticing scents coming from the parlor. If she wasn't mistaken, she smelled frying fatback and hot biscuits.

She paused outside the doorway to the parlor, then peeked in. Alice Mellin was bent over the fireplace, poking at the fire with a poker.

"Morning, Alice," Letty said.

Alice looked up.

"Oh! Good Morning, ma'am. Breakfast is—"

"Not ma'am...Letty...please."

Alice flushed. "Yes, ma—...I mean, Letty."

"Something sure smells good," Letty said.

Alice beamed in spite of herself.

"Thank you. It's ready when you are."

"I'll be right back," Letty said.

Alice nodded, then turned back to her cooking, while Letty made a run for the back door. They'd dug a well and built an outhouse before they'd dug footing for the house, and that was where she headed. At the time, it had seemed reasonable to put it a distance from the back door, but this morning she was doubting the wisdom. Still, no one wanted to be greeted with the scent of an outhouse while enjoying the view. There was nothing to be done but make a run for it. She noticed, as she stepped off the porch, T-Bone was already there, nosing around the door. She hoped a skunk hadn't taken shelter from the weather where she intended to pee.

Water splashed up on the legs of her pants as she ran, while the falling rain dampened her long, curly hair and poured down the back of her neck. By the time she made it to the outhouse, she was soaked. T-Bone was whining and woofed softly as she reached for the door.

"Is it a skunk?" she asked.

The pup didn't have much to say on the subject other than offer up another woof.

Letty rolled her eyes.

"I can't believe I was waiting for an answer," she mumbled as she yanked the door open.

Seconds later, she stifled a scream. A young girl about the age of ten was huddled on the seat. Her stringy, blonde hair was plastered against her head and face, and her sodden clothes clung to her frail, little body.

"Lord have mercy!" Letty squealed. "Where did you come from?"

The little girl started to cry.

"Oh, well, for pity's sake, don't cry," Letty said, then pointed at the two-holer seat. "Scoot over. We'll talk about all of this later."

The little girl stood abruptly and started to run.

Letty grabbed her arm.

"Wait, honey, wait. I just gotta use the facilities. I'm not gonna hurt you."

The little girl turned her face to the wall, giving Letty the privacy she needed.

"Dang it," she muttered as she undid her belt to lower her pants. "I could'a just stood outside in the yard and peed my pants and gotten the same results," she said, as she tried to peel down the wet clothes from her skin.

The wooden seat was cold against her bare backside as she sat. The raindrops echoed inside the small outhouse like bullets against the wood. The scent of human waste, green wood, and nearly a week's worth of rain produced an overwhelming smell. She wondered how long the little girl had been in here and figured she must have been bad off to choose the outhouse instead of coming to the house.

Letty eyed the little girl's thin body as well as the scratches and bruises visible on the back of her neck and frowned as she did her business, then pulled up her pants. The child appeared to be in pretty sad shape.

"You okay?" she asked and laid her hand on the little girl's shoulder.

The child flinched then cowered.

"Not another one," Letty muttered, thinking of Alice, then she patted the child gently on the back and took her by the hand.

"Are you hungry?"

The child hesitated, then nodded without looking up.

"So, let's go find us some breakfast, what do you say?"

The child took a deep breath, then exhaled slowly.

"We won't hurt you," Letty added, then led the child out of the outhouse into the rain. "Let's run," she said but soon found out that wasn't feasible. One of the child's ankles was bruised and swollen. "Oh, honey, I'm sorry. I didn't know you were hurt. Here. Put your arms around my neck, and I'll carry you."

Ignoring the rain running down the back of her shirt, Letty bent down and picked her up. When the little girl's arms curled around her neck, an odd, almost comforting feeling swept through her. She'd never been around kids in her life, and yet this felt so right.

Conscious of the shivering child and the continuing downpour, she hurried as fast as she could toward the house. Halfway there, she looked up to see Eulis coming out the back door. He bolted off the porch and into the rain, coming toward them on the run.

"For the love of God, Leticia...what's happened here?" he asked.

"She was in the outhouse," Letty said. "Her ankle is hurt."

"Here, give her to me," Eulis said and took the child out of Letty's arms before either one could argue. "Get on inside out of the rain," he ordered. "We're right behind you."

Letty could see that the child was beyond caring who had her, just as long as she didn't have to walk. Satisfied that something constructive was being done, she made a run for the porch. Inside the house, she pulled off her muddy boots at the door and ran through the rooms to the parlor where Alice was cooking breakfast.

"Alice! Alice! Go get some dry rags and a quilt. And hurry!"

Alice looked wild-eyed but did as she was told, running upstairs as quickly as she could manage to move. By the time she got back, Eulis was there and kneeling by the fire. At first, she didn't see the child, then when she did, was horrified by her condition.

"Oh, Lordy! What's happened here?" she asked, as she began helping Letty strip the child of her sodden clothes.

Eulis quickly turned away, removed the food from the fireplace, then added another log. The women spread the child's clothes out to dry, then dried her off and wrapped her in the quilt.

"What's her name?" Alice asked.

Letty shrugged. "She won't talk to me."

Alice sat down flat on the floor, then pulled the little girl into her lap and began to rock her in a gentle, comforting way.

"You must be freezing," she said softly, as she pulled the girl close. "I'll bet your mama and papa are near out of their mind, wondering where you've gone. Did you get lost?"

"No."

It was the first word to come out of her mouth, and it startled them all.

"So... what's your name, darling," Alice asked.

The little girl didn't answer but looked at the healing wounds on Alice's face instead.

"Did you fall in the water, too?" the girl asked.

Letty stifled a gasp. This didn't sound good.

"No, honey, but is that what happened to you?" Alice asked.

"Yes."

"Did your mama and daddy fall in the water, too?" Letty asked.

"Uh-huh...and my big brother, Dave."

Eulis squatted down in front of Alice and the child.

"How did you get out of the water?" he asked.

"Dave pushed me onto a log. When the log got caught in some rocks, I climbed off."

"Good girl," Letty murmured.

"Did Dave get out of the water?" Eulis asked.

The little girl hid her face.

"The water swallowed them," she said softly. "It swallowed them all."

"Oh dear," Alice whispered and rocked a little faster.

Letty put her hand on the child. "My name is Letty. What's yours?"

"Katie. My name is Katie Samuels."

Eulis groaned softly.

"Was your papa's name James?"

The answer was barely above a whisper.

"Yes."

"Well. Well then," Eulis said and got up and walked out of the room.

Letty followed.

"Eulis...did you know the family?"

"Yes. They had a claim just below the Cherry Creek crossing. You remember...they had a wagon they slept in instead of tents like most of the others."

"Oh, Lord," Letty said and shivered suddenly.

Eulis frowned. "Go change your clothes before you get sick."

"Does she have any other family?" Letty asked.

"Not that I know of," Eulis said.

Letty straightened her shoulders, then set her jaw.

"You need to go tell those men who are building our cots to build another one and make it quick. We can't have that child sleeping on the floor. And if there are any more blankets to be had at the general store, get some."

Eulis arched an eyebrow.

"Reckon we oughta put out the word that we're takin' in strays?"

Letty turned on him, her eyes flashing angrily.

"What would you have me do...turn her back out in the rain?"

Eulis sighed. "Course not. I was just tryin' to make a joke that wasn't all that funny. Sorry."

"Have Alice cook up some more food. I'll be down as soon as I change."

She strode out of the room with her head high and leading with her chin.

Eulis watched her go and stifled another sigh. There was one thing for sure—living with Letty kept life interesting.

7

rich man, poor man, beggar man, thief, doctor, lawyer, MERCHANT

Milton Feasley had measured up the last of his coffee and flour into one pound sacks and was stacking them on the shelves. A pound of coffee could last a family a good while if they used the grounds more than once, which most of them did. But a pound of flour could be used up in one baking. Still, it was the only way he knew how to fairly distribute the stores he had left. Once these sold, he and everyone else in Denver City would be doing without until the next freight wagon got through. If this infernal rain didn't stop, the citizens of Denver City were going to be giving him a hard time.

He picked up a feather duster, although dust on his goods was the last of his worries. What with the rain they'd been having, it would more likely be mold and not dust gathering on his shelves.

The bell jingled over the door, signaling the arrival of a customer. Milton laid the feather duster aside as he recognized the man coming in, but it was what he saw through the window that brightened his day.

The stagecoach was pulling into town, which meant that if it could get through, then so would the freight wagons. One was due in tomorrow. It seemed he had worried all for nothing. However, the customer who'd come in was obviously nervous. When Milton saw him take off his hat and then shuffle his feet, he knew what was coming. Carl was probably going to ask for credit. These days, it seemed he took in far less money for the goods that went out.

"Howdy, Carl, what can I do for you, today?"

Carl Mithers was a small man with thin, red hair and dark hollow eyes. Like most of the other residents of Denver City, he'd come hoping to find his fortune. Instead, he'd found hardship and hunger even more severe than what had driven him out of Ireland.

"I'll be needin' a few things today."

"Yeah, like what?" Milton asked.

"Some coffee and some flour...and maybe some of yer fine beans."

"Got any color?" Milton asked.

Carl ducked his head. "I lost me poke in the flood, I did, and was hopin' ye'd stand me for some credit...just 'til the rains be lettin' up, ye understand."

"Your claim is washed out and you know it," Milton said.

Carl shook his head. "No, no, tisn't true. I'm not one of those pannin' fer color, I'm not. It's just that me claim is on t'other side of the creek."

This was news to Milton. It changed his attitude enough to give Carl a chance.

"I see. Well then, I reckon we'll give it a try. Just don't let your debt get bigger than you can handle."

"Yes, sir. I'm thankin' you kindly, sir," Carl said.

Milton went about filling the man's order, while the occupants of the stagecoach were unloading.

One passenger in particular, a dandy by the name of Judge Joshua Dean, stepped out of the coach to find himself instantly ankle deep in the mud of Denver City's main street.

* * *

The stench of fresh horse manure wafted up Judge Dean's nostrils as his first foot sank into the mud. He cursed beneath his breath as his other foot sank even deeper.

"Hey, mister, here's your bag!"

He looked up just as the driver tossed his satchel down from the top of the coach, then staggered as he was forced to catch it, himself.

Muttering beneath his breath about the lack of class and social niceties in this godforsaken place, he made his way to the uneven planks of the wooden sidewalk and tried not to think of the elegance of the life he'd left behind. He had to keep reminding himself of his moral views and why he was now living in such a fashion.

He was deep in thought when a man walked out of the doorway in front of him. The man showed no signs of moving, so Dean stepped aside, and as he did, noted the sign on the door, *Hair Cut Here.*

Don't these barbarians show that's called a Barber Shop?

Then he sighed. There were days when he wondered if he'd ever be able to feel comfortable in such a low-class, plebeian life.

"I say, sir...where might I find the sheriff's office?"

His soft, southern drawl belied the steel of his will and manner.

The freshly shorn man pointed across the street—across fifty yards of mud and ruts.

"Of course," Dean drawled and looked down at his shoes. They were already ruined. He supposed it hardly mattered he must tread in that disgusting mess again. "Oh...one more thing, my good man!"

The man stopped and turned around. "Yeah?"

"I assume there's a hotel in this place?"

"Yep."

When the man wasn't forthcoming with anything more, Joshua Dean was forced to continue their conversation.

"And where might this hotel be?" he asked.

The man pointed. "Down yonder on the other side of the gamblin' parlor."

"Thank you," Dean said and shifted his satchel to his other hand before turning in that direction. He'd taken a half-dozen steps when the man from the barber shop called out to him.

"It won't do no good to walk all that way down there," he said.

Dean frowned as he turned around.

"And why, pray tell, would that be?"

"Cause there ain't no empty rooms. The flood displaced a whole bunch of people. There ain't no rooms to be had anywhere in town."

Joshua Dean arched an eyebrow. It was the only outward sign he gave of his dismay. He eyed the stagecoach and it's driver and then made a quick decision and waved him down.

"I say...when are you leaving Denver City?" he asked.

"Just as soon as we can get some food and a fresh team."

Dean handed him his satchel.

"Put this back on the coach. I'll be traveling on with you."

"Yes, sir," the driver said.

Dean dug a dollar out of his pocket and handed it to the driver.

"Do not leave without me."

The driver pocketed the money. "Yes, sir."

Having satisfied that concern, the judge eyed the street and the mud, and then stifled his dismay and stepped off the sidewalk and headed toward the sheriff's office. A few minutes later, and all the muddier for the trip, he was at the door.

Sheriff Rodney Ham looked up as the door opened.

"Howdy. How can I help you?"

Joshua Dean took off his hat.

"I'm Judge Dean."

Rodney Ham stood up.

"Well now...didn't think you'd make it in this fast."

"Where's the man who's waiting to stand trial?"

"In there," Ham said and pointed toward a door behind his desk.

"What did he do?" Dean asked.

"Uh...beat up his wife, I reckon."

Dean frowned. "Is she dead?"

"No, but—"

"Do you mean to tell me that I was summoned all the way out here just because a man and his wife had a fight?" The judge's nostrils flared. He looked down at his shoes and the legs of his pants, then back up at the sheriff.

"Well, yeah, but you should have seen his—"

"Sir! It is not against the law for a man to lay hand on his wife. In fact, I believe it is no one's business how a man and woman conduct their personal lives within the bonds of matrimony."

"Well now...their baby died, too," the sheriff said.

Dean's eyes narrowed. "Did he kill the child?"

"No, but the doctor reckoned it starved to death."

"That is hardly the duty of a husband," Dean snapped. "It is the mother whose business it is to suckle her child. If this is all you have to say for this man, then I'm telling you to release him at once."

Sheriff Ham frowned. "The people ain't gonna like it none that—"

"I don't care what the *people* in this godforsaken place think," Joshua Dean snapped. "I've given you my decision. Let him go!"

The sheriff shook his head as he reached for the cell key.

"All I got to say to you is, it's a damn good thing you're leavin' because when people find out what you've done, they'd most likely be hankerin' to string you up, instead of old George."

Judge Dean's heart skipped a beat. He'd witnessed the brutality of this country and its people more than once. He had no intention of staying around to witness this outcome.

"Are you threatening me?" he asked.

The sheriff frowned. "I reckon you've talked enough for both of us. I ain't got nothin' more to say to you."

He turned his back on the judge and headed for the jail cell.

* * *

George Mellin was lying on his cot. When the door opened, he sat up. But when the sheriff unlocked the cell and swung the door wide, he stood abruptly.

"What's goin' on here?" he asked.

Sheriff Ham pointed to the dandy in the other room.

"That there's the judge. He said to let you go, so I'm lettin' you go."

George grinned. It seemed his world had taken a turn for the better. He grabbed his hat and bolted, afraid someone would change their mind before he got to the door.

"Thank you, sir," George said, as he moved past the judge.

Joshua Dean nodded once without ever looking at the man, settled his hat a little firmer on his head, and walked out as abruptly as he'd entered.

The stage driver was loading a trunk onto the top of the coach when he arrived. Without comment, he climbed up into the coach, chose a seat by the window, and then leaned back and closed his eyes.

The sooner he left this place, the better.

* * *

The next morning, unaware of her husband's release, Alice was cooking breakfast while keeping an eye on the child who sat quietly in a corner with the quilt pulled tight beneath her chin. Katie answered when questioned and ate when food was put in front of her, but as yet, had not responded normally.

Even so, her appearance into the household had brightened Alice Mellin's outlook on life. She had latched onto the little girl with a ferocity that would have made a mama bear proud, even taking her to her bed last night in case she might awaken with nightmares from her ordeal.

Alice hadn't thought once of George, who, she believed, was still sitting in jail awaiting the arrival of a judge. The only thing really wrong in her life at the moment was that Baby Mary had yet to be buried. She fretted constantly about the Denver City cemetery and the fact it was so close to the rising flood waters.

Letty had made an offhand suggestion to Alice that she might prefer to choose a burial site up on their mountain, somewhere near the trees beyond the house. Alice had jumped on the offer. The problems that existed down in the cemetery did not exist this high up the mountain. Drainage was good, and no longer than the grave would be opened, accumulating water was not a problem.

Alice had been subdued and tearful.

"I don't know as how I'll ever be able to thank you people for your help," she said.

"Thanks aren't necessary," Letty said and gave her a quick hug.

Eulis had stayed in the background of the conversation, leaving the women to work out the issue on their own, but once the decision had been made, it was Eulis who had taken a shovel in hand and headed for the edge of the clearing in the back of their house to dig a grave.

Letty watched him as he walked away and was struck by how life sometimes come full circle. Back in Lizard Flats, before they'd begun their religious odyssey across the territories, Eulis had dug plenty of graves. In fact, if one ever got dug, he was the man who'd done it—and all for a bottle of whiskey. But today, it was to ease a grieving mother's pain.

The man made her very proud.

* * *

The drizzle was soft against Eulis's face as he walked into the trees. He walked slowly, searching the area for a place that seemed proper. It seemed a good idea to dig near a big tree. Even if this child would never grow to climb a tree, or see the sunshine, or take relief in the cool, dark shade, it seemed right to lay her to rest where she might have played.

He chunked the shovel into the earth, testing to make sure he wasn't digging into roots. When the shovel sank easily into the dark, wet earth, Eulis grunted with satisfaction and began to dig.

T-Bone had followed Eulis to the edge of the clearing, and once Eulis stopped, the pup trotted off to do his own exploration. Every so often, Eulis heard him bark, but other than the sound of spade to earth and the raindrops on the leaves above his head, the place was silent.

He couldn't imagine Alice Mellin's distress or sadness, but he knew what it was like to lose his family. He knew how empty and afraid he'd felt when his own had been killed. He'd lived with the fear and loneliness ever since —until Letty. She strengthened him without anything but her faith and presence.

One hour passed, then another, until he'd managed to dig a decent opening. He was just cleaning up the corners of the grave site when T-Bone appeared.

"Woof."

Eulis looked up and grinned.

"Hello, to you, too," he said.

T-Bone whined a couple of times, then offered another woof.

"Yeah, I hear you, but there'll be no squirrel huntin' today."

T-Bone wagged his tail one more time, then bounded off into the woods.

Eulis glanced back down at the grave, then shouldered the shovel and started back to the house. He was going to have to use his horse to bring the coffin up here. It was too slick and muddy to take the wagon down, but he figured he could tie the little coffin onto the saddle and lead the horse down the path that stretched from the back of the house.

He was halfway across the yard when T-Bone came running out of the trees. It took Eulis a few seconds to realize the pup had something in his mouth.

"Hey, T-Bone. Come here, boy."

Now that the pup had Eulis's attention, he had no intention of giving up his prize. Every time Eulis got close, the pup darted just out of reach. Finally, Eulis had enough. He was tired and wet and still had a baby to bury. Whatever it was that T-Bone had dug up, he could have.

He picked the shovel back up and went to the house, but he was too wet and filthy to go inside. Instead, he stood in the open doorway calling Letty's name.

She soon came running. Concern etched her face as she saw him.

"Eulis! You're soaked clear through. Come in and get some dry clothes."

"Not yet," he said. "I've yet to go get the baby. Reckon I'll go now while I'm still wet, instead of goin' later and ruining another set of clothes."

Letty frowned. "I don't want you to get sick."

He grinned. "Letty. It's me, Eulis. Remember? I've passed out and slept in worse weather dozens of times. Remember when them kids back in Lizard Flats doused me with sorghum molasses after I'd passed out drunk. I woke up with ants biting me all over. And the night I passed out in the snow. And the day—"

"Okay, okay." Letty rolled her eyes. "I get your point. So, do you want me to go with you into town?"

"Naw...I'll just tie the coffin onto the saddle and walk it up."

"What about a preacher to say words?" Letty asked.

Eulis held out his arms.

"Won't I do?"

Letty hesitated, then sighed.

"I been tryin' to put that part of our lives behind us," she muttered.

Eulis frowned. “Why’s that, girl? Ain’t nothin’ to be ashamed of. Just think, if everything hadn’t happened the way it had, we’d both still be back in Lizard Flats.”

Letty shuddered.

“I guess you’re right. You say the words over that baby’s grave, Eulis, and I’ll be proud to stand beside you when you do.”

“Tell Alice I’ll be back soon.”

“We’ll be ready,” Letty said.

Eulis stepped off the porch and headed for the small shed where the horses were stabled.

Within a few minutes, he had his horse saddled and was headed down the mountain into town. His heart was heavy with regret for the circumstances that had ended the little baby’s life and sad for Alice Mellin who was still saddled with a brute for a husband.

* * *

Milton Feasley was trying to sweep the latest collection of mud from the front of his store when he looked up and saw Eulis Potter riding in from the south end of town. He paused, watching the tall, homely man and thinking to himself that Potter was damned lucky. That wife of his was something of a hellcat, but she was pretty as she could be—and tough. Lord, but that woman was tough. He’d been part of the crowd that had watched her take a bullwhip to George Mellin. And just the other day, she’d stood down that nest of women right here in his store, who’d judged her and found her wanting. He’d heard she’d taken in Mellin’s wife. It was generous of her, but the way he looked at it, she could afford it. Then just this morning he’d heard someone say the Samuels family had drowned in the flood, except for their little girl, Katie. The gossip was that Letty Potter had taken in the child, as well. He wondered what Eulis thought about all those strange women settling in at his fancy new house, then waved as Eulis rode past.

"I got them blankets put aside for you just like you asked!" Milton called out.

"I'll pick 'em up later," Eulis said and continued down main street toward the livery stable.

Milton wondered what the Potters and Alice thought about the judge turning George loose, and then decided it wasn't any of his business to pass on the news.

The street was a quagmire of mud. The ruts that weren't rained out were a good foot deep and full of water. Even the smelter at the far end of town had shut down for the simple fact it was impossible to pull a loaded ore wagon through this mess. But the arrival of the stagecoach yesterday had been a delightful surprise. It meant the freighters shouldn't be far behind.

Milton gave the sidewalk a last sweep with his broom, then went inside. It didn't pay to stay out long, what with so many idle people lingering inside his store. Most were pretty hard up, and he didn't trust them not to pocket his goods without paying.

He was busy filling the banker's list when Eulis rode back past the store, so he didn't see the little coffin tied to the back of the horse. Even if he had, he wouldn't have given it much thought. Life was hard. Some lived. Some died. It was just the way it was.

* * *

Eulis met Robert Lee at the far end of town. Robert Lee had come in to purchase some coffee and salt. With mining at a halt all over, he was at loose ends, too. But when he saw the tiny coffin tied to Eulis's saddle, his smile died.

"What's goin' on?"

"Takin' this little girl up the mountain to bury. Her mama is stayin' with us for a while."

Robert Lee's voice softened.

"What happened to her?"

"Starved to death," Eulis said shortly. "Her daddy is the man Letty took a bullwhip to."

An odd expression spread over Robert Lee's face, but Eulis didn't notice.

"I heard somethin' about that man today," Robert Lee said.

"Like what?" Eulis asked.

"That judge they were waitin' for came in on the stage and told Sheriff Ham to let him go."

Eulis froze, then shook his head. "Gawd...don't go and tell Letty. She'll have a big enough fit when she finds out on her own."

"Yeah...you're probably right."

"I reckon I'd better be gettin' on home," Eulis said. "Still got to have a buryin' for this little one."

Robert Lee glanced at the tiny, rough-hewn coffin, then looked up the mountain. He wouldn't let himself think past a baby's funeral. No need torturing himself about the woman who lived up there.

"Mind if I tag along?" Robert Lee asked. "Just to pay my respects to the mother and all?"

Eulis smiled, pleased that Robert Lee would think of that.

"That would be just fine. The mama's name is Alice Mellin. She'll be real honored you wanted to come."

Robert Lee fell in single file behind Eulis's horse. The silence between them was one of reverence. There was nothing to be said that was more important than the little box riding on Eulis's saddle. The absence of bird song and squirrel chatter seemed to indicate that even the animals sensed the solemnness of the procession.

About halfway up, the drizzle stopped. An easy breeze appeared, slipping lightly between the water-laden leaves, sending a shower of droplets flying to the forest floor. As it continued to blow, the thick gray layer of rain clouds seemed to thin, then dissipate, as they blew faster and faster across the sky.

T-Bone came running to meet them when they were about two hundred yards from the top. He barked once, then fell into step beside Eulis and trotted quietly beside him all the way to the house.

To Eulis's surprise, Letty, Alice, and little Katie were all sitting on the front steps. Eulis took notice of the fact Letty was even wearing a dress and realized that she was doing this burying thing as proper as she knew how.

Robert Lee tried not to stare, but he'd never seen Letty in anything but men's pants and shirts, and seeing her all soft and feminine like this made him feel weak at the knees. Still, the seriousness of the day was enough to help him maintain his composure.

When the men came to a stop, Alice stood up. Her face was streaked with tears, but her expression was stoic. She lifted her chin.

"Lead the way," she said. "We'll follow."

Eulis nodded at her, then caught Letty's gaze. Without saying a word, she knew he was pleased with the way she had dressed.

Robert Lee was speechless. Before, he'd been taken by her intensity and strength, but today was the first time he'd seen her and thought "woman". He didn't know whether he was coming or going, and decided his wisest strategy would be to keep this visit short. Pay his respects to the grieving mother, meet the little girl they'd taken in, and say hello and goodbye to Letty, all at the same time. He dismounted, tied his horse to the hitching post, and took the other side of the horse's bridle as he and Eulis walked the horse to the back of the house where the grave had been dug.

Alice took Katie's hand as they stepped off the porch.

"Will you walk with me?" she asked softly.

Katie nodded solemnly. She knew what dying meant. She'd witnessed her whole family's demise. For the first time since her arrival, she met Alice's gaze without flinching.

Letty brought up the rear, unable to look at the little coffin without remembering those few precious moments when she'd held Baby Mary in her own arms. Her heart was aching for the waste of precious life and could only imagine what Alice was feeling.

When they reached the grave site, Robert Lee held the horse while Eulis untied the coffin. Together, they took a rope and lowered it into the hole.

It wasn't until the little box was resting at the bottom of the hole that Alice started to cry—softly, but steadily—shoulders shaking—clutching her belly as if remembering she'd held her baby there far longer than she'd ever held her in her arms.

Katie looked nervous and leaned against Alice, then ducked her head and closed her eyes.

The back of Letty's throat was burning from unshed tears. She knew if she ever let out a sob, she'd never be able to stop crying.

Robert Lee saw her distress and had to walk away into the trees to keep from putting his arms around her.

Eulis cleared his throat, then began a simple eulogy.

"Lord...this here's Baby Mary Elizabeth Mellin. She didn't have much of a chance here on earth, but I reckon she gave her mama a lot of joy. We don't want to give her up, but we're a trustin' that You know what You're doin', so here she is. And...if You don't mind... Baby Mary's mama is in need of some of Your strength. Amen."

"Amen," Letty echoed, then swiped at her face with both hands, angry she'd lost control of her emotions.

Eulis picked up the shovel and began covering up the grave. No one spoke. No one moved. It took far less time to put the dirt back than it had to dig it out. Eulis was tapping the back of his shovel over the small mound of earth when Robert Lee re-appeared, carrying a small wooden cross.

He handed it to Eulis without looking up, then stood with his hands in his pockets and his gaze on the ground.

Letty had been touched by Eulis's words and the tenderness with which he'd spoken, but when Robert Lee came back carrying that small cross, she looked past her own tears to the ones on the gunslinger's face.

The tiny cross was fashioned from two small limbs tied together with rawhide. The ends of the cross had been whittled to small white points, as had the end Eulis pushed into the ground.

Eulis gave the cross a final tap with the shovel, then stepped back to eye his work.

"There now," he said.

It was over.

8

rich man, poor man, beggar man, thief, doctor, lawyer, merchant, CHIEF

The rains finally ended with the burial of Alice Mellin's child. Two days later, the sadness Letty had felt at the funeral still caught her off guard now and then, although her sadness was nothing to Alice's grief. She knew Alice was devastated, but she gave no outward sign of it. In truth, the arrival of Katie Samuels to the family had been a lifesaver for Alice. She'd transferred her motherly instincts to Katie without a hitch, giving Katie the stability she so desperately needed.

Yesterday, they'd received word that the furniture they'd had the carpenter make was finished and ready to be picked up. Eulis had taken the wagon into town and loaded up the hand-made cots, as well as the table and benches. They were nothing like the fancy pieces Letty had ordered from back East, but they would do to tide them over until the real furniture arrived.

Last night, it had been a small piece of heaven to have the cots to sleep on, rather than the floor. Sitting down at a table to eat seemed the ultimate in luxury.

Eulis had also called the miners back to work and resumed his routine.

The flood waters were receding, which was a huge relief to all, including the banker, Amos Trueblood, who was thankful not to have to move the money and gold.

Dr. Warren and his wife Mildred gave up their tent and went home, thankful for the comfort of their simple life. The water damage was minimal, with only minor repairs needed inside.

After Baby Mary's funeral, Robert Lee had exiled himself to the cabin. He'd had some uneasy nights of sleep, which had resulted in taking extra precautions in guarding the mine. He didn't know what was happening, but every day he felt an impending feeling of doom. It was something he knew better than to ignore.

Now and then Eulis thought about telling Letty and Alice about George's release, but they didn't ask, and he figured the more time passed, the better off they'd all be when they heard he'd been set free.

T-Bone continued to sleep inside at night and never strayed far from the house during the day. Wherever Letty went, T-Bone wasn't far behind. Only now and then did he disappear into the trees, and when he did, often came back with something in his mouth, which he promptly buried near the back steps. No one paid any attention to his comings and goings, which was unfortunate, because T-Bone was the only member of the Potter family who knew they were not alone.

*   *   *

Letty lay in their bed, watching Eulis dressing for the mine. He thought she was still asleep. She didn't let on that she wasn't. It gave her time to study the man who was her husband without scrutiny.

He wasn't a handsome man by any means, but he was sure and steady, and she owed him her life. She pulled the covers up beneath her nose to hide a smile as she remembered the stunts they'd pulled while traveling through the territories, preaching the Word of God. It had all been done in good faith and with a true heart, but there were several couples out there who did not know they'd been married by the town drunk of Lizard Flats, or that the so-called preacher's companion had been a fifty-cent whore. She didn't suppose it much mattered. God knew what was in everyone's heart, no matter what a piece of paper said.

She remembered the night she and Eulis had exchanged their own vows while snowed in at their cabin in the valley. If she had it all to do over again, she wouldn't hesitate.

Eulis pulled his shirt over his head, then began tucking it into the waistband of his pants as he turned around. When he realized Letty was not only awake, but watching him dress, he grinned.

"Good mornin', wife."

Letty pushed back the covers and smiled as she sat up. "Good morning, husband."

"That has a right nice ring to it," he said softly.

Letty nodded, then sniffed the air.

"Alice is cookin' breakfast."

"Yeah, I been smellin' it for some time now."

Letty arched an eyebrow.

"Are you still sorry I hired her to cook?"

Eulis's grin widened.

"I ain't right sure how to answer that without gettin' myself in trouble. If I say yes, then you're gonna think I like her cookin' better than yours. If I say no, then you'll most likely feel obliged to make changes, which are unnecessary as far as I'm concerned."

"Good answer," Letty said and then laughed. "Pour me a cup of coffee when you get down there. I'll be right along."

"Sure thing," Eulis said and winked at her before he left the room.

Letty dressed quickly, choosing a clean pair of pants and a shirt, then quickly braided her hair. She sat down on the side of the bed to pull on her boots, then stomped each one firmly as she stood. A quick trip to the outhouse and she'd be ready to face the day.

Until the arrival of Letty's fancy cookstove, they were still cooking in the parlor, but the hand-made table and benches made serving meals much easier.

"Good morning, Alice," Letty said, as she came striding into the room.

Katie was playing beneath a window on the east side of the room. Sunbeams danced around her in the new light of day, making it appear as if she were surrounded in gold dust. It seemed an appropriate sight in this place where gold was worshiped more highly than God.

But Letty knew different. She was rich—richer than even her wildest dreams—and yet she could not buy respectability. Most of the time she didn't care, but once in a while it might have been nice to know she wasn't constantly being judged and found wanting. She'd been so conscious of living a life that was not proper she didn't realize most of the dislike from the citizens of Denver City was based on jealousy, not a lack of respect. However, the world within these walls was where she felt safe, and she took none of it for granted.

"Morning, Letty," Alice said. "Breakfast is 'bout ready. I made some flapjacks, but it's the last of our flour."

"If you'll make a list, I'll see about filling it later this morning."

Alice nodded, then glanced toward Katie, before returning to her cooking.

Letty saw the look and was happy. Taking in this child had been the saving of both Alice and Katie. They were getting strength from each other's presence.

"I'm going to the outhouse," Letty said. "Be right back."

She strode out of the house with purpose, enjoying the early sunlight and the fact the long-sodden earth was finally beginning to firm. She side-stepped a couple of puddles at the door to the outhouse and then went inside and quickly did her business.

When she came out, she saw Eulis leading his horse from the shed. He'd already saddled him up and was moving toward the back porch, obviously led by the scent of Alice's flapjacks.

When he saw Letty coming across the yard, he tied the horse to a porch post and started toward her.

T-Bone was lying on the bottom steps, but when he saw Letty emerge from the outhouse, he jumped up to follow Eulis.

Letty smiled at the sight of her two favorite males, and was thinking what to do with her day when the first shot rang out.

T-Bone yelped, tucked his tail between his legs, and ran for the porch.

Letty saw the shock on Eulis's face, then the blooming stain of red appearing on the front of his shirt.

She screamed out his name, then started running.

Halfway there, another shot rang out, hitting him in the arm. When she was less than ten yards from where he stood, the third shot burned past her head and hit Eulis right above the knee.

His leg buckled as he was reaching for Letty.

Letty kept screaming Eulis's name as she watched him drop. Within seconds, she threw herself across his body in a futile effort to protect him, as she scanned the boundary of the trees.

Eulis's hand clutched her arm. She looked down, and in that moment, everything seemed to move in slow motion.

The tears in his eyes were startling. She'd never seen Eulis cry. His lips were moving, but he wasn't making any sounds.

"Eulis! Eulis! Don't you die," Letty cried. "Don't you die on me!"

He blinked—so slow she thought he would never open his eyelids again—then he looked up, straight into her eyes.

Her face was the last thing he saw.

Letty heard the breath leave his body and wanted to go with him. This wasn't right! It wasn't fair! Just when she'd found someone to love—once again they were taken away.

She lowered her head, and for a moment, they were touching, cheek to cheek. She could feel the stubble of whiskers on his face. It was then she rocked back on her heels and screamed.

The word "no" was ripped out of her throat to be repeated over and over until, in her grief, she lost the enunciation of the word.

The back door flew open. Alice emerged on the run, took one look at the scene before her and gasped. There was a huge hole in Eulis's chest. She didn't have to feel for his pulse to know he was dead. And she knew that, as good a man as Eulis Potter had been, there was nothing more to be done for him. It was Letty who was still in danger.

Alice bounded off the porch and grabbed Letty by the arm.

"Get up, Letty, get up! We've got to get inside!"

Letty wouldn't stop screaming, and she wouldn't let go.

Alice glanced nervously toward the trees and tightened her grip on Letty's arm.

"They'll kill you, too! Let go, let go!"

Unprepared for Alice's strength, Letty felt herself being pulled backward. Before she knew it, she was on her knees and being dragged toward the porch.

"Stop, oh God...please stop! I can't leave him there!"

Alice turned, her face twisted into a fierce grimace as she screamed back at the woman who'd saved her life.

"He's dead! He's dead just like my baby and there's nothing that can be done. Get up, damn it! Don't make me have to bury the both of you!"

Alice pulled again, and this time Letty went, stumbling and crying as they ran.

Once they were inside, Alice slammed the door shut behind them, then dragged her into a corner.

"Katie! Come away from the windows," Alice cried.

The little girl ran to Alice and hid her face against Alice's breasts.

"Lord, oh Lord," Alice muttered, as she stood between

Letty and the door.

An hour passed while Eulis's blood ran out of his body, soaking into the dirt beside the back steps. Letty cried until her throat was so raw she couldn't swallow. It wasn't until Alice knelt beside her and put a wet rag on her face that she began to regain a sense of herself. The pain in her chest was so great it hurt to breathe, but breathe she still did.

"There now, there now," Alice murmured as she wiped the hot tears from Letty's face.

Letty shuddered. She couldn't think, but she could feel. She looked down at her hands and the front of her clothes. They were stained with Eulis's blood. A hot, sweeping flush swept up, from her gut to her head, but it wasn't pain she was feeling, it was rage. Someone had taken away what had been good and gentle in her life. She shoved Alice's hands away from her face, then held out her hand.

"Help me up."

Alice did so, but was far more nervous around this Letty, than the one who'd been grieving. When Letty strode out of the room and headed upstairs, Alice quickly followed, with Katie, who'd taken to sucking her thumb, at her heels.

"What are you doing?" Alice asked.

"I'm getting the rifle."

Alice wrung her hands. "You'd better tell the sheriff to—"

Letty's gaze was cold as she looked at Alice.

"You tell the sheriff whatever you want. I'm going after the man who killed my husband."

Alice gasped and clasped her hands to her heart.

"Letty...dear...you can't! That's too dangerous for a woman!"

Letty turned on her then. Her eyes were swimming in tears, but they never fell.

"He would do it for me. Pack me some food. I don't know when I'll be back."

Alice's face crumpled, then she began to wail.

"You'll die! You'll die, too, and then what will become of Katie and me?"

"I'm not the one who's going to die next," she said.

The cold, still tone of Letty's voice made Alice shudder. She was beginning to understand the true depth of this woman's strength. Without another word, she ran downstairs to pack up the uneaten food, and when Letty came down the stairs, she handed it to her without a word. Letty carried it outside and packed it into the saddlebags on Eulis's horse.

T-Bone came slinking around the corner of the house, whining his own brand of sorrow.

Letty glanced down.

"You comin' with me?" she asked.

T-Bone whined, then stood at Letty's said as she checked the rifle. It was loaded. She added her extra ammunition to the other saddlebag and mounted up. Alice was standing on the porch.

"There's money under my bed to buy food. I'll be back before you get it eaten up," Letty said.

"You'd better be," Alice muttered, then bit her lip and pointed to Eulis.

"What do you want me to do?"

"Bury him," Letty said and turned the horse's head, then rode toward the trees. The ground was still soft enough that whoever had been hiding out there would have had to leave tracks. She felt no fear as she rode, confidant that, whoever had fired the shots could have stormed the house at any time. Since they had not, she took it to mean they were gone.

But it didn't matter. He could run, but he couldn't hide from Letty Potter's rage.

* * *

Robert Lee had ridden shotgun into town with a wagon-load of ore, but they'd gotten stuck twice before pulling out of the valley. He'd made the decision that they'd begun mining too soon, so after delivering the wagon to the smelter, he'd told the men not to come back for a couple of days until the ground had time to dry out some more.

He had signed off on the wagon and was on his way outside to find Eulis and give him the news, when a man he knew only as Cecil walked into the smelter office.

Cecil saw Robert Lee and quickly took off his hat.

"Hello there, Robert Lee. Sorry to hear about your boss. He was a right good man."

Robert Lee froze, staring at the man as if he'd lost his mind.

"What the hell are you talking about?"

Cecil stared back in shock, then looked away.

"Say, I'm sorry. I reckoned that you knew."

Robert Lee grabbed him by the shoulders.

"I said...what the hell are you talking about?"

Cecil pulled out of Robert Lee's grasp and took a quick step backward.

"Eulis Potter was gunned down in his own yard this morning. The woman who works for them came into town to get the sheriff."

Robert Lee felt his blood run cold. He tried to form words, but it seemed they just wouldn't come. It wasn't until Cecil started to walk away he finally asked.

"What about Letty? What about Mrs. Potter?"

Cecil shrugged.

"Can't say what happened to her."

Robert Lee's mind went blank. He walked out of the smelter office, got on his horse, and rode down main street, then headed up the road to their house. The road was too steep for his horse to run, and he wouldn't let himself panic. Surely, if Letty had been a victim, Alice would have mentioned that, as well.

When he finally got to the house and dismounted, his legs were shaking so hard he could barely stand up. He moved up the steps, took a deep breath and then walked in the front door without knocking, calling out Letty's name as he went.

Alice came running from the back of the house with her hand to her heart, fearing the killer had returned. When she realized it was Robert Lee, she began to cry with relief.

"Thank God that it's you," she said, and sobbed anew.

"Is it true? Is Eulis dead?"

"Yes, dear God, it was awful," she said and covered her face with her apron.

Robert Lee grabbed her by the shoulders—his voice so tight with fear he could barely make himself heard.

"Letty...did they shoot Letty, too?"

Alice dropped her apron as she shook her head.

"Lord no, but I thought they might. She threw herself on top of Eulis. I could tell he was gone, but I couldn't get her off. She kept screaming and screaming."

The thought of Letty's anguish was like a knife to his heart.

"Where is she?" he asked, looking up to the second floor. "Is she in her room?"

Alice started crying again.

"If only she was!" Alice said.

Robert Lee frowned.

"Then were is she?"

"She went after him," Alice said. "Made me pack up some food for her while she went to get the rifle. I tried to stop her, but she rode off like a madwoman."

Fear struck Robert Lee anew.

"Jesus! Which way did she go?"

Alice pointed into the trees at the back of the house.

"The shots came from back there. She rode into the trees with T-Bone. I haven't seen her since."

Robert Lee felt sick.

"How long ago?"

"Two or three hours, I think."

He swore softly, then strode out of the house, untied his horse, and mounted on the run. He saw the dark stain of blood in the earth as he circled the house, then looked past it to the sight of Letty's tracks. He couldn't focus on the dead when there was still a life that might be saved.

* * *

George Mellin had been staking out the Potter house ever since his release from jail. The first time he'd seen his wife come out of the back door of the house, he thought he was dreaming. It wasn't until he'd seen her several more times he realized she was living there. He didn't know how it had happened, but the fact she was living in luxury in that big, fine house, while he was forced to make cold camp alone in the woods, only added to his anger.

He'd seen Letty Potter coming and going many times. It had given him a sense of power to know he could kill her and be done with it at any time. But that didn't seem like payback enough. If she died, then she wouldn't suffer, and he wanted her to suffer.

It had finally dawned on him that the best way to hurt Letty Potter was to take away the thing she loved most, which he knew was her man. He'd had to deal with their damned dog nosing around his camp and more than once awakened to discover the dog had carried something off. Thanks to that dog, he didn't even have a hat anymore.

He'd started to shoot the pup, but then realized he couldn't shoot it without alerting the Potters to his presence. After that, he'd tried to catch it but failed miserably. It would be a simple matter to slit its throat, but he hadn't been able to get close enough to grab him.

So, he'd watched and watched the house for the perfect moment, waiting until both Eulis and Letty were outside at the same time, because he wanted Letty Potter to watch her husband die. He wanted her on her knees, the same way she'd put him. Then today, it had happened.

He'd been up since before dawn and moved to his watching place a few yards into the trees surrounding the back of the yard. When he'd seen Eulis Potter emerge from the house and go toward the horse shed, he stood up. The dog knew he was out there, but he'd been in the vicinity for so long now the dog took his presence for granted. For that reason, no alarm was sounded.

He'd waited impatiently, willing Letty Potter to come out before her husband left for the mines. He'd been disappointed before, but something told him today was the day.

When he saw her come out of the house and walk to the outhouse, it had been all he could do not to shout. At last he was going to get his revenge.

He waited impatiently, his hands shaking a bit as he kept the rifle to his shoulder. He saw Letty Potter come out of the outhouse. When she started toward the house and Eulis was still nowhere in sight, he began to panic.

"No, no," he muttered. "Come on, damn it. Get your lazy ass out of that shed."

Then Eulis appeared, leading his horse.

At that point, George knew everything he'd planned was going to happen—now. He shifted the butt of the rifle firmly against his shoulder and squinted carefully as he looked down the sight. He couldn't see Letty's face, but he knew she was smiling. He could tell by the look on her husband's face.

When Eulis started toward her, he held his breath and tightened his grip on the trigger. One pull. That was all it would take, and yet, he waited. Not yet. Not yet.

When the rifle fired, George was almost as surprised as Eulis Potter looked. He saw the blood stain blossoming at the front of the man's chest. For a few seconds, he was so taken with what he'd done he didn't move. But then Eulis didn't fall, and in a fit of panic, he began to reload the rifle.

Seconds later, he took aim again, but in his haste, missed the broad shape of Eulis's chest and hit him in the arm. He reloaded again without conscious thought and fired without taking aim. The third shot hit Eulis in the leg.

After Potter fell, George lowered his rifle and watched.

Letty Potter was screaming. The pain in her voice was what he'd wanted to hear. For a few moments, he just stood, taking great satisfaction in seeing her grief. It was the payback he'd promised himself she would get for whipping him in the street like a dog.

It wasn't until he'd seen Alice running out of the house that he'd come out of his trance. Alice's vehemence in getting Letty to safety fostered the notion of shooting her, too, then he changed his mind. He'd gotten out of jail once with no punishment. He didn't relish staying around to test his luck a second time.

While Alice was dragging Letty up the back steps, he turned and ran. His cold camp was about a half mile down the backside of the mountain. He had nothing to his name but what he'd managed to steal after he'd been released, so it didn't take long to pack it all up. There was an old man working a small mine about a quarter a mile further down the mountain. He had a horse. George needed a horse. It would be a simple enough matter to take it.

9

TO THE DEATH

If it hadn't been for T-Bone, Letty might have ridden right past the place where the killer had staked them out. But when the dog suddenly stopped and began to run in small circles behind a thicket of undergrowth, she dismounted, then knelt.

There was a small square of linen caught in the top of a bush and a deep depression behind the trees, as well as a large amount of footprints. The bit of cloth was obviously part of the packing used to load a rifle, and from the depth of the area behind the trees, it appeared the killer had been watching them for some time.

She stood abruptly, looking back toward the house and realized if she took three steps to the right, she had a clear view of the back porch. Her focus shifted to the man lying on the ground near the back porch.

"Oh, Eulis," she whispered, then dropped her head and clutched her belly as a fresh wave of pain threatened to send her to her knees.

It was the thought of catching the man responsible for this tragedy that kept her going. So she gritted her teeth, rubbed the tears from her eyes, and began scanning the floor of the forest for more footprints. She soon found his trail. As she looked up at the wall of trees before her, she couldn't help wondering if he was somewhere nearby, watching her struggling with shock and with grief.

T-Bone whined.

She looked down at the dog, then pointed into the trees.

"Find him, boy! Find him!"

T-Bone seemed to sense the urgency in her voice and took off with his nose to ground. Letty didn't know the pup was just following a well-traveled path—one he'd taken every day into George Mellin's camp.

Letty quickly mounted and followed with an eye to the trail. There was no way to tell how long the killer had been gone, but she didn't want to waste any daylight in her search.

Within fifteen minutes, she rode into what had obviously been someone's cold camp. Again, she dismounted. A shelter of sorts had been built from limbs and pine boughs, although no fires had been made. She found a rabbit snare but no sign of fur or bones. There was also a long indentation in the earth beneath some trees, with pine boughs and leaves as a cushion. She walked onto it, then kicked out in anger, sending pine needles and leaves flying. The bastard had slept here. When she found him, she promised herself his next sleep would be permanent.

After a thorough search of the area, it didn't appear he had plans of coming back. When she found a new set of footprints leading farther down the mountain, she went back to her horse, mounted up, and whistled for T-Bone.

The pup fell into step behind the horse as Letty continued on. The density of trees lessened as they descended, and she soon began seeing signs of old, long-abandoned campsites, as well as a few abandoned mine shafts. She knew them as places where men had searched for, then given up on, their dreams.

The signs of habitation were also a sign she must be close to the base of the mountain. This intensified her eyeing the underbrush, to make sure she wasn't riding into an ambush. T-Bone was running ahead of her now with his nose in the air, on the trail of something new.

When she rode out of a stand of trees into a small clearing and saw an old man lying on the ground beside a small lean-to, she pulled back on the reins, bringing her horse to a halt.

Grabbing her rifle as she dismounted, she ran to where the old man was lying. There was a spilled bucket of grain near his right leg and what appeared to be a half-eaten biscuit clutched in his left hand.

Just for a second, she saw Eulis again, and as she did, her vision blurred with a fresh set of tears. Swallowing back a sob as she knelt, she felt for his pulse. There was none. It was then she saw the crack in the back of his skull.

He was dead.

His body was cold to the touch, and when she lifted his hand, it felt stiff. People who'd just died were still supple. She'd seen enough dead people in her life to know a definite amount of time had passed since this man had taken his last breath. It meant her killer was, most likely, a good distance ahead.

Again, she began to look for the killer's footprints, only this time, it seemed he'd disappeared into thin air. It wasn't until she began searching the other outbuildings she realized the old man had owned a horse. Only the horse was gone. This changed everything. Now the killer was mounted, as well.

After a few more minutes of trying to make sense of the tracks coming and going from the house, she found what appeared to be a fresh trail, moving west.

So he wasn't going to Denver City. She wasn't familiar enough with the surrounding area to know what lay west of the burgeoning town, other than more mountains, but if she kept on going, she was bound to find out.

For the first time since she'd ridden away from her home, she got scared. What if she lost the trail? A horse was a horse. How could she tell one's trail from another? How would she ever live with herself again if she let a man get away with Eulis's murder?

Determined not to be defeated, she convinced herself there was surely something she was missing, so she retraced her steps around the old man's place. It wasn't until she went back into the stable she noticed a difference in the tracks. The horse was missing a shoe on its right hoof.

She grunted in satisfaction. That was what she'd needed to find. She wouldn't look back at the old man—there was nothing she could do for him now but try and find the person responsible for his death. So she mounted up—ignoring the gut-wrenching pain in her chest—refusing to acknowledge that when this journey was over, Eulis would not be waiting for her at the end.

"Come on, T-Bone. Let's go."

The dog barked, and then they disappeared into the trees.

* * *

Robert Lee could tell by the deterioration of the tracks he'd been following he was at least three hours, maybe four, behind Letty. As he'd ridden away from the house, he'd taken some comfort in the knowledge the pup was with her. He would be some protection against animals or humans, but completely useless against a man with a gun.

He found the stalker's camp as easily as Letty had and was somewhat surprised, then impressed, with her ability to track. She'd moved unerringly with the footprints that were descending the back side of the mountain.

Later, when he rode into the old man's camp and found him dead and a horse obviously missing, he realized the stakes had gone higher. The killer was no longer on foot. But unlike Letty, he saw immediately that the stolen horse was missing a shoe. This would make it much easier to track, although the prints of Letty's horse were now mixed with those of the killer. All he could do was follow and pray he didn't get there too late.

* * *

For hours, George rode with a cocky assurance, unaware he was being followed. He made no effort to hide his tracks and stopped once for more than an hour to water the horse at a small creek. At that time, he dug into his stolen food and ate the piece of fried fatback that had been in a skillet on the old man's stove, as well as some cold johnnycake. Later, as the horse was resting, he felt a pain in his belly and quickly took to the bushes, leaving a calling card of his own without bothering to bury it.

After raiding the old man's place, he was now in possession of a horse, food, and a bedroll. When night came, he would be sitting pretty. He still had some cold johnnycake and a couple of pieces of jerky, a large piece of flint for building fires, and a good-sized piece of uncooked fatback, wrapped in a piece of thin, greasy cloth. He had a half-sack of dry beans and about three pounds of cornmeal, a spoon, and a couple of small pots, well-blackened from many outdoor fires. For a man who'd been without nothing, he felt a great sense of well-being.

It wasn't until he saw how far the sun had moved into the west he resumed his trek. Although he'd made good time since the shooting, he wanted to be farther away before he made camp for the night. He mounted up, eyed the sky once more, then kicked the old horse in the flanks.

Within three hours it was dark, and George was sitting beside his campfire, eating the last of the fatback he'd cooked. A small pan of beans was simmering at the side of the fire. By morning they would be cooked through and through. He would be able to eat from the pot, then pack it up, saving the cold beans for travel.

When he'd first made his escape, his intent had been to just keep riding west, but the farther he rode from Denver City, the more convinced he became that the smartest thing for him might be to backtrack and go home to Boston. At least there, he'd had a trade. He'd never liked fishing or spending every waking hour out on the ocean, but right now, it seemed far more appealing than the past year he'd lived through.

Later, with a belly full of johnnycake and jerky, he spread his bedroll by the fire, pulled the loaded rifle up close to his chest, and covered himself with the old man's blankets. They smelled of wood smoke and body sweat, but it was more than he'd had last night. Within minutes, he was fast asleep.

* * *

Darkness came with Letty still in the saddle. The rage that had carried her this far was burning strong and steady. Every uneven jolt of the horse's hoof to ground was a pain she welcomed. She needed a physical pain to match her emotions—something that would give her the balance she needed to stay focused. The luxury of grief would come later, when she watched Eulis's killer die.

The later it got, the more she debated with herself about making camp for the night. But when it became apparent there would be a full moon tonight, she changed her mind. She couldn't track in the dark, but she was going to take a chance that the killer wouldn't change direction, and if she kept going, eventually she would smell the smoke from his campfire.

And so she rode, ignoring the aches in her muscles and the hungry growl from her belly. The thought of putting food in her mouth turned her stomach. She needed to stay focused on the task at hand. Stopping meant thinking, and thinking meant remembering, and remembering meant reliving the shock and the acceptance of death she'd seen on Eulis's sweet face.

Several times she was forced to slow down. The land through which she was riding was wild and at night, dangerous. The valley was wide and long, nestled between two snow-capped peaks. But her instincts led her to keep following the creek that wound through the middle, believing that, when the killer decided to make camp, like anyone else, he would want easy access to water.

Sometime around midnight she dismounted to water her horse and give him time to graze. When she swung out of the saddle and put her boots on the ground, her strength and willpower faded into nothing. The bloodstains on her clothes had long since dried and looked black in the moonlight, and when she finally laid her hand on the dark stain across her breast, she dropped her head and sobbed. It was a sobering fact to know his blood was the only thing of him she had left.

T-Bone's ears were on point—his nose was to the wind. The hair on his back had been raised for the better part of an hour, and ever so often he let out a low, warning growl. Letty wouldn't let herself think of the wildlife that might be watching. She didn't have time to be afraid of a four-footed devil, when the one for which she searched walked on two legs.

She had taken a cold flapjack from the pack Alice had made for her and was absently feeding it to T-Bone while listening to the sound of her horse eating grass. There was a repetitive crunch as the horse bit down, then a tearing sound, as it pulled off a bite of the thick, lush growth. The grass around the creek was already over ankle high. Letty knew it would be higher than her waist by mid-summer. It was a fine country, rich in all the things that counted, including that damnable gold.

Only once, when she heard a sudden, shrill, high-pitched scream, did she panic. Even though it sounded like the screams of a dying woman, she knew it wasn't human. It was a cougar and still some distance away. Nervously, she reached toward the butt of the rifle. It wasn't until she felt the warmth of the wood beneath her fingers, she finally relaxed.

T-Bone growled what she assumed was another warning. She reached down and patted his head, murmuring softly until she felt the hair on his back finally relax.

And so time passed. She didn't know how long she'd been smelling wood smoke, but when it finally sank in, her heart skipped a beat. Everything around her, from the sound of the wind in the grass to the water running in the creek beside them, faded in the background of her consciousness. She went suddenly still—cocked her head to one side—and then closed her eyes, concentrating on nothing but her sense of smell. Adrenaline shot through her, heightening every sensation. She began to turn in a clock-wise direction, intent on locating the direction from which the smoke was coming. It wasn't until she felt the wind on her face and the smoke up her nose, she realized what had happened.

Somehow, in the dark, she had ridden past the killer's camp. The scent of smoke was faint. From the way the wind was blowing, there was no telling how far back the camp had been made, but she was going to find out. She mounted quickly, whispered a command to her dog, and began to backtrack.

A short while later, she realized the smell of smoke was growing stronger. Within minutes, she'd ridden close enough she could see the flames of his campfire through the trees. At that point, she stopped, dismounted, then tied her horse to the branches of a tree along the creek bank.

She pulled the rifle from the scabbard, then put her hand on T-Bone's head. The pup sensed her anxiety and whined softly. She felt the muscles of his back trembling beneath the palm of her hand and gave him a quick pat. With her rifle in one hand, a knife in her boot, and her dog at her side, she walked away from her horse and into the camp.

The light from the fire was so much brighter than the moonlight by which she'd been traveling, that she saw everything quite clearly. The shape of the man lying beneath an old blanket was long and large. From where she was standing, she could see the end of a rifle barrel beneath his blanket near the back of his head.

Since she'd walked in from the backside of the fire, she had yet to see his face, but it didn't matter. She was almost as positive as a person could be this man was the killer she'd been tracking—still she needed to make sure.

The man's horse was tethered some twenty yards away, but when she noticed it was standing on three legs and favoring the front hoof on the right—the one that was missing a shoe—she knew she'd found her man.

She took a deep breath, and without giving herself time to panic, pointed at T-Bone. Although he never moved his gaze from her face, he sat down, quivering with tension but sensing the need to obey.

Letty moved quietly, taking care with every step, until she was only inches from the man's head. Without moving the blanket, she reached down and silently slid his rifle from beneath the blanket. Clutching his weapon in her left hand, she backed up until she was out of the circle of light, then laid the gun in the grass. The man was snoring loudly, completely unaware he was no longer alone, yet she could barely hear the sounds for the thunder of her own heartbeat in her ears.

She eyed the layout of the camp, noting a large stack of firewood he'd obviously gathered before bedding down for the night. Tightening her grip on her rifle, she picked up a large stick and from where she was standing, tossed it into the fire.

It hit the flames with a thud, scattering sparks and burning embers in all directions, including the man's hair and blanket.

"What the hell?" he shouted, as he sat up in his bed and began beating at the blanket, trying to put out the flames.

He didn't know Letty was there until he heard something growl. Believing it to be a wolf or a bear, he went for his rifle, then saw Letty Potter at the same time he realized his rifle was gone.

She looked like something out of a nightmare, with the flames from his campfire highlighting the bone structure of her face. Her gaze was as steady as the gun she had aimed at his heart. But it was the bloodstains on her clothes and the glitter in her eyes that told him he would not see tomorrow.

"You!" Letty muttered, shocked to learn it was George Mellin who she'd been trailing all along, and yet at the same time, it began to make a sick kind of sense.

She wanted him dead now—she wanted to see him take his last breath, just as she'd watched Eulis die. But she needed him to suffer, too—to know that his physical pain was as sharp as the one in her gut.

George was immobile, frozen from fear.

Letty knew he was scared, but it wasn't enough. Without talking, she picked up another stick from the woodpile and threw it into the already blazing fire.

Again, the sparks flew outward, this time singeing George's hair and skin and burning more holes in his blanket. He cried out in pain and terror and began to beat at the flames when suddenly, Letty warned him.

"If you move again, I'll shoot you where you sit."

George's eyes widened in disbelief.

"I'm on fire," he cried.

"Not yet, you're not...but you will be," Letty promised.

George writhed beneath the blanket as a small fire began to spread there near his feet.

"Please," he begged. "You don't understand. You shouldn't a done what you did. No man deserves to be whipped like a dog in front of his friends."

"No *man* does to his family, what you did, you bastard...you coward...you sorry-ass, back-stabbing son-of-a-bitch. But the flogging wasn't about your wife, Alice. She's a grown woman. The way I looked at it, she could have spoke up for herself. It was about your baby. She died in my arms. Died before she had a chance to live. That's why I whipped your ass, and I'd do it again."

George groaned. The hole in the blanket was burning a little larger as it continued to spread. He felt the heat catching onto his pant legs and knew it was just a matter of time before he burst into flames.

"Please," he begged. "You can't do this to a—"

Letty lifted the rifle to her shoulder.

"Shut up," she said softly.

George groaned as his bladder gave way.

Letty took a step closer.

"You should have killed me, too," she said softly, then pulled the trigger.

The scent of gunpowder was suddenly up her nose as the kick of the rifle made her stagger.

When the echo of the shot had faded away, George Mellin was still sitting, with the burning blanket in his lap and a bloody hole between his eyebrows.

Letty shuddered, then lowered the rifle and took several steps backward until she felt the bark of a tree at her back. She slumped, then slid downward until she was sitting flat on the ground with the rifle at her feet.

A few yards away, the blanket finally burst into flames. She watched it catch on George's pants, then his shirt, then watched his face disappear behind a column of swiftly rising smoke.

Mellin was aflame.

Nearby, his horse whinnied nervously. The smell of burning flesh sent it into a panic. It reared backward on the rope, then suddenly tore free from its tether and disappeared into the night, running at a full gallop.

* * *

Robert Lee's horse was lathered in sweat, its breathing hard and labored. Ever since he'd come off the mountain into the wide, verdant valley, he'd been riding in fear. When dark came, he kept imagining he was riding past Letty's body, lying somewhere out of sight in the grass.

In his mind's eye, he kept seeing the dark, blood-stained earth at the back of the Potter house, imagining he could hear the sound of Letty's screams.

Eulis Potter had been a good man—better than most. Robert Lee owed him in a way he'd never owed a man before. He'd been hired to protect the Potter mine, but had been unable to protect the Potters. That dug at him like a burr beneath the skin, pushing him on when good sense bade him stop for the night.

He had been in the valley, for what seemed like hours, hearing nothing but the sounds of his horse's breathing and the steady rhythm of its hooves upon the ground. His body was tense, his eyes burning from trying to see what the night was hiding.

Only a short while earlier, he'd stopped long enough to water his horse at the creek and mounted back up as soon as the horse had drunk its fill. He was riding without caution, flying through the moonlit valley as if he could see in the dark.

Suddenly, a shot rang out in the night, echoing within the valley until the sound was too distorted to discern its origin.

He reined in his horse, his heart hammering, frantically searching the darkness, waiting for another round to be fired, but there was nothing. Then, within a minute or two of the shot, he became aware of another sound—one he'd heard plenty of times before—but usually at his back.

A horse was running, coming his way fast.

He drew his gun, wrapped the reins around his hand a little tighter, and waited.

Suddenly, it appeared, almost upon him before he could react. With nothing but moonlight by which to see, it was still obvious the horse was running from fear. Its head was up, its nostrils widely distended. When it saw them, the horse squealed out a warning. Robert Lee's horse squealed back, and it was all he could do to stay seated as the runaway horse dashed past.

In those few seconds, it came close enough Robert Lee imagined he could smell its fear. At that point, he also saw the horse was riderless, which only heightened his panic.

Once he had his own mount under control, he urged it forward in the direction from which the horse had been running. Within a couple of minutes, he could see fire, and the closer he got, the more his horror grew.

He rode into the camp at a gallop, dismounting with his gun drawn and landing in a run. Letty's dog came out of the darkness, barking and growling. The campfire was ablaze, but he wouldn't look in it for fear of losing his night vision.

He dropped to a crouch, scanning the area for signs of a struggle and at first, saw nothing. The dog was still growling.

"Hush, boy," he said. "You know who I am."

At the sound of Robert Lee's voice, T-Bone went silent. As he did, Robert Lee suddenly focused on the fire and the body within it, then at the woman beyond, sprawled lifelessly on the ground and leaning against a tree.

"Oh, Jesus," he said softly and walked toward her.

At first, he wasn't sure if she was alive or dead. Her gaze was fixed, her face expressionless. The large, black stains on her clothes were obviously dried blood. He couldn't tell if it was hers. His legs were shaking as he knelt at her side. When he reached out and touched the side of her face, she didn't blink, but she was warm —blessedly warm—and her skin was soft—so soft to the touch.

"Letty, it's me, Robert Lee. Are you hurt?"

She didn't answer.

He moved closer, then slid an arm around her shoulders and pulled her against his chest. Her hair was in wild disarray—her clothes covered in dried blood and dust—and yet, because she was alive, she seemed beautiful.

Her pup was back beside her now, lying silently at her feet with a paw on her knees, as if pleading with her to get up. If only the dog could talk.

Robert Lee cradled her head against his forearm, then he pulled her into his lap and began to rock her where they sat. He wouldn't look at the fire—trying not to think of what she'd been through—or what must be going through her mind—then wondering if she had a mind left with which to think. He'd been afraid a few times before in his life but never as scared as he was at this moment.

"Letty...darlin'...you got to talk to me now. I can't help you none if you don't say where it hurts."

He felt her shudder, then heard her moan. When he looked, tears were rolling down her face. As he watched, she blinked—so slowly at first he thought she was falling asleep. Then she shuddered again, and this time when she blinked, he saw her eyes come into focus.

The first thing she saw was the fire before her. A cold, almost satisfied expression came and went on her face, but when she looked up at him, she was weeping.

"Robert Lee? Is it you?"

He cupped her head gently, then began brushing the hair from her forehead and her face.

"Yes, ma'am, it's me. Are you hurt?"

Her features crumpled.

"Oh, Robert Lee...he killed Eulis...my Eulis is dead."

Tears burned at the back of Robert Lee's throat.

"I know, girl...I know."

Her hands curled into fists as her gaze shifted once more to the flames.

"He's burning in hell, Robert Lee."

The rage in her voice made him shiver. This woman who held his heart would make an incomparable ally but a formidable enemy. He was suddenly grateful they were on the same side.

"I see that."

To his surprise, she pushed away from his arms and then dragged herself up. Swaying slightly, she moved back to the stack of firewood and picked up another stick. One after the other, she threw them all on the burning pyre until flames were higher than her head and wild, renegade sparks were flying up, up, up into the darkness.

Robert Lee didn't intervene. He understood the need for revenge. God knew this woman had done a hell of a job getting hers.

It wasn't until she'd thrown the last stick on the fire he moved to her side, with nothing but a touch of his hand on her shoulder to let her know he was there.

She turned then, and the look on her face was one of calm resolve.

"Letty."

"What?"

"Did you know him...the man who shot your man?"

"George Mellin."

Robert Lee flinched.

"You talkin' about Miz Alice's husband?"

"Yes."

He stared back into the fire. The implications of this revelation were such it could drive someone mad—if that same someone was assigning the blame.

If he'd never walked out into their valley looking for work, they might have never moved into town to the hotel. And if they hadn't been in that hotel, they would have never known Alice Mellin, or gotten involved in her tragedy—or felt the need to intervene on her behalf.

George Mellin would have continued on his way. Letty would never have felt impelled to take a bullwhip to the man, the grudge the man obviously bore her would never have evolved, and Eulis Potter would not be dead.

Robert Lee's father had often said, if wishes were horses, then beggars would ride, but he'd learned long ago wishing for something didn't change the truth.

There was nothing more to be said.

10

PROMISES KEPT

Letty kept the fire going all night, dragging limbs and brush and anything she could find that would burn. The higher the flames, the easier it became for her to breathe without wanting to scream. Her hair was singed at the ends and her eyes were raw and red-rimmed from the heat and burning ash. Her hands and arms were so bruised and scratched, they looked like she'd fought a bear and won, but she was impervious to pain. She refused to stop, no matter how many times Robert Lee tried to coax her to rest. Finally, he gave up the fight and followed the creek to where she'd tied her horse and walked it back to George Mellin's camp.

T-Bone shadowed every step Letty took, from going into the trees after more firewood, to standing watch at the fire as it burned.

When Robert Lee came back with her horse, Letty staggered to the saddlebags and dragged out the food Alice had packed for her. She pulled a piece of jerky from the pack and handed it to Robert Lee, then she dropped to her knees and began feeding the last of the cold flapjacks to T-Bone.

Robert Lee was dumbfounded. He didn't know what to make of this woman. She was in shock and so weary she could hardly put one foot in front of the other, and yet she was still taking care of those around her.

"Letty...ma'am...please. I sure wish you would eat somethin', too."

"No food," she said shortly and handed T-Bone another piece of flapjack.

"You could at least rest a bit."

"I can't rest. The fire will go out."

"No. I promise I won't let it."

Letty dropped the last of the flapjack in front of T-Bone and then stood up, wiping her shaky hands on her pant legs as she turned toward the fire. If a person hadn't known there was a body in there, it would have been impossible to tell. But Letty knew it, and in her mind, she still saw him, sitting there breathing when her Eulis was dead.

"He's still there," she said and wiped a hand across her brow.

Robert Lee frowned. Letty sounded like a woman out of her mind. He knew grief could do a thing like that. What he didn't know was if she'd come out of this with her sanity intact.

He took her by the arms and gently gave her a shake.

"Letty...Letty...look at me."

Her eyes were burning, and she'd inhaled wood smoke for so long she felt light-headed. Having to focus on Robert Lee was more difficult than he could imagine.

"What?"

Robert Lee cupped her face with his hands, gently rubbing his thumbs along the edge of her jaw.

"He's dead. You know he's dead...don't you?"

Letty frowned at him as if he'd lost his mind, then pushed his hands away.

"Hell yes, he's dead, Robert Lee. I oughta know. I put a lead ball right through the middle of his forehead before I set him on fire."

The hair crawled on the back of Robert Lee's neck. He hadn't known that. In fact, now that he thought about it, he'd been so worried about her safety he hadn't taken time to think about how George Mellin came to be burning. Just the fact it wasn't Letty who'd been on fire had been all he'd cared about. But this bit of information set his teeth on edge.

"You shot him," he said.

She frowned at him.

"That's what I said, didn't I?"

"Did he shoot at you?"

"No. I took his rifle away while he was still asleep."

Robert Lee took a couple of steps backward, then sat down on a stump before he made a fool of himself and fainted.

"You walked up on him in the dark? You took his rifle?"

"What would you have done? Waited until he woke up and then had a shoot-out? I'm sorry, but I didn't have the luxury."

"What do you mean?" Robert Lee asked.

"There's one shot in a loaded rifle."

Robert Lee knew he was missing something, but he still didn't know what.

"Well, yes, ma'am, I know that."

Letty picked up another stick and threw it on the fire. Sparks rose toward the heavens like smoke up a chimney.

"So I didn't want him shooting back at me if I missed, cause I don't know how to reload."

Robert Lee grunted as if he'd been kicked in the gut.

"You took off after a killer with one shot. You rode all day and most of the night, not knowing where the hell you were going or who you were after?"

Letty looked down at him and then nodded.

"What if you'd missed?" he asked.

A muscle jerked in her jaw as she licked her fire-burned lips.

"But, I didn't."

Then she turned away from him to stare into the fire.

Robert Lee put his hands on his knees and then took a slow, deep breath. He'd seen some things in his life, but this woman beat them all. When he thought he could stand without stumbling, he got up and walked into the woods.

Letty knew he was gone, but his whereabouts were of no concern to her. When he finally reappeared, he was carrying an arm load of deadwood. He dropped it at her feet, then went back for more.

It wasn't until daylight, when Letty could finally see, that she let the fire go out.

* * *

She was sitting on the ground with her knees against her chest and her hands over her face. T-Bone was lying beside her. To Robert Lee's knowledge, the dog hadn't taken its eyes off of her since she sat down, and she hadn't moved in over an hour. He wanted her to talk but was scared of what might come out of her mouth.

The morning sun shown down on the harsh reality of last night. The fire was nothing but a pile of warm ashes. From where Robert Lee was sitting, he could see what appeared to be a charred skull and some bones. The scent of smoke had dissipated drastically, but Robert Lee knew he would never forget the scent of burning wood and flesh, or the flash of fire in a grieving woman's eyes.

Across the creek, a doe slipped out of the trees, then lifted her head, tentatively sniffing the air. Finally, the need for water overcame her caution, and she moved down to the creek to drink. A small spotted fawn followed, taking short, tentative steps.

He watched until they'd drunk their fill and moved back into the woods. At that point, his belly growled. Except for the piece of jerky Letty had given him, he hadn't eaten in more than thirty-six hours, but he'd gone far longer without food and in far worse situations. An empty belly now and then was good for the soul.

* * *

Letty was numb. Her rage had burned out with George Mellin's fire. She didn't want to move. She didn't want to ride all the way back to Denver City. She didn't know why in God's name George Mellin hadn't killed her, too. It wasn't fair that she'd been left behind.

Sensing her turmoil, T-Bone stood up, then licked her ear.

She raised her head to shoo him away and instead, found herself staring into the half-grown pup's brown eyes. For the space of one heartbeat, she felt the pup's distress as sharply as she felt her own.

"Oh, T-Bone, what am I going to do without him?"

Then she put her arms around the pup's neck and started to cry.

T-Bone whined softly.

Letty patted him on the head, then pushed herself upright. She swayed shakily, then seemed to get her bearings, and began digging through Mellin's things. After nosing around, she picked up a large cloth sack and turned it upside down. The food and cookware he'd stolen from the old man tumbled out into the dirt.

Robert Lee heard the commotion and turned around just in time to see Letty move toward the fire. He stood abruptly, and started toward her.

"Letty!"

She didn't stop until she reached the ashes. To his horror, she began digging the bones out of the ashes and putting them in the sack. It was just as he feared—she'd finally lost her mind. He grabbed her arm and pulled her back.

"Letty! What the hell are you doing?"

She shrugged out of his grasp and picked up the skull.

"I'm taking Eulis's killer to the sheriff."

Surely, she didn't believe this man was still breathing. This was worse than he feared.

"Letty! He's dead, I tell you. He's dead."

She looked at him as if he'd suddenly become simple.

"We've already been through this, Robert Lee. I know that. But, for God's sake, it doesn't change what he did to Eulis...or to that old man he robbed. I intend for the people of Denver City to know that this killer paid for what he did."

Robert Lee was so relieved to know her wits were still about her he took the sack from her hands and then held it open.

Letty exhaled slowly. For the first time since his arrival last night, she became fully aware of what he'd done. Despite all the hours that had passed and the miles she'd traveled, Robert Lee had found her.

She looked down at his hands—at the long, slender fingers holding the old flour sack—remembering how quick he was on the draw and how steady they were now. His eyes were narrowed with determination and there was a jut to his jaw she'd seen only once before—the day he'd stepped between her and the sheriff after she'd taken a whip to Alice's husband.

She took a slow, deep breath, and then met his steady gaze. "I don't think I've mentioned this before, but I'm right glad you happened along."

Robert Lee gritted his teeth to stop himself from saying what was on his heart and just nodded.

T-Bone barked.

They turned to look at what had set him off and were just in time to see a raccoon waddling from the water back toward the trees.

"Leave him be," Letty said, and the dog sat down at her feet.

Without another word between them, Letty piled what was left of George's bones into the sack. Together, they saddled up and began the long journey home.

* * *

It was just after daybreak of the next day when Letty Potter rode into Denver City. Several noticed her arrival, as well as the tall, dark-haired man riding behind her. Her dog was trotting beside her horse with his head up and his tongue dangling out the side of his mouth.

Her hair was pulled back from her face and fastened at the nape of her neck with a piece of rawhide. The long, dark strands were uneven where the lengths had burned. Her skin was scratched and raw, and the old bloodstains on her clothes added to the drama of her appearance. Everyone knew her husband had been killed and she'd disappeared soon after. Some claimed she'd thrown herself off a cliff from the grief. Others swore she'd surely been done in by her husband's killer.

Her reappearance in town put rest to the gossip of her demise. However, they could tell something big was amiss. The lack of expression on her face sent tongues to wagging, and by the time she had ridden through town and dismounted in front of the sheriff's office, a small crowd was gathering behind her.

Sheriff Hamm came out to see what was happening just as Letty was tying up her horse. Like those gathering in the street, he'd supposed they'd never see her again—certainly not alive—yet here she was.

He'd learned of Potter's murder from Alice Mellin and had followed a trail of tracks away from the murder site all the way down the backside of the mountain to where they'd found the old man.

By the time they'd carried the old man's body back to Denver City, it was dark. He knew Letty Potter had ridden away from her home, supposedly after her husband's killer. It was his opinion she would be the next victim.

The next morning, he'd deputized a couple of down-on-their-luck prospectors and tried to pick up the trail from the old man's cabin. They followed it until they rode into a valley and came upon a large herd of elk. Upon their arrival, the herd bolted. Whatever tracks had been left by horses and men were gone, trampled beneath the hooves of the massive herd. Still, they tried for some time to pick up the trail, but were finally forced to give up, and rode back to Denver City.

The last thing Hamm ever expected to see was this woman tying up her horse in front of his office. He walked out with bravado, eyeing the dog who was sniffing his boots, and then stared at Robert Lee, who was quietly sitting on his horse. The fact the man hadn't dismounted seemed strange, but Hamm let the thought slide and shifted his focus to Letty Potter.

Her clothes were stained with blood and dirt, and the smell of wood smoke was strong about her. He thought she stumbled as she reached toward the saddle and untied an old flour sack, but then he changed his mind when she grabbed it firmly and turned around. He tried to meet her gaze but couldn't get past the guilt of coming back to Denver City without her or her husband's killer.

"Miz. Potter, I'm right sorry about your loss."

Letty didn't comment. Instead, she untied the sack and turned it upside down, dumping the contents at the sheriff's feet.

The charred bones clattered as they fell onto the wood planks, while the skull took an odd roll, coming to a stop at the toes of his boots.

"Godallmighty!" Hamm cried and jumped back as if he'd been burned. "What in hell have you done?"

"Brought back my husband's killer. I'm done with him. You can do what you will."

She dropped the sack, whistled at her dog, and mounted her horse.

"Wait! Where do you think you're going?" Hamm yelled.

Letty looked up the mountain where the roof of her house was barely visible. Her eyes filled with tears, then spilled over, running silently down her face.

"I reckon I'm going home, now," she said.

The crowd was deadly silent. Hamm didn't know what to think. The bones had their own truth to tell, but he didn't have enough facts to let this all go.

He was reaching for his pistol when he heard a distinct and familiar click. Robert Lee was holding a gun aimed at his chest.

"Don't even think it," Robert Lee said softly. "Miz Letty...you head on home now. I'll be along soon."

Letty didn't acknowledge that she'd heard him, but she did ride away.

Hamm was furious. This didn't look good, him letting a woman like her ride in and dump bones at his feet without some explanation. Then, having her hired gunslinger pull a weapon on him in front of all these people set his teeth on edge.

"I don't care if you got two guns trained on me. I need some answers," he said, then pointed at the skull. "There's a hole in this here skull."

"That would be where Miz Potter shot her husband's killer," Robert Lee said.

There was a collective gasp from the crowd of people as they all moved closer for a better look.

"Well, then," Hamm sputtered. "If she shot the man, then how did his body get burned?"

"That would be because she set him on fire."

All the color in Hamm's face went south. His mouth was moving, but he couldn't get the air to form words.

"Who is he?" someone shouted.

Robert Lee fixed the sheriff with a hard, angry stare.

"Ask the sheriff, here," Robert Lee said. "He's the one who let him go free."

Hamm reeled as if he'd been punched in the gut. He stared down at the pitiful pile of bones, unable to believe what he was seeing.

"What's he talking about?" A woman cried.

Hamm sputtered, then took a deep breath and quickly shifted the blame.

"Don't look at me," he said loudly. "It weren't me who said to let him go. It was that judge...Judge Joshua Dean, he called himself. He wouldn't even let me keep the man over for trial. He just walked in my office and ordered me to let the man go."

Unaware of the history behind the story, the same woman called out again.

"Let who go?" she asked.

Hamm bit his lip.

Robert Lee pointed with the barrel of his gun.

"George Mellin, and that there's what's left of him. He

killed Eulis Potter, an unarmed man, standing in his own yard. Miz Potter didn't do anything but get justice for her man." He started to holster his pistol, then thought better of it and added. "One more thing. If I hear one unkind word said about that woman, I will take it real personal...you hear? There aren't many men, let alone a lone woman, do what she just did. She rode the saddle for nigh on to twenty straight hours, riding hard through the dark in unfamiliar land, with one shot in a rifle she didn't know how to reload. That's the kind of woman a man would lay down his life for...which is what Eulis Potter did. It don't matter whether you agree with her method. She just did what was right."

Hamm was speechless, but the crowd was not. By the time Robert Lee had ridden out of sight, the story of Letty Potter's prowess had spread through half the town.

Letty didn't know and didn't care. The easy part of her life was over. The hard part was learning how to live without Eulis at her side.

* * *

Katie Samuels was playing in the dirt near the front steps when she heard someone coming up the trail. She saw the horse, recognized the riders, and went running into the house.

"Mama Alice, Mama Alice...Miz Letty and Robert Lee are back!"

"Thank you, Lord," Alice cried and wiped her hands on the front of her apron as she ran from the house. But when she saw Letty's face and the condition of her clothes, she was almost afraid to ask what she'd done.

"Letty...Letty...thank God you're home," Alice said, as Letty slid off the horse.

The reins slid out of Letty's hands to fall dangling to the ground. Robert Lee grabbed her around the waist, steadying her stride before she fell.

Alice gasped, then put a hand to her mouth. Her eyes were wide—questioning.

Robert Lee shook his head slightly, then tightened his grip on Letty.

"Come on now, Letty. Let me help you in the house. You made it this far. Just a little bit farther to go."

Letty swayed against him, then looked up. When she saw Alice, their gazes locked.

"Where is he?" Letty asked.

Alice sighed, then bit her lip.

"I laid him out in his coffin in the living room. A man is digging his grave right now. I'm right glad you made it back in time to see him put to rest. Did you catch who did it? Did you learn his name?"

Letty sighed. She hadn't thought past seeking revenge for Eulis, but this was going to be a thing Alice would have to learn to bear.

"Yes, I know his name," Letty said.

Alice waited.

Letty looked down at her boots, then back up at Alice.

"It was George...your husband...and I'm right sorry to tell you that I killed him dead."

Alice's face flushed, then turned pale as a sheet as she covered her mouth to keep from screaming. Overwhelmed with guilt for what had happened, she fell to her knees and wrapped her arms around Letty's legs.

"Lord, God...I am so blessed sorry. It's all my fault. I should never have stayed and put you and your family in this danger."

"Get up," Letty said. "It's not your fault Eulis is dead. George killed him, not you. It's something that happened, and it's something we will get through."

Then Letty looked past Alice to the front door. He was on the other side of those walls—waiting for her to tell him goodbye.

Robert Lee felt sick. He didn't think Letty would survive this. She hadn't eaten or slept in days. Now, the thought she was going to have to face her husband's funeral seemed a torture she shouldn't have to endure.

"Letty?"

"I can do this," she said softly and started up the steps.

"At least let me—"

Letty stopped, then spoke without looking back.

"I need to do this alone."

Alice sat down on the front steps and covered her face with her apron.

Katie slid beneath Mama Alice's arm and hid her face in her new mama's lap.

Robert Lee didn't move.

T-Bone laid down near the steps.

Letty walked into the house, then quietly closed the door behind her.

No one moved. No one looked at the other.

A pair of butterflies flitted through the morning sunlight, landing briefly on the porch rail, before flying off in search of blossoms from which to feed. An eagle appeared just above the treetops north of the house, causing a flock of feeding birds to take flight.

Between one heartbeat and the next, Robert Lee heard the sound, and at first, thought it was the wind in the trees, only there was no wind. It rose in pitch with the rhythm of his pulse until the pain in the sound pierced his soul. Hearing her grieve like this was almost more than he could bear.

"Ah, God," he muttered.

T-Bone cocked an ear toward the door, his nose quivering. When Letty began to sob in earnest, the pup lifted his head and began to howl.

Robert Lee wanted to howl, too. Instead, he held the reins of Letty's horse while she went about the business of dealing with a broken heart.

11

ASHES TO ASHES

They dug the grave at the back of the house, in the clearing near the trees, a few yards from Baby Mary. A steady stream of people had been coming since daylight, filling the yard to wait for the services to start. They didn't all know Eulis Potter, but they'd all heard about what his widow had done to avenge his death. They wanted to see the woman with ice in her veins.

Women arrived bringing food to feed the gathering afterward, giving them an excuse to go into the fine house. They'd expected more in the way of luxurious furnishings, but still found enough to foster envy. Few of them had ever spoken to the infamous Letty Potter, although they all knew who she was. Today was their chance for a first hand view of Denver City's richest woman.

Alice and Letty had shared a moment when they embraced in mutual grief, and then Alice had washed Letty's hair, bathed her as if she'd been a child, dressed her in a clean, simple dress, then coaxed her into sitting in a chair beside Eulis's coffin. People filed by to pay their respects to Mr. Potter and to get an up close look at the woman who was now his widow.

Letty saw none of it—heard none of it—felt none of it—not the touches of condolence or the words of sympathy—not even the curious looks. She was gratefully, blessedly numb. It wasn't until Robert Lee appeared that she was pulled back to the reality of what had yet to be done.

Robert Lee didn't speak, but when a small man with a weathered face began nailing the lid on Eulis's coffin, she grabbed him by the hand. With every blow of the hammer, Letty's grip tightened. By the time the man was done, Robert Lee could no longer feel his fingers.

The men who worked in the Potter mine walked single file into the living room, murmuring their uneasy condolences to a woman most of them feared. When Robert Lee gave them a nod, they shouldered Eulis's coffin and started out the door.

Robert Lee leaned down and whispered in Letty's ear.

"It's time to go now. Will you let me walk with you, ma'am?"

Letty frowned, then looked up.

"Robert Lee?

"Yes, ma'am. We need to go now."

"Oh. Yes. Of course," she said.

He helped her up and kept a firm grip on her elbow as he escorted her out the door.

She fell into step behind the coffin without notice of the crowd watching her pass, or of the people who fell into step behind her.

She was remembering the days back in Lizard Flats when she'd demanded a nightly bath in hot water that Eulis had to carry up to her room—and the night he'd turned himself into a preacher and baptized her in a moss-covered watering trough down at the livery.

All the months they'd traveled through the territories on the Amen Trail, preaching and singing and marrying and burying under the identity of a dead preacher from back East.

The nights they'd spent alone on the prairie—and the morning they woke up in the middle of a buffalo herd, certain that was the day they were going to die.

Then last winter, the fear she'd felt when they got snowed in at the abandoned cabin, convinced that Eulis was going to die from smallpox—facing down a starving wolf, then killing it with a stick of firewood.

The day she'd discovered the hidden gold mine behind a wall in the cabin, and the shock, then delight on Eulis's face, knowing their lives were forever going to change.

Everything was a jumble in her mind—all the times they'd laughed and all the times they'd fought and the days she'd wept in frustration.

The times Eulis was always there to hold her hand.

As they were lowering his coffin in the grave, she was remembering the tenderness in his voice when they'd exchanged wedding vows beneath the glow of a moon, and the first time they'd made love.

He'd treated her—a fifty-cent whore—like something special—until she'd begun to believe that she was.

He'd been everything she'd ever wanted. Their time together had been far too brief, but she knew if she had it to do over again, she wouldn't change a thing—except the way she'd dealt with George Mellin.

She would never have taken a bullwhip to him. She would have shot him where he stood. Then Eulis would still be alive, and she wouldn't be wishing she could join him in that grave.

* * *

With the absence of a preacher, Dr. Warren offered to read a passage from the bible. Letty didn't hear a word of what was said.

In her mind, she was watching Eulis preaching over Baby Mary's grave, hearing the sorrow in his voice as he gave the final prayer, then watching as he began filling up the hole, letting the dirt fall gently on top of the little box until he was done.

Someone squeezed her hand. She looked up. It was Robert Lee. Then she frowned. He'd been at Baby Mary's service, too. He'd made the cross they'd put on her grave, and here he was again. Eulis had been so certain this man was good. It seemed he'd been right.

"Mrs. Potter?"

She shivered as Dr. Warren laid a hand on her arm.

"Here, ma'am, please hold out your hands. It would be proper if you drop the first handful."

Letty shivered, assailed by the musty smell of damp earth, the scent of green wood, and the stench of death awaiting her blessing.

She opened her fingers, watching the dirt fall into the hole. It splattered on top of the green wood like raindrops, then one after the other, the mourners filed past, picking up a handful of earth from the pile, then dropping it into the grave, as she had done.

Letty stood without moving until they had all passed, then watched as the rest of the earth was shoveled on top of the pine box. Once they were done, Robert Lee led her back to the house. Alice had set up a chair for her near the fireplace in the parlor. She put a plate of food in her lap and then frowned when Letty handed it back to her without comment.

Alice leaned down until she was eye to eye with Letty, then lowered her voice to an angry whisper.

"You can't die with him, so don't bother to try. Trust me, Missy. I know."

Letty blinked. Their gazes locked, first in understanding, then with tears.

Alice squeezed Letty's hands, then kissed her briefly on the forehead.

"This, too, shall pass," she said softly and walked away, carrying the plate Letty had refused.

The food that had been brought to the home quickly disappeared as the hungry horde descended on the makeshift tables set up outside. They ate their way through two hours of food and gossip, and then convinced that they'd seen all of the drama to be had that day, went back down the mountain the same way they'd come up.

Robert Lee had a self-appointed mission of his own. Until Letty Potter came to herself, he was going to make certain she had a life and a business to come back to. He didn't have to convince the hired hands to go back to work. They showed up at the mine the next day and fell to working as if they owned the place themselves. Part of it had to do with their pride in working for a woman like Letty Potter, and the other part had to do with their fear of her and how she dealt with being crossed. Nobody wanted to make her mad and nobody wanted to see her cry. It was a good arrangement for all those involved.

* * *

A week into Letty's self-imposed isolation in her bedroom, her long-awaited furniture from back East finally arrived. Five wagons full of everything from furniture to linens to silverware and Letty couldn't have cared less. She was sitting on a small stool at the bedroom window when Katie came running up the stairs calling her name. Letty frowned, angry at being disturbed.

From where she was sitting, she could see the freshly turned earth mounded over Eulis's grave. In the back of her mind, she knew he would be disgusted with the way she was acting. She could almost hear him telling her to get up and get over it. Even though she knew that withdrawing from life was not helping her situation, she couldn't find a reason to care.

"Letty! Letty! Mama Alice said for you to come down quick!"

Letty turned toward the door.

"Why?"

"Our furniture! It's here! It's here!"

Two things struck Letty. The first was that little Katie, who'd suffered a loss much worse than Letty's, was already willing to give her allegiance to another woman, and the second was that she'd claimed this house as her own.

Letty had needed a purpose to face the day. It seemed that purpose had arrived. She got up from the stool and smoothed her hands down the front of her dress.

"Is that so?" Letty asked.

"Yes! Come see! There are five wagons full of crates. Mama Alice said we'll be living in a palace tonight."

Letty grinned, and then the moment she did, felt guilt for allowing joy, no matter how small, into her heart. She followed the little girl down the stairs and then out onto the front porch. The freighters had already tied down their teams and were prying the crates apart.

The first piece they unpacked was a wardrobe. Letty recognized it as one of the pieces Eulis had picked out. The elaborate carvings of oak leaves and acorns, as well as the red and gold stenciling on the doors looked like something out of a dream. They'd had no idea when they'd ordered the furnishings months ago he would not be here to see their arrival.

"Oh Eulis...you were right," Letty whispered. "The things are truly grand."

"Where do you want this, ma'am?" one of the men asked.

"Upstairs. First room on the right."

Up they went, and down they came until, one by one, all the crates were unpacked and the furniture was in place. The china Letty had ordered was still packed and in a crate in the kitchen. It would be up to her and Alice to put it in the cupboard.

There was also a large stack of linens, including bedding, tablecloths, and napkins to be put away. There was a large chest of silverware sitting on the sideboard. Letty had looked in it twice, still struggling with the reality this opulence belonged to her.

Alice's favorite piece, the wood cookstove, had been set up in the kitchen. The stove and stovepipe were shiny black, and the stove had a warming shelf and a large cooking surface. There was a small, ornate box beside the stove meant to hold kindling, and Alice immediately sent Katie outside to bring some in. She had not cooked on anything this fine since she'd left Boston three years earlier and couldn't wait to start a fire and cook a meal.

When they began unpacking the crate with the cooking pots and china, Letty's enthusiasm ended. The more homey the house became, the more she resented the fact Eulis would never share it with her. Without explaining herself, she left the room and headed for the back yard. She needed to talk to Eulis.

T-Bone fell into step beside her. He was growing so fast Letty could touch the top of his head without bending over anymore. When they reached the grave site, Letty paused, bracing herself for this confrontation. It had been bearing on her mind ever since she'd watched him take his last breath.

There was a small stump beside the wooden marker bearing Eulis's name. She didn't know Robert Lee had put it there for her, and if she had, would have been puzzled by his continuing concern. Still, she was grateful for its presence.

T-Bone plopped down beside the stump. Letty sat on it, then leaned forward, resting her elbows on her knees. Just looking at his name on the marker brought tears to her eyes. She cleared her throat, smoothed down the bits of hair that had come out of her braid, and licked her lips.

"It's me," she said. "I reckon you're doing fine. Wish I could say the same."

A large, fat robin sailed out of a nearby tree and then perched on Eulis's marker. Letty frowned.

"Is that supposed to be some sign that you're hearing me now?"

The bird tilted its head sideways, peering at her with a tiny black eye.

Letty sighed. "Listen to me...I must sound like some crazy woman...talking to a bird and all. Anyway, that's not why I came. I wanted to tell you that the furniture finally came." Her voice broke, but she kept on going.

"Those pieces you picked out are real pretty. I hate to admit it, but you were right about them all along."

The robin flew out of sight.

Letty sighed. "I guess it wasn't you after all." Then her chin began to tremble. "I'm sorry, Eulis. I'm as sorry as I can be. George Mellin was the man who killed you. If I hadn't interfered in his life, you would still be alive."

Tears were rolling down her face as she wiped her nose on the back of her hand.

"I never could mind my own business, could I? Anyway... I just wanted you to know I never meant for you to suffer for what I did, and that the man paid and paid dearly."

A breeze lifted the fringe of hair away from her forehead as she briefly closed her eyes. In her mind, she could almost see Eulis standing there, smiling at her in that slow, easy way he had. But when she opened her eyes, the fantasy was gone.

"Well, I guess I'll be going now. If you get the time and aren't too mad at me, I wouldn't mind if you said a prayer for me. For a man who couldn't read all that much, you were real good at praying."

She stood then, glancing down one more time at the marker with his name. Her shoulders slumped, but as she turned away and started back to the house, she straightened her back and lifted her chin. She'd been beaten down, but she owed it to Eulis to get up. She still carried his name, and even if she didn't want to—even if it hurt her heart every day for the rest of her life—she was going to do right by him and make his name a name of which to be proud.

* * *

Two weeks came and went and Letty began to resume something of a daily routine. She went into town when supplies were needed and with some help from Amos Trueblood, her banker, began keeping a decent set of books on her mine, which still showed no signs of playing out. For all intents and purposes, Letty Potter was worth more than she could spend in three lifetimes.

The flood that had washed all of the gold deposits out of Cherry Creek had long subsided, and new pockets were being found daily.

For some of the prospectors, it meant relocating a bit father downstream, and for others, they rediscovered new color on their old claims.

Robert and Mary Whiteside had finally come down off the mountain, but their fate had drastically changed. Before, they'd been getting color almost every day, but now they had nothing. They'd had to ask for credit at Milton Feasley's general store.

Mary had offered the suggestion that they go back to Philadelphia. Instead of giving Robert an excuse to pack it in, it had angered him. He'd taken it as failure on his part to provide for his family, and every day afterward without gold in the pan, he became more and more depressed.

* * *

Mary Whiteside had awakened this morning with a cramp in her neck and a centipede crawling on top of her blanket. She'd screamed in fright, as much as in anger for being put in such a precarious place. In frustration, she'd told Robert she wasn't going to the creek this morning and stayed in camp to put a pot of beans on to cook. Robert felt sorry for her and offered to go hunting to put some meat in the pot. Mary had pouted her way through breakfast, and when Robert left camp, she wouldn't tell him goodbye.

Now, hours later, the beans were almost done and Robert still wasn't back. She gave the bubbling beans a quick stir, then replaced the lid on the pot and looked up toward the woods. Robert should have been back a long time ago. She was on the verge of working up a new fuss when she heard a gunshot.

"It's about time," she mumbled to herself and hoped he'd shot them a rabbit or maybe a squirrel.

She waited for a few moments, then when Robert didn't appear, she put a couple of sticks on the fire so it wouldn't go out and started into the trees. He was probably in there cleaning his kill now. If he had it skinned and gutted, she'd take it right back to camp and put it on a spit. There was a little salt left in the sack which would make the meat right tasty.

Humming to herself, she walked a few yards into the trees and was somewhat surprised when she still hadn't spied him. Now she was wondering if he'd missed his shot and moved farther away from camp. He'd done that once before, and she'd had to spend a good two hours by herself in camp in the dark before he'd appeared. She didn't want to have to do that again. If he missed his shot, the beans would do fine.

"Robert! Robert! Where are you?" she called, but he didn't answer. "Dang man," she muttered, pausing with her hands on her hips as she squinted through the trees.

"Roobbberrrt!"

Still no answer. It wasn't until a few more minutes had passed she realized she was the only thing in the woods making any sound. There were no bird calls, no squirrel chatter—even the breeze seemed to have lain. A sick feeling turned in the pit of her stomach, not unlike the night they'd almost drowned in the flood. She called out again, only this time her voice cracked.

"Robert? Robert?"

A black snake slithered out of the underbrush and across her path. Normally, the sight wouldn't bother her, but the anxiety she was already feeling raised superstitions. She watched as the snake slithered away and convinced herself it was some kind of sign.

Now that her anxiety had turned to true fear, she began running up the hill, then backtracking the way she'd come, running west, then east. Up, then down. Backward, then forward, dodging small limbs, while others slapped her face. Wild berry vines, just past blooming, grabbed at her clothes, ripping the homespun, as well as her skin, and leaving stinging droplets of blood behind.

Finally, she found him at their old campsite near the creek, sitting with his back against a tree. He'd dropped his pistol near his right leg, right after he'd pulled the trigger and shot himself through the head. The shot had gone in one ear and out the other, and flies were already gathering on the blood trail down the left side of his face.

Mary gasped in disbelief, then fell to her knees and covered her face as she let out a wail. Then she looked at her husband and began to scream.

Men prospecting upstream heard her, but by the time they found her, she was wading up and down in the creek and babbling hysterically. She'd dug deep bloody gouges in her face and was pulling at her hair. When they tried to help her, she fought them like a woman possessed.

One of the men had the foresight to knock her out, while the others ran for help. By the time Sheriff Hamm arrived, Mary Whiteside had come to and was weeping softly at the edge of the water.

They carried Robert's body into town and laid him out at the blacksmith. These days, the blacksmith was making as much money building coffins as he was shoeing horses and mules. He calmly began to cut some pine boards.

Mary Whiteside was taken to the doctor's house. She wept quietly as he applied a mint salve to her face, while Mildred made her some tea. She'd wanted Robert to take her home to Philadelphia, instead, he had sent her to hell.

* * *

Letty was in the general store when a man came in, full of the story and of himself, claiming he'd saved Robert Whiteside's wife from drowning herself in Cherry Creek. The story didn't seem likely, considering the fact that Cherry Creek was less than four feet deep, but when Letty heard that Robert Whiteside had killed himself, she reckoned she knew how the woman must feel.

"Hey, mister...where did they take Mrs. Whiteside?"

"She's at the doctor's house," he said and then flushed when he realized who he was talking to. "Say...I was real sorry about your husband, Miz. Potter."

"Thank you," she said shortly, gathered up her purchases and headed out the door.

She drove the wagon up the street to Dr. Warren's house, then knocked on the front door.

Mildred answered.

"Come in, Letty. Angus is with a patient right now. He can see you in a while if you're a mind to wait."

"I didn't come to see him. I came to see Mrs. Whiteside."

Mildred shook her head sadly.

"Poor woman...looks like she tried to do herself in. She's in a bad way, she is." Then she realized the connection between Letty and Mary Whiteside and paled. "I'm sorry. I wasn't thinking."

"Not a problem," Letty said. "Life does go on...even when it pisses us off to no end."

Mildred blinked. She wasn't used to ladies using such language, but then she remembered Letty Potter never claimed to be a lady.

"I'll tell Angus you're here," Mildred said.

Letty waited.

A few minutes later, Angus came out of his office, eyed Letty with a professional stare, judged her as sad, but sound, and greeted her as such.

"You're looking well," he said.

Letty nodded. "I'm still breathing. Reckon I might talk to Mrs. Whiteside a minute?"

Angus sighed. "It can't hurt. Maybe you can say something to her that will help. Lord knows you understand what she's going through."

"Thanks," Letty said, and even as she was opening the door to the office, she wondered what the hell she was doing.

Mary Whiteside was sitting on the side of the examining table, staring down at the floor. Her face looked like she'd been slapped by a bobcat and come out the loser. Her eyes were red-rimmed and swollen, and there was a thin stream of snot running down the side of her lip.

Letty grabbed the hem of Mary's dress and yanked it up over her knees, wiped Mary's nose, and then dropped the skirt.

Startled by the feel of air on her bare limbs, Mary looked up.

"Snot," Letty said, pointing at Mary's nose.

Mary blinked. "What did you say?"

Letty pointed again. "You had snot on your lip. I wiped it off."

"Oh." She blinked again. "My Robert killed himself today."

Letty nodded. "I heard. Damn selfish of him, don't you think?"

Mary gasped. "How dare you come in here and—"

"What?" Letty leaned forward, placing her hands on either side of Mary's legs, until she could see her own reflection in the woman's eyes. "Don't get all indignant on me, now, and try to tell me you haven't thought the same damn thing. Just because you were having a run of bad luck, doesn't mean you walk out on your partner like that. Dying is one thing. Killing yourself is another. He ran out on you, woman. I understand your shock, and I understand your pain. But damn it, lady, he left you high and dry without a care for what you might have to do to keep yourself alive. You don't need to grieve for someone who'd do that to you."

Mary frowned. Despite this woman's ravings, she was making some sense.

"So, you've said your piece," Mary muttered. "I don't need someone like you rubbing salt in the wound."

Letty's anger shifted, as she laid a hand on Mary's knee.

"I didn't come to rub salt," she said softly. "I came to take you home."

Mary's eyes widened. "We had a tent. It washed away in the flood."

"I wasn't talking about your camp, I'm talking about my house. There are empty rooms. You're welcome to one."

Mary's lips went slack.

"I'm what?"

"Welcome to come stay with Alice and Katie and me."

"But I can't pay."

Letty frowned. "I'm not running a hotel. I'm just offering you a room in my house."

"But what will I do?" she asked.

"Well...Alice cooks and looks after Katie." She eyed the woman closer. "Are you coming or not?"

Mary fidgeted slightly, then picked up the hem of her dress and blew her nose soundly.

"I can grow just about anything. If you've got some seeds and such, I can make a vegetable garden. Mama had a fine vegetable garden back in Philadelphia. I used to help her with it."

"We'll get some seeds," Letty said. "In the meantime, is there anything you need to get from your camp?"

Mary thought of the beans she'd left cooking on the fire and Robert's axe he'd left leaning against a tree.

"No."

"No matter," Letty said. "All of us up at the house are like you. Clothes can be replaced." Then her voice softened. "It's the people we lose that we think we can't live without." Just for a moment, her chin quivered. "Trouble is...despite everything we do to the contrary, we somehow keep breathing...so...are you coming with me or not?"

Mary slid off the examining table and picked up the small tin of salve the doctor had given her to put on her face.

"I reckon I'd be much obliged," Mary said and then shuddered. "I have to see to burying my man."

"I know something about that," Letty said. "Follow me."

And she did.

12

A REASON TO CARE

Within a week of Mary Whiteside's arrival, the townspeople had begun referring to the fancy home on the hill as the Hen House. Letty supposed it was because of all the females living there.

Mary Whiteside fell into the routine easier than she would have believed. Having a roof over her head and a clean bed to sleep in every night was a big inducement to adapt. There was also the fact Mary Whiteside could read —and read quite well. With Alice's approval, Mary took it upon herself to begin giving Katie daily lessons. The trio of newcomers bonded quickly. It was Letty who still held herself back, even though it was her home and money providing their care. There was a part of her that didn't trust life enough to take another chance at being happy. She was satisfied with just being okay.

But, like every good thing, it must eventually come to an end. For Letty, it ended on a Thursday, just before noon, and in a way that put what she thought was important into sharp perspective.

* * *

Noah Shaffer was one of the first men Eulis had hired when they'd opened the mine, so when Letty saw him riding up to the house at a fast clip, she thought little of it. Robert Lee often sent one of them to ask her instructions as to how she might want them to proceed. But when Noah rode up to the front porch in an all out gallop, she realized it wasn't a normal visit.

"Miz Potter! You need to come quick. Robert Lee went and got himself shot."

Letty felt the blood draining out of her face. She opened her mouth, but couldn't find the air to talk.

"He's at Doc Warren's right now. Doc sent me to tell you."

By this time, Alice had come out on the porch. Her face was sweaty and flushed from baking bread, and the front of her apron was white with flour. She took one look at the shock on Letty's face, then grabbed her by the arm and gave her a shake.

"Breathe, woman!" Alice cried.

Letty leaned against the porch rail to keep from falling.

"What happened?" Letty asked.

Noah pulled off his hat as he began to recite the news.

"Robert Lee was going into the bank when robbers came running out, making off with the money. Amos Trueblood came out all bloody and yelling he'd just been robbed. Robert Lee went and shot both men dead in the street, but not before one of them put a shot in him."

"Oh, Lord," Letty muttered.

"Is it bad?" Alice asked.

"I couldn't rightly say, ma'am," Noah said. "I was to meet up with him at the smelter, but when I heard what happened, I went straight to the Doc's. He was laid out on Doc's table when I got there, and I didn't see him talking."

Letty bolted off the porch.

"You can't ride in those clothes," Alice yelled. "Go change."

Since Letty rarely left the house these days, she had taken to wearing dresses again, but she ignored Alice's orders as she made a run for the shed.

"Where are you going?" Alice cried.

"To saddle my horse," Letty called.

"I'll do it for you, ma'am," Noah said, and rode past her to the shed. By the time she got there, he had a bridle and a saddle blanket on the horse and was reaching for the saddle.

Moments later, Letty hitched up her skirts and mounted without care that her skirt and petticoats were bunched up around her waist, and her legs were bare clear to her knees.

She kicked the horse in the flanks and away they went.

"Oh, Law!" Alice cried, when she saw Letty's bare flesh, and covered her face with her apron.

Letty rode down the mountain without thought for decorum, begging God all the way there to spare Robert Lee. The streets were awash with people who'd heard about the robbery. Some had gathered on corners to rehash the gossip, while others had moved to the blacksmith shop to get a look at the two dead men.

There were plenty who saw Letty Potter come riding into town with her hair flying and her skirts up around her waist. They all saw her bare legs and bouncing bosom, but no one had the guts to voice an opinion as to the wisdom of such a stunt.

Letty got to the doctor's office, but when she dismounted, she found herself shaking so hard she didn't think she could walk.

Mildred had seen her coming and ran out to meet her.

"Lawsy sakes, Miz Potter, your limbs were showing," she cried, as Letty tied her horse to the rail.

Letty grabbed Mildred's arm.

"Tell me he's not dead."

"How 'bout if I tell you, myself," Robert Lee said, as he walked out of the house.

Letty took one look at his face, saw the sling over his shoulder and the bandage on his arm right before her eyes rolled back in her head. She was out before she hit the ground.

"Damn it," Robert Lee muttered and bolted off the porch.

"Oh my!" Mildred gasped and ran into the house, calling her husband's name.

Letty came to almost as fast as she'd passed out. Robert Lee was kneeling at her side and cradling her head in his lap.

"What happened?" she mumbled, as she pushed herself upright.

"I reckon you fainted, ma'am," he said softly, regretting the fact he no longer had an excuse to be touching her.

"I don't faint," she said, then pointed to his arm. "Are you all right?"

He grinned slowly. "Except for a hole in my shoulder, I'm just fine."

"I fail to see the humor in this," Letty said. "You could have been killed."

Her fear and anger surprised him. His expression stilled.

"There are far too many times in my life when that has sure been the case. Today was no different. However, if you don't mind my sayin', I am right glad it isn't so."

His soft voice rattled across Letty's senses. She looked up into his dark, solemn eyes and swallowed nervously.

"Well...of course, I am, too."

At that point, Dr. Warren came running out of the house.

"What's going on out here?" he cried, as he ran down the steps.

"She fainted," Robert Lee said.

Letty glared. "I don't faint."

Robert Lee frowned. His shoulder was hurting something fierce and he wasn't in the frame of mind to let Letty get away with the lie.

"You know, Doc, she must be right. I guess I just mistook her fainting when it must have been disgust. I reckon when she saw my ugly mug, she closed her eyes from the sight, and then fell on her ass because she couldn't see where she was going."

The doctor swallowed what sounded like a small snort of glee as Letty gasped. Robert Lee had just mentioned her backside and made fun of her at the same time. She pointed her finger in his face.

"It's not polite to talk about women's body parts."

"No one ever accused me of having manners," Robert Lee drawled.

Letty fidgeted. "I didn't faint, I guess I was just...just... relieved and uh...afraid."

"There's nothing to be afraid of," he said softly.

Letty didn't know why, but she suddenly felt as if he was saying one thing but meaning another. It threw her off kilter even more.

"Well, I—" Letty stuttered, then held up a hand. "Oh... never mind, just somebody please help me up."

Dr. Warren took her by the arm and helped her up while Robert Lee kept his distance. Once Letty was up, she began brushing the dust from her dress and muttering beneath her breath.

"I swear...scared me half to...don't know what...high and dry...damn guns."

Robert Lee ignored her fussing because he couldn't fix what was wrong with her anymore than he could fix what was wrong with himself. She was at a loss without her husband, and he was drowning in his own love for her.

"I gotta go find my horse," he said and then shook the doctor's hand. "I appreciate you fixing me up."

"My pleasure, Robert Lee. Take care of yourself, and if you have any trouble with that shoulder, you come back to see me."

"All right," Robert Lee said and waited until the doctor had gone back in the house before he turned to Letty.

"Where is your horse?" she asked.

"He was at the hitching rail at the bank, although when all the shooting started, people and horses went everywhere. I hope he's still there."

Even as he was saying it, Noah Shaffer was riding up, leading Robert Lee's horse.

"It sure is good to see you standin'," Noah said, as he dismounted and handed Robert Lee the reins.

"Yeah, I'm encouraged by the fact, myself," Robert Lee said. "I reckon I'll be heading on back to the mine now."

"Oh no, you aren't," Letty said. "You're coming home with me. You're going to need some help with changing bandages and such."

Robert Lee didn't know if the shock he was feeling showed on his face, but there was no way in hell he was going to spend a single night under the same roof with this woman.

"No, ma'am, I'm not. I've been shot before, in far worse situations, and without a fine cabin or a horse to get me out of the weather."

Letty wouldn't let it go. "But what if—"

"Ma'am." Robert Lee balked. "I appreciate you more than you will ever know, and I understand your kindness, but I'm going home."

Having declared himself, he grabbed the saddle-horn with his good arm and swung up into the saddle. Noah handed him the reins. His stubbornness cost him. Holding on so hard his knuckles turned white—he bowed his head until he could control his breathing, then looked at Letty.

"I'm available if you need me," he told her, then said to Noah. "It's time we got back."

"Yes, sir," Noah said.

Together, they rode out of town. Letty watched until she could no longer see them, then mounted her horse and went home.

Alice was on the porch, anxiously awaiting news.

"Oh, Letty! Thank goodness you're back! How is Robert Lee?"

"I suppose he's just fine...he said he was fine, and who am I to argue," she snapped and led her horse toward the shed.

That night when she went upstairs to go to bed, she changed into her nightgown, then walked to the window overlooking the backyard.

The quarter moon appeared in the sky like a tear in the fabric of heaven, partially hidden by the constantly moving clouds. She tried, without success, to pinpoint Eulis's grave. It was strange, knowing it was there, but not being able to see it. She'd had no idea how much she'd depended on him until he was no longer there. Talking to him, even when she couldn't see him, seemed to help.

"Well, you probably already know this, but I thought I'd let you know Robert Lee went and got himself shot today." She paused for a bit, thinking out what she needed to get off her chest. "I got mad at him. That wasn't right, was it?" She sighed, then tunneled her fingers through her hair. "I don't know what I was thinking, but when Noah Shaffer rode up and told us he'd been shot, well, you can imagine what I thought. I thought about you. You went and died on me. I guess I was afraid he would, too. That's crazy, isn't it? I don't know why I'm acting like this. I took care of myself for all those years without anybody's help...except maybe yours. You did make sure I had my hot bath water when I wanted it, didn't you?"

The wind was rising. It rattled the panes in the window enough she flinched.

"It looks like we might get ourselves a storm tonight, which reminds me...I've been wondering about digging a root cellar. Probably should have put one under the house. I'll think on it some."

She looked up at the sky again, then back down at the darkness and reluctantly laid the flat of her hand on the window.

"Good night, Eulis. I miss you. Thanks for listening."

* * *

As Letty had predicted, a thunderstorm swept through the area, moving at a wild, frantic pace and leaving an inch of rain behind. It muddied up the streets and roads some, but nothing that couldn't be traversed.

She woke up with the feeling something important needed to be done. It took her a few moments to remember about Robert Lee getting shot. Her instincts were to ride out and check on him, make sure he hadn't come down with a fever, or was in terrible pain and unable to tend to his own needs.

But, she didn't. In fact, she was a little uncertain as how to proceed with Robert Lee. In a way, he'd done something no other man had ever been able to do—he'd intimidated her—a lot.

* * *

A few days later, a couple of freight wagons arrived, which was a big relief to Milton Feasley's customers. He'd been out of coffee for more than a month, and while they were accustomed to doing without many things, coffee was something they didn't want to give up.

Milton had hired a couple of men to help the driver unload his goods, and they were in the act of carrying them through the store to the storeroom, when another customer entered the store.

Milton looked up and frowned. It was Delia, the whore from the hotel. He'd availed himself of her services a couple of times, but there was a fine line between her accommodating him, and him being able to accommodate her. He hurried to the counter, then glanced nervously around.

"Miss Delia?"

Delia Carter knew she was crossing a line, but she needed food just like the rest of Denver City's fine citizens. She laid a list in front of Milton and dared him to make an issue of it.

Milton cleared his throat and picked up the list.

"Coffee...cornmeal...beans?" He scanned the rest of the items she'd written down and then frowned. "I didn't realize you had access to a cookstove."

Delia smiled coolly, when she really wanted to slap his face. "Like everyone else, I require food to live. I do not live in the hotel. It's just where I do my business, remember?"

Milton flushed nervously. He didn't particularly want it known he had taken advantage of her services. He decided the best way to deal with it was to get her list filled and get her out of the store as soon as possible.

"I'll be getting these for you right now. If you want to wait out—"

"I'll be right here." Delia glared.

Milton flushed.

"Yes, of course. I won't be long."

"I'll just bet," Delia muttered, as he began scurrying about the store.

"Sometimes, they just grate on your last nerve, don't they?"

Delia flinched and then turned around, surprised a woman was actually speaking to her. When she saw who it was, her surprise deepened.

"Mrs. Potter?"

"Call me Letty," she said and smiled. "My husband and I lived across the hall from you a while back. Maybe you remember?"

Delia flushed. "Yes, ma'am, I remember. I'm real sorry about your husband and all. I would have come to the services, but I knew it wouldn't be proper. Still, you have my sympathies."

Letty nodded.

"Thank you." Then she pointed toward the new crates being unpacked in the back room. "Did you come for coffee, too?"

"Yes, ma'am."

Letty smiled again. "Your name is Delia, isn't it?"

"Yes, ma'am. Delia Carter."

"Where are you from?"

Delia rolled her eyes. "You name it."

Letty understood. She eyed her closer, guessing her age at about twenty, maybe twenty two. She was a tall, pretty girl with auburn hair and blue eyes. Her skin was smooth and clear, but there was a hard look in her eyes Letty recognized. The young woman had no trust left in her.

Milton came scurrying by, eyed Letty nervously, then glared at Delia, as if she were overstepping her bounds by even speaking to Denver City's richest woman.

Letty saw the look and glared back at Milton, startling him to the point he got flustered and dropped the bag of beans he'd been carrying. It hit the floor with a splat and burst open, sending dry speckled beans in every direction.

"Oh! I'm so sorry!" Milton gasped and ran for a broom and pan to scoop them up. They had to be washed anyway, so he didn't figure they'd come to any harm.

"We'll get out of your way for a bit," Letty said. She smiled at Delia and pointed toward the corner of the store where the fabrics were kept. "Join me...will you?"

Delia was more than surprised. She was shocked.

"Thank you, ma'am, but I don't think it would be—"

Letty took her by the arm and all but dragged her away from the counter.

"Don't look so startled," Letty said. "I have something to ask you." She put her hands on her hips and eyed the young woman from head to toe. "Do you like what you're doing?"

Delia frowned. "If you're about to preach at me, ma'am, then I'd just as soon you kept your thoughts to yourself. You've obviously never been in my position, or you wouldn't ask a question like that?"

Letty led with her chin and kept talking.

"That's just it, honey...I have been in your position...for years back in the Kansas territories...in a watering hole in Lizard Flats called The White Dove Saloon."

Delia's lips went slack. Her eyes widened in disbelief.

"I don't get it. If this is true, then why are you telling me?"

"Because I thought if you were interested, you might consider changing your occupation."

A muscle jerked near Delia's left eye, but her voice never wavered.

"I didn't choose my occupation. It chose me. Believe me, not a day goes by I don't wish the redskins had killed me, too, when they killed my ma and pa."

"Where were you when this happened?" Letty asked.

"We'd just crossed the Mississippi."

"How did you get away?"

"I wasn't in camp when they attacked." Tears suddenly pooled in Delia's eyes and rolled down her face unchecked. "I hid when I heard the war cries. Then I heard Mama screaming and closed my eyes. When I woke up, it was night and they were gone. They scalped my folks and took the wagon and horses. A pair of French trappers found me."

Letty hurt for the child Delia had been. Their lives were too similar to ignore.

"How old were you?"

"Ten."

"Lord," Letty muttered, then a thought occurred. "How old were you when they started messing with you?"

"Ten."

Letty folded her arms across her breasts and stared Delia straight in the face.

"I have an offer to make."

"What?"

"If you want...I'm offering you a way out of the life you're living."

Delia frowned. She'd been wise to the ways of the world for far too long to trust anyone or anything.

"Oh yeah...and what do you want in return?" she asked.

"Nothing," Letty said.

Delia's heart skipped a beat. If the woman was serious, this just might turn out to be the best day of her life.

"Why would you do this?" Delia whispered.

"Because someone did it for me," Letty said softly, thinking of Eulis.

"I don't understand," Delia said and then started to cry.

"You don't have to understand. You just have to make a decision to give up this life for another."

"But what will I do?" Delia said. "I don't know any other way."

"Something will come to you," Letty said.

"Are you sure?" Delia asked.

"I'm rich as sin," Letty said. "Might as well do something useful with it."

Delia threw her arms around Letty's neck and hugged her fiercely. Letty smiled and patted her on the back.

"So, how long will it take you to pack?"

"About five minutes," Delia said.

"My wagon's out front. I'll be in it, waiting."

"Oh, Lord, oh, Lord," Delia muttered and then ran out of the store without looking back.

Milton was just finishing the last items on Delia's list when he saw her run out.

"Hey! You forgot your things!" he yelled.

"Put them in with my stuff," Letty said.

"But she didn't pay me yet," Milton whined.

"Add it to my bill. I'll pay for both."

Milton's eyes bugged.

"Well now, Miz Potter...are you sure you want to—"

"Milton!"

"Yes, ma'am?"

"Mind your own business."

He blinked.

"Yes, ma'am."

* * *

It was with no small amount of distress the men of Denver City learned of Delia's escape. It took a few days for the news to spread that another hen had been added to the Hen House at the top of the hill above the city.

But by then, Delia was settling in just fine, and with Alice's help, was learning how to bake bread.

Robert Lee heard about Letty's latest stunt but kept his opinions to himself. Personally, he believed Letty kept gathering the lost around her because she felt as lost as the females she'd taken in.

His shoulder continued to heal without problems. Within a month after the shooting, he pronounced himself fit, discarded the sling, and began practicing his draw, making sure he didn't lose the one skill that had kept him alive all these years.

13

BEYOND HER WILDEST DREAMS

It was Sunday when Letty decided she'd ride out to the mine and check on Robert Lee. More than three weeks had passed since he'd been shot, and during that time, he'd been by the house twice to give her updates on the situation at the mine. Once to tell her they'd blasted into a whole new vein that seemed even richer than the first, and the second time to tell her Noah Shaffer quit and went back home to Louisiana. Both times he'd been cordial, but there was a reserve within him she just didn't understand. She had fretted over it to the point she was beginning to lose sleep. She feared she'd somehow hurt his feelings, and she intended to do whatever it took to get back to the friendly relationship they'd once observed.

The weather was warm, unlike the last five days when the men she'd hired had dug her a cellar. A carpenter had come yesterday and put a door on it. Now, they were ready for anything.

The day was sunny. The scent of chicken frying in the kitchen drifted up the stairwell as she dressed in a pair of pants and a shirt. She pulled her hair away from her face and tied it at the back of her neck with a length of ribbon.

But when she sat down on the side of the bed and leaned over to put on her boots, the room began to spin around her.

Immediately, she straightened and grabbed the bedspread to keep from sliding onto the floor. It took a few moments for the room to settle. Shaken by the unexpected weakness, Letty sat, waiting to see if it happened again. When it did not, she wiped a shaky hand across her forehead, feeling to see if she was coming down with a fever. Her forehead was cool to the touch.

"Good grief," she muttered and leaned down to put on her other boot.

As before, the room began to spin like a top. She managed to get her foot into the other boot, then grabbed onto the bedpost to keep from falling on her face.

What's happening to me? I was fine at breakfast, although the eggs Alice fried did taste a bit off.

She'd suffered food poisoning once before when she'd eaten some bad meat and didn't relish a repeat of that event. Wondering if anyone else in the house was feeling ill effects, she managed to get herself downstairs, then headed for the kitchen.

Alice was standing at the stove, taking pieces of fried chicken from a large cast iron pot. Delia was moving from the kitchen to the dining room, setting the table with Letty's good dishes. Through the window, Letty could see Katie with Mary Whiteside bringing up a fresh pail of water from their dug well. No one seemed the worse for wear, so she decided not to mention it. The last thing she wanted was for Alice to start fussing.

"That chicken smells good," Letty said.

"It's mite near done," Alice said. "You could carry that plate of cornbread to the table."

Letty reached for the plate, then staggered.

Alice saw her stumble and grabbed her before she fell.

"Here now," Alice said and sat her down on a stool beside the window. "Are you all right?"

Letty shuddered. Suddenly the scent of cooking chicken didn't smell so good after all.

"I don't think so," Letty said. "I'm thinking the eggs I had for breakfast might have been a bit off."

Alice frowned. "I got them from Milton Feasley yesterday. He said Georgia Bennet brought them in fresh that morning. Besides, we all ate eggs this morning and no one else is ailing. Do you hurt anywhere?"

"No. Just a little dizzy," Letty said. "I'll just sit here a bit until the room stops spinning."

Alice frowned, eyeing Letty's pallor, as well as her clothes—a sign she planned to go riding.

"You stay by the window. There's a good breeze blowing."

"Yes, I believe I will," Letty said.

Alice went back to her cooking, but ever so often looked at Letty, her frown deepening with every glance.

"I see you're planning to go somewhere. Do you think that's wise, considering how you feel?" Alice asked.

"I intended to ride out to the mine and check on Robert Lee, but I suppose now I'll wait and see how I feel after we eat dinner."

Alice nodded approvingly.

"Do you reckon we'll have enough chicken that you could put back two or three pieces for Robert Lee?" Letty asked.

"Of course," Alice said. "I fried up two big hens. There should be plenty...and fresh cornbread, too."

"Good," Letty said. "I know he'll appreciate your fine cooking."

Alice beamed as she continued to take up the rest of the chicken.

Mary Whiteside and little Katie came in the back door with the bucket of fresh water as Delia came in from the dining room.

Delia glanced at Letty, then stopped and stared.

"You're sick."

Letty shrugged.

"It's nothing. Just a little bit dizzy."

"You're white as a sheet," Delia said.

Mary hurried to the sideboard, got a clean glass and filled it full of fresh water.

"Here now," she said, handing Letty the water. "Drink up while it's still cool from the well."

A little embarrassed by all of the female attention, Letty nodded her thanks and took a quick sip. Within seconds of it hitting her stomach, she knew it had been a mistake. She made a dash for the back door and barely made it to the edge of the porch before everything in her stomach came up.

Someone was holding her around the waist, while another was wiping her face with a wet cloth. She could hear little Katie's nervous whisper, asking if Miz Letty was going to die. Letty wanted to assure her that she was just fine, but she couldn't draw breath long enough to talk before another spasm hit. By the time she was finished, she was of the opinion that little Katie could be right. Never in her life had she felt so miserable.

"I think I'll just sit out here for a bit," Letty said, as Alice helped her to a chair near the edge of the porch where the breeze blew strongest. "You all go on ahead and eat your dinner. I couldn't eat a bite."

Alice frowned.

Delia stared.

Mary Whiteside set her jaw.

Katie began to cry.

"Here now," Alice said, gathering Katie up into her arms. "Miz Letty isn't dying. She's just a bit under the weather today. Let's go on in the house and give her some space. Okay?"

Katie nodded but didn't seem all that convinced. She hid her face against Alice's bosom, afraid she was about to witness another death.

Letty could hear the women whispering among themselves as they went back into the house. She was thankful for their concern but too queasy to dwell on it.

T-Bone came out from under the porch and sat down at her feet, staring up at her with a brown, soulful stare.

Letty laid a hand on his head with an absent touch, as she leaned back in the chair and closed her eyes, letting her body go limp.

The breeze was fairly stiff, and the cool mountain air blowing against her face felt wonderful. It didn't appear she was going to ride out to the mine after all. She hated to think about Robert Lee not getting any of Alice's fine chicken and cornbread. She'd have Alice save it for a while anyway. There was always the chance he'd ride by.

She sat for a bit, letting her thoughts wander as her stomach slowly settled. Finally, she opened her eyes and as she did, caught a glimpse of the cross marking Eulis's grave. Without thinking, she got up from her chair, stepped off the porch and headed for the stump. The urge to talk to Eulis was strong.

Columbines were blooming along the edge of the path, their pale, rosy blooms dangled from the fragile stems like tiny bells. A pair of robins were fussing over a green woolly caterpillar, and a small gray squirrel was digging near a clump of rocks, searching for nuts it had buried last fall. T-Bone's presence made the squirrel nervous, and it disappeared up a tree.

The peacefulness of the moment was, for Letty, bittersweet. It was the kind of scene Eulis would have loved, and she felt more than a little anger that fate had taken him away.

When she reached his grave, she eased herself down onto the stump, and as she did, realized she was shaking.

"Lord, Eulis, what's the matter with me? I'm carrying on like some helpless female, and you and I both know I'm anything but that."

Her complaint seemed out of place within the peacefulness, and since it was obvious Eulis wasn't going to answer, Letty decided to shut up. For a while, she just sat, watching a tiny trail of ants marching from somewhere beneath the stump to an anthill on the other side of the white cross bearing Eulis's name and trying to concentrate on anything but the constant rumble in her belly.

As she sat, a quiet enveloped her. The shaking eased. Her stomach settled. She closed her eyes and drew a deep, cleansing breath, and as she did, a realization dawned.

Eulis had been gone for more than two months. There had been so much turmoil in her life afterward she hadn't given the normal functions of her body a single thought, but she was thinking about them now. Not once since Eulis had died, had she had her monthly flow.

Suddenly, she stood, her gaze frantic, her heart pounding in disbelief. Her vision blurred as she gazed down at the cross on Eulis's grave.

"Oh, Eulis...Eulis...can it be? Here I've been thinking you went off and left me all alone." Her voice began to shake as she laid her hands across the flat of her belly. "I'm not sure about this, because...well...I haven't been in this situation before...but I just realized we might be having a baby." She sat back down on the stump, stared at the bulge of bare earth over his grave and started to cry. "All I have to say is...it's not fair."

It took a few minutes of bawling aloud before she could finish what she needed to say. The ants were still in the midst of their march, but the robins had flown away and the squirrel was still up a tree. Letty shuddered, overwhelmed from the realization and from the new wave of grief. Eulis was gone, but he'd left a bit of himself behind. She didn't have to see Dr. Warren to be told, there was a knowing deep in her heart. She was truly going to have a baby.

She came off the stump and went down on her knees, then fell forward, embracing the bulge of brown earth that blanketed her man. She lay there, numb to everything but the knowledge she was coming to accept. Eulis was gone, but he'd given her the one thing she'd believed was beyond her.

"Thank you, Eulis...thank you from the bottom of my heart."

She never heard the sounds of someone approaching on horseback or the thump of his boots hitting dirt as he dismounted on the run. It wasn't until he was on his knees beside her and pulling her up into his arms she realized she was no longer alone.

* * *

Robert Lee had awakened with Letty on his mind. It wasn't anything unusual, because she haunted his thoughts during the day, as well as his dreams at night. Still, for some reason, today felt different.

He'd purposefully kept his distance over the last few weeks, knowing it was safer if she was angry with him, than if she was overly sympathetic regarding his gunshot wound. Yet, for some reason, his need to see her today was stronger than his fear of revealing too many of his feelings. And so he'd saddled up after tending his chores and ridden into town. He'd killed time at the saloon, bought some needed supplies, and ridden by the blacksmith to have a loose shoe replaced on his horse's right hoof. Each time he stopped for a task, his gaze was drawn to the fine house just visible on the hill above Denver City. It was almost noon. He knew if he rode in during mealtime, they would invite him to eat. It would be a good excuse to spend some time in Letty's presence but with the distraction of all the other women to keep his manners in place. Once his horse had been shod, he headed for the road that led to Letty.

He'd smelled fried chicken as he was riding up to the front of the house. The windows were open and the curtains were blowing in the breeze. He could hear the sound of laughter and recognized little Katie's voice, as well as Alice's. He knew Mary Whiteside only slightly but was getting to know her better with each trip. He knew Miss Delia all too well, but in deference to her new lifestyle, pretended she was a new acquaintance.

However, despite the surfeit of females living in the house, his interest lay with only one. It was the fierce warrior-woman with the long brown, hair and clear, blue eyes who haunted him, and it was her he'd come to see.

He started to dismount when he realized T-Bone was standing at the corner of the house, watching him in a strange, quiet fashion. Usually the dog came running, anxious for a pat on the head or a piece of jerky.

"Hey, boy," he said softly and clucked his tongue, thinking the dog would come.

Instead, T-Bone turned and disappeared around the corner of the house. He thought nothing of it until the dog reappeared, again with that watchful stare. This time, Robert Lee remembered that wherever T-Bone was, Letty wouldn't be far away. He settled back into the saddle and rode around the corner of the house, thinking he would find Letty at some job in the back yard.

At first, he didn't see her, then when he did, his heart came up in his throat. She was face down on the ground at Eulis's grave, and from where he was sitting, appeared to be unconscious.

He spurred his horse forward, riding toward her at a lope. By the time he dismounted, he could tell she was crying. The sound tore straight through him as he ran toward her. Without a word, he lifted her up into his arms.

* * *

Letty was startled to find herself upright and cradled against Robert Lee's broad chest.

"Robert Lee?"

He carried her to the stump, then sat her down gently before dropping to one knee.

"Are you hurt? Did you fall?" he asked.

Letty sighed and, without thinking, cupped the side of his face with her hand.

"I didn't fall," she said gently. "I suppose you could say I was indulging myself with a good cry."

The touch of her hand on his face struck him dumb. For a moment, he couldn't think—couldn't speak—couldn't breathe. It wasn't until she dropped her hand in her lap that he came to his senses.

"Oh," he said awkwardly, then stood up and stepped back. "I didn't mean to intrude. I'll just ride on—"

"You'll do no such thing," Letty said and held out her hand. "Help me up," she said and then grabbed his hand before he could think to pull back and hefted herself upright. "Lord, I'm shaking like an aspen."

"Are you ill?"

Letty grimaced, shading her eyes with her hand as she looked up.

"I have been a bit under the weather this morning and would appreciate a ride back to the house."

Robert Lee was surprised by the request but more than happy to oblige.

"Yes, ma'am," he said softly and helped her mount. "Just hold onto the horn. I'll walk you back myself."

"Thank you," Letty said, thankful she wouldn't have to make the trek back on her own.

Robert Lee gave her a nervous glance before starting toward the house at a slow, easy pace. The rocking motion of the horse didn't sit all that well with Letty, but it was still better than making the walk back of her own volition.

"I'd be happy to ride down and get Dr. Warren," Robert Lee said.

"There's no need," Letty said and lifted the heavy fall of her hair away from her neck.

Robert Lee frowned. "But you said you weren't well."

Letty sighed. It seemed odd that Robert Lee was going to be the first one she told, but she had to start somewhere and he was the closest.

"Well, if this morning is any indication, I reckon I've got a few more months of being sick ahead of me," she said.

Robert Lee paused, then turned around and looked her square in the face. There was a glitter in her eyes he'd never seen before and a softening to the sternness around her mouth.

"What are you saying?"

"That I'm with child." Her chin quivered just the least little bit, but she didn't give way to the tears in her voice. "I was just giving Eulis the good news. He didn't have much to say on the subject, but you know how he is. Even when he's happiest, he's still a quiet man."

Robert Lee's heart stuttered to a stop, then started back up so suddenly it hurt the inside of his chest. He looked at her body, picturing the way it was going to change and was instantly ashamed that he was jealous of a dead man.

But then he smiled, and as he did, Letty was startled by the way it changed his face. It was the first time she'd actually seen Robert Lee as the man he was and not just an employee and a friend. It also struck her that, for a man who'd lived such a hard and dangerous life, he was actually quite handsome.

"I'm proud for you, ma'am," he said softly. "It must give you a real good feeling to know Eulis is still with you after all."

Letty thought about it a moment, then nodded.

"You're right, Robert Lee. You put a good name to the feeling that's in me. I'm sad my baby will never know its father. Still, I've had a dream all my life of one day I'd be sitting out on the back porch of my house with my child at my feet, watching the sun go down and the moon come up. And as the darkness comes to the land, we'd be listening for the first call of the whippoorwill. I used to do that with my mama before she died. Then, after the way my life turned out, I never thought I'd get to do it with one of my own."

Robert Lee heard the longing in her voice and wanted to weep. Instead, he pulled his hat down a little lower over his forehead and urged the horse forward. With every step that brought them closer to the house, Letty

Potter was growing farther and farther away from him, and there was nothing he could do about it.

* * *

Within the month, everyone in Denver City knew the Widow Potter was carrying her dead husband's baby. Even the hardest of men were touched by the situation.

After a quick examination, Dr. Warren pronounced Letty and her baby healthy and forbid her to ride until after the baby was born. For Letty, it was a small price to pay for the joy of becoming a mother. At first, she'd been uneasy, afraid Alice would be upset, maybe even envious, that she was having a baby when Alice's was dead. But she wasn't. It was Letty's first lesson in knowing how the heart of a mother can work. Alice had taken Katie into her life as readily as she'd accepted the baby to whom she'd given birth. One had been taken away, but another had been given. Life wasn't easy. Raising a child to adulthood was even harder. Alice knew that firsthand. Letty prayed to God it was something she would never have to face.

* * *

Letty's pregnancy had, in an odd way, eased Robert Lee's yearnings. He still cared for her—dreamed of her, yearned for her. But he was well aware that her entire being was focused on nothing but the baby she was carrying. Because she couldn't ride out to the mine anymore, he made a habit of stopping by the house more often. The ease of the routine into which they'd settled was pleasing to both. Letty didn't realize how much she'd come to look forward to Robert Lee's visits until he'd gone three days without stopping by.

* * *

Letty stared at her growing girth in the full-length mirror in her bedroom, then turned sideways and cupped her hands beneath her belly to test her size from that angle as well.

"Amazing," she muttered, slowly smiling as she patted her belly. "Come on, Little Bit, it's time we started our day."

She moved out of her room and headed down the stairs, taking care to hold onto the railing as she descended. Once light on her feet, she now moved at a slower and awkward gait.

* * *

The imminent arrival of a baby in the house sent every female hormone into overdrive. Alice was piecing a baby quilt. Delia was saving and hand-hemming flour sacks to be used for diapers. Mary Whiteside had traded a traveling salesman a nugget of gold for two skeins of cotton yarn to knit the baby a bonnet.

Even little Katie had involved herself. With Alice's help, she was making a rag doll for the baby out of a couple of handkerchiefs and a stocking.

And, unknown to all the women in the Hen House, Robert Lee was making a gift of his own. He'd built a cradle out of hickory, honed it down to a smooth, satin sheen, and spent his nights carving figures into the headboard by candle light. He'd finished the little bird he'd put in the center of the design and was working on a small rabbit. He had plans to put a turtle on the other side to balance the image and let himself dream of tiny fingers tracing the shapes of what he was carving into the wood. When he was deep into the dream, he imagined himself teaching the baby the animals' names, even hearing a small, baby voice trying to repeat the words.

* * *

Letty was all the way down the stairs and moving through the parlor into the kitchen before she realized the house was completely silent. With so many women in residence, it wasn't often the house felt like this.

"Hello," she called. "Where is everybody?"

A floor board creaked behind her. She turned, expecting to see one of the women, but there was no one there.

"Probably out in the vegetable garden," she said and headed toward the kitchen.

The screen door squeaked as she walked out onto the porch. T-Bone was noticeably absent, and the women were nowhere to be seen.

14

TWICE A HERO

After calling for several minutes with no answer, Letty began to feel uneasy. She circled the house, thinking they might have gone into the woods to look for berries, but when she went back into the house and searched the kitchen, the berry basket and both bowls they might have taken were still on the shelf.

She turned and gazed out the window toward the forest, hoping to see the women emerging from an early-morning walk—certain wherever they were, T-Bone would be running in circles around Katie, waiting for her to toss a stick for him to fetch.

Lost in her muse, she stared out the window for several moments, trying to shake a feeling of unease. It wasn't until a bird flew past her line of vision she shook off the feeling of malaise and decided to look for them in earnest. She was all the way across the kitchen and reaching for the screen when she saw the first drop of blood.

It was the size of a pea and almost lost in the shadow of the threshold. Startled, she went down on her knees and touched it with the tip of her finger. It was still sticky.

Breath caught in the back of her throat. When she looked up, she saw a trail of blood drops leading all the way out the door and off the porch. By the time she dragged herself to her feet, she was trying not to panic. There were all kinds of reasons why the blood could be there. Children got nose bleeds, and Alice was known to nick her fingers now and then when peeling vegetables.

She sidestepped the drops and then followed them out the door and off the porch. It took her a few moments to find the small droplets in the grass, but when she did, she continued to follow them. She was halfway across the yard when she realized the door to the root cellar was open and the blood trail seemed to be leading in that direction.

She couldn't imagine why they would all be in the cellar at once, or why they hadn't answered when she'd called before, but her heart was lighter as she started toward it.

"T-Bone! T-Bone!" She whistled sharply, expecting the dog to come bounding up the steps. When he didn't, she couldn't help frowning. Whatever was going on still didn't feel right.

She was less than twenty feet from the cellar when a man emerged and started toward her. Letty was so startled by his appearance it took her a few moments to realize he was holding a gun on her.

He waved the gun in her face as he grinned.

"Well, well now...I was just comin' to get you. After all, you're the belle of the ball."

Instinctively, Letty cupped her hands across the swell of her belly and took a step back. Even from where she was standing, the stranger's stench was evident. A few seconds later, she doubled up her fists as she stared down the barrel of the gun.

"What have you done with my family?"

He laughed, revealing a mouth full of broken and rotting teeth.

"They're all fine…just a little tied up right now," he said and waved the gun at her again. "You and me got some business to do. If you're real good, I might be persuaded to turn everyone loose."

"What do you want?" she asked.

"Want? What do I want?"

Letty shuddered. The flat, almost vacant stare on his face was more frightening than if he was screaming at her.

"You can have anything on the place. You want a horse? Some food? Just take it and go."

The man's eyes narrowed as his smile disappeared.

"Now, now…it's not all that simple, missy."

It was at this point, Letty realized part of the stains on his hands were blood—almost as red as the drops she'd seen on the porch. She didn't want to think of who he'd hurt—maybe beyond redemption. Despite the fear roiling in her belly, she remembered something she'd learned the hard way a long time ago. Never let them see your fear. Never let them see you cry.

"Then speak your peace and get off my property," she snapped.

The stranger was startled by her behavior. He was the one with the gun. He was the one in charge. She was supposed to be crying. She was supposed to be scared.

"You're not the one callin' the shots," he said shortly. "Shut up and get over here."

"Or what?" Letty asked.

Again, the man felt as if he was losing some ground. This wasn't the way it was supposed to be.

"Or I'll do more than bloody that dark-haired bitch's nose."

Letty hid a shiver. So Delia was the one he'd hurt.

"I want to see my friends," she said. "Show me they're all okay and then we'll talk."

A long string of curses spilled into the air between them as he pulled back his jacket and took another pistol out of the waist of his pants. Without taking a breath, he fired into the ground right in front of where Letty was standing. Dirt showered up onto the hem of her dress, but she didn't move.

"Is that supposed to reassure me you're the kind of man who keeps his word?"

"Damn it all to hell, woman. Shut up! Shut up! Just don't talk. I'm the one who's talking. I'm the one with a gun. You don't talk. You don't do anything but what I tell you."

Letty swallowed past a knot in her throat. It was all she could do to maintain eye contact with him, but she knew his kind. Showing fear would feed into his power. It was the last thing she intended to do. So she stood without moving or talking, waiting to see what happened next.

"They say you're rich. Are you rich, lady?"

"Yes."

He giggled.

The sound turned Letty's stomach.

"Well then...here's the deal. You share some of the wealth, and I'll see about lettin' them bitches down in the cellar go free. How much money you reckon you got in the house?"

"Maybe ten or twelve dollars."

His eyes bugged. "What the hell are you doing...trying to play me for a fool? You got money. Lots of money and don't say you don't cause I know better. You're the woman who went and struck gold, so where is it?"

She pointed toward town.

"Down yonder in that bank, and in a bank in Philadelphia and in another bank in New York City, and in a bank in Boston."

A drop of spittle slid from the corner of the man's mouth as his nostrils flared.

"You're lyin'!"

"No, I'm not."

"Why would you put your money in all them banks so far away?"

"So people like you couldn't get their filthy hands on it."

He reeled as if he'd been slapped. Before Letty could

react, he had crossed the distance between them and put a knife to her throat.

The coppery scent of fresh blood went up her nostrils, as did the rotten smell coming from his body. She couldn't bring herself to look directly at his face for fear he'd see the terror she was trying to hide.

"I'll teach you to smart-mouth me," he said and gave her a back-handed blow to the face.

Letty dropped to her knees as blood spurted inside her mouth. She bent over and spat blood into the dirt. The skin on her face burned, as if he'd pushed her too close to a fire.

"Now get up!" he yelled and grabbed her by the hair, dragging her to her feet. "You and me are goin' inside that fancy house of yours and get me some money...a lot of money. If I find out you been lyin' to me, I'll shoot you where you stand."

Letty didn't argue for fear if he hit her again, the baby might suffer. With one last glance toward the cellar, she let the man drag her toward the house.

* * *

Robert Lee was hitching a team of mules to an ore wagon when one of the miners yelled out.

"Hey! Look there! Ain't that Miz Letty's dog?"

Robert Lee looked up to see the huge brown and white dog coming toward the mine at a lope. Although the dog had been here many times before, he'd never before come alone. Robert Lee dropped the harness and stepped out from behind the wagon for a better look.

Moments later, the dog ran up to him, then dropped at Robert Lee's feet. Robert Lee's stomach rolled when he realized there was a long bloody cut on the dog's back leg. Even though he knew Letty had been forbidden to ride until after the baby was born, that didn't mean she was beyond defying orders. He stood up, searching the valley for sight of her, but saw nothing.

"Something's not right," he said and pointed to one of the men. "Harness up the team and go ahead and take that load into town. I'm going to Miz Letty's house to check on them."

"Sure thing, boss," the man said and picked up the harness as Robert Lee mounted his horse.

Before he knew it, T-Bone was back, running at his side. He spurred his horse and leaned into the ride as his horse broke into a gallop. Everything went through his mind and none of it was good, but he wouldn't give in to the fear.

He rode hard. By the time he got to town, his horse was heaving for breath. Flecks of lather from the horse blew onto the legs of his pants as he rode, and he could hear the heavy groan from his near-spent mount. He knew the animal was almost past going, and yet he didn't dare slow down for fear whatever was going on, he would arrive too late to help.

When he rode through town at a hard gallop, several people stopped, curious as to what was happening. More than one yelled out as he passed by, but he didn't take time to answer. His gaze was fixed on the roof of Letty's fine house that sat on the hill above the town.

Less than two hundred yards from the house, he heard a gunshot and immediately reined in his mount. The trembling horse was wild-eyed and snorting as he sat, listening for a second shot. He knew the women had a rifle, which Letty kept loaded. But the shot he'd heard was from a handgun, not a rifle, and as far as he knew, there wasn't one on the place.

He spurred his horse forward and rode into the yard at a gallop. He didn't know what was happening, but he sensed Letty was in danger. He dismounted quickly, pulled his gun and started running around the side of the house, taking care to stay concealed until he knew for sure what was wrong. When he saw the man holding a gun on Letty, something inside him snapped. Without thought for anything but Letty, he walked out into the yard with his gun drawn.

"Let her go!" Robert Lee yelled.

* * *

When Letty heard Robert Lee's voice, she went weak with relief. Even when the stranger pulled hard on her hair and yanked her backward, she didn't panic—not even when he used her body for a shield and put a gun to her head.

"I'll shoot her!" the man screamed. "I will! I'll shoot her dead!"

Robert Lee fixed his gaze on Letty and spoke to her, as if the man wasn't even there.

"Are you all right?"

"Yes," Letty said, unable to hide the quaver of fear in her voice.

"Get back! Get back!" the stranger screamed.

Robert Lee's voice didn't falter, nor did his gaze as he kept coming closer.

"Do you trust me?" he asked softly.

Letty swallowed nervously, then answered.

"Yes."

"Close your eyes. No matter what you hear, keep them closed."

She shut her eyes as the stranger began yelling at Robert Lee.

"Listen here...you can't—"

The gunshot was loud—the scent of gunpowder strong in Letty's nose. Something wet hit the side of her face at the same time she fell free. In shock, she staggered. Even though she couldn't see him, she knew it was Robert Lee who caught her before she fell.

"It's me, it's me," he said softly. "Keep your eyes closed and just listen to the sound of my voice."

He scooped Letty up in his arms and carried her into the house, then set her down in a chair. She heard him pouring water into a basin. When she felt a wet rag on her face, she flinched.

"It's just water, honey," Robert Lee said. "It's just water."

He didn't tell her that he was washing the dead man's blood off of her face, and she didn't ask. He just kept wiping and rinsing until it was all gone.

"Where are the others?" Robert Lee asked. "Where's Alice and Mary and Delia...where's little Katie?"

Letty shivered as his thumb traced the curve of her cheek, unaware he was rubbing off a rather large splatter of blood.

"I think they're in the cellar. He was coming out of the cellar when I saw him. I woke up and couldn't find anyone. T-Bone was gone and the women were gone and—"

"T-Bone came after me," Robert Lee said.

Surprised by the news, Letty opened her eyes before she thought, only to find Robert Lee's face only inches away from hers. Mesmerized by the sight, she froze.

When he realized she was watching him, his first instinct was to pull back. It wasn't until he saw his own reflection in her eyes he knew he was close to losing control.

"I, uh...."

Letty grabbed his hand, took the wet rag from him and tossed it into the basin.

"You saved my life," she said softly.

"I only—"

Letty put her fingers across his mouth, silencing whatever he'd been going to say. At that point, the baby kicked. Letty winced, then, still holding his hand, laid it palm down on the swell of her belly.

"Feel that?" she asked.

Robert Lee was so stunned he had forgotten to breathe, but then he felt a solid little thump against his palm and grunted as if he'd been kicked.

"Lord," he said softly, then leaned forward, resting his forehead against Letty's forehead, feeling the warmth of her breath on his face. "Does that hurt?"

"No."

"My baby and I are alive because of you."

Tears blurred his vision. He tried to pull away, but Letty wouldn't let go.

"Please...Letty...don't do this."

"Don't do what, Robert Lee?"

"You're just upset and—"

"Hell yes, I'm upset," she said. "But I'm not dead." Her voice broke. "My mama and papa are dead. Eulis is dead. That piece of shit who was trying to pass himself off as a man is dead. But I'm not and my baby's not...and you're not dead either, Robert Lee. I don't know what I've done to hurt your feelings, but whatever it is, I'm right sorry."

Robert Lee groaned, then pushed away from where Letty was standing and turned his back on her.

"You didn't hurt my feelings."

"Then why have you been so...so...cold?"

He turned abruptly.

"Cold is hardly the word I would use to describe my feelings for you."

Letty's mouth opened, but the words didn't come. Slowly, understanding dawned.

"Oh...Robert Lee, I—

"Don't say it," he muttered. "Don't say anything. You sit down. I'm going to go see if the women are in the root cellar. If you're a mind to keep talking, then say a prayer to that God of yours they're all still alive."

With that, he strode out of the kitchen with his jaw set and his shoulders hunched against a blow that never came.

Letty stood abruptly. Startled by her revelation, she didn't know what to do, but then the baby kicked again, and her answer came. She watched Robert Lee from the kitchen window, praying as she'd never prayed before.

"Please, God, You know my heart and You know I've done wrong. But please don't let the girls be harmed. Please, Lord. You took Eulis from me. Don't take them, too."

Robert Lee disappeared down in the cellar.

Her eyes were burning with unshed tears.

* * *

Alice saw Robert Lee first. Even though she was bound and gagged, she started to cry as he untied her.

"Oh, Law...you're a sight for sore eyes," she said. "We heard gunshots! What happened? Is Letty all right?"

"Letty's fine," Robert Lee said and took out his knife and cut the bindings at Mary's ankles.

Little Katie was bound and gagged and lying face down. He picked her up and deposited her in Alice's lap before untying her. She was so traumatized she wasn't crying.

Delia seemed to be the worse for wear. There was blood all over the front of her clothes. When he untied the gag that had been on her mouth, he saw she'd also been beaten. His hands were gentle as he pulled the bindings from her face and hands.

"He hit you," Robert Lee said, lightly touching the side of Delia's swollen nose. "Can you breathe through it?"

There were tears in her eyes as she nodded.

"Good," he said. "Maybe it's not broken."

As soon as Delia's hands were free, she put both hands to her face and traced the shape of her features, thankful they felt almost normal. From the way her head and face were throbbing, she had imagined the worst.

"I'll carry Katie," Robert Lee said. "Can you ladies make it up the steps?"

The trio stood, wincing as the feeling began to come back into their arms and legs.

"Let's get out of here," Robert Lee said and led the way up and out of the cellar.

* * *

The longer Robert Lee stayed down in the cellar, the more frightened Letty became. She was at the point of going to see for herself when T-Bone suddenly appeared from the forest and hobbled toward the cellar. Letty remembered then what Robert Lee had said—that the pup had come after him.

She swallowed past a knot in her throat. Twice now that dog had helped save her, too. Once from a rattlesnake—and now from a snake with two legs. And from what she could see, the dog was injured.

Then she saw Robert Lee emerging from the cellar carrying little Katie in his arms. She held her breath, waiting, praying—then they came up one by one with Alice in the lead, then Mary, and finally Delia.

Letty's eyes were burning as she headed for the door. When the women saw her, they ran past Robert Lee with their arms outstretched. When they got to Letty, they embraced her, smothering her with their cries of relief.

Letty never looked down at the body of the man who'd held them hostage, nor did the women as they clung to each other, laughing, crying, then embracing each other again.

Robert Lee handed Katie to Alice.

"I'm going down to get the sheriff," he said and rode out of the yard without looking back.

"What's wrong with Robert Lee?" Alice asked.

Letty couldn't look at him without feeling a sharp pain near her heart. He'd asked if she trusted him. She'd answered yes without hesitation. But was it just trust—or was it something more she felt for this man?

"I reckon he's a bit upset at having to shoot that man," Mary offered, eyeing the dead man near the steps.

"Alice, you and Katie go on in the house," Delia said. "She doesn't need to be seeing this."

Alice gathered the little girl up and hurried inside.

Delia, on the other hand, had no problem with the body at her feet.

"Damn shame you can't kill a man twice," she muttered, then kicked at the bottom of his shoe before stepping up on the porch.

Mary put her arm around Letty's shoulders and urged her up the steps.

"Come on, darlin'. You need to get off your feet. This has been a bad morning all around."

"Did he harm any of you?" Letty asked. "Did he touch you in a—"

"Shush now," Mary said. "None of that happened, so don't fuss. He might have thought about it, but it didn't happen. He just kept talking about your gold mine and your money."

Letty frowned. She'd never dreamed how much trouble it could be to be rich.

* * *

They buried the stranger in the town cemetery without knowing his name. Someone carved the words *greedy bastard* on his tombstone. It seemed to fit the situation.

The incident was, for a while, all the gossip down in town, and then like everything, it was superceded by an even greater event.

The territories had been hearing rumblings of discord for some time between the northern and southern states regarding many things, most of which hinged on the aspect of slavery. What with having to worry about droughts, prairie fires, Indian raids, and generally surviving in an unforgiving land, people had paid little mind to suppositions.

However, the last freight wagons to come through had brought news no one could ignore.

The southern states had seceded from the Union of the United States of America.

They were at war.

* * *

Letty shut down the mine. She had more money than she could ever spend in two lifetimes, and now that the country was at war, moving gold bars or large amounts of money from one place to another was impossible. Breaking men's backs for the accumulation of more wealth seemed redundant, especially since she'd learned firsthand the reality of what happened to people who were filthy rich.

Without asking what anyone thought, Robert Lee had packed up his belongings and moved into a tent at the edge of the woods near Letty's home.

Letty didn't know what to think. Robert Lee kept watch on the women, but he kept his distance. She had to satisfy herself with glimpses of him from time to time and tell herself that whatever was not happening between them was for the best.

The townspeople whispered among themselves about Robert Lee's new home, but no one had the guts to tease him to his face. Even if they had, it wouldn't have changed a thing. Robert Lee wasn't going to let another man lay a harsh hand on Letty or any of the women living in her house.

Within a month of Robert Lee's arrival at the Hen House, the war was all the gossip. Men began to take sides. It wasn't unusual for a brawl to break out at a saloon over who was in the right—the north or the south.

Letty was beyond caring one way or the other. All of her days and nights were focused on the impending birth of her baby.

Even though she chose to ignore a war that seemed too far away to consider, the war came to her, just the same.

15

SOLDIERS AND PATRIOTS

In his other life, Carson Mylam had been a banker. But that was before his country separated itself into north of the Mason-Dixon line and south of the Mason-Dixon line. After that, he and thousands of other men entered the ranks of the Union army. Thanks to his father's money and influence, Carson skipped training and skill, and upon taking the oath of office, became Major Mylam. Only problem was, Carson Mylam's expertise lay in money —acquiring it and saving it. He didn't know the butt from the barrel of a gun.

However, it had come to the attention of his government that one of the largest depositors in Mylam's bank in Philadelphia was also the largest depositor in a bank in Boston, as well as one in New York City. It was of no consequence to the officers the depositor happened to be a woman. Seeing as how the country was at war, Mylam's superiors decided to use him where he could best serve. Wars cost money. It seemed only fitting one of the richest women in the country would want to donate to the war effort. The fact that she lived all the way out in the unsettled western territories was a little inconvenient.

But Major Carson Mylam had been given a choice—pack his bags and head west, or saddle his horse and head south.

He'd opted for the territories. By the time he finally reached Denver City, he'd convinced himself it hadn't been a cowardly choice. The hardships he'd endured were far beyond what his cultured life in Philadelphia had been. He'd eaten food cooked over a campfire, ridden in stagecoaches that had been robbed, been rained on, narrowly missed being struck by lightning, and come face to face with unfriendly Indians. Had he been alone, he would have died on the spot. Being in the midst of travelers who'd been born and bred on the frontier had been guidance enough to keep him in one piece. After all of that, he expected the rest of his trip would be simple.

He presented himself at the Denver City bank with a letter of reference and a request to meet with one Mrs. Leticia Potter, owner of the famous Potter gold mines. It came as a shock to learn she'd shut them down, and when he learned she'd been widowed only months earlier and was now carrying her dead husband's child, he was in a quandary. It seemed a bit hard-hearted to present a business proposition to a woman in mourning. Still, there was the war to consider—and in war time, everyone had to sacrifice.

He took a room at the hotel across the street from the bank and made arrangements to hire a horse and pay a visit to Mrs. Potter first thing in the morning. He didn't know word had already reached Letty a stranger was in town asking about her, or that Robert Lee was lying in wait.

* * *

In Philadelphia, Carson was accustomed to walking to work or, in winter months, having one of his men drive him to the bank in the family buggy. Still, he certainly knew how to ride, and the horse he'd hired from the livery seemed amenable enough. The owner of the livery had pointed out the big house sitting on the mountain above Denver City, as well as the road leading to it. Carson mounted and rode off, well aware of the fine figure he cut in the Union officer's uniform.

However, the dark blue uniform with its bright gold buttons and braid did nothing for Robert Lee's attitude. He wouldn't have cared if the man had been sporting wings and carrying a letter from God. Visitors had to go through him to get to Letty Potter.

* * *

Letty had known since yesterday a man from back East had come to Denver City to see her. She couldn't help remembering the last man from back East who'd come to see her had died—on top of her—in her bed. That he'd been a preacher seemed to have magnified the problem. Had it not been for Eulis, she didn't know what might have happened to her. Eulis was no longer here to back her up, but considering the size of her belly and the formidable presence of the gunslinger camped out on the edge of her property, she wasn't expecting problems.

* * *

Robert Lee had been up since before sunrise. His tent was roomy enough for him to stand up in, should the need arise, but he rarely spent any time in it other than to sleep. He had a small table set up beneath a tree outside the tent where he kept a basin and a bucket of water. Every other day he shaved. Today would have been an off day, but since he'd heard about the man who'd come to find Letty Potter, he hadn't been able to rest easy, so he'd passed part of the time waiting by giving himself a shave.

His lack of trust in his fellow man had been magnified a thousand times by his feelings for Letty. Never in his life had he felt so helpless, yet been so driven to be near her. He kept remembering the day he'd first seen her. He'd walked all the way to the mine from Denver City. It had been one of the lowest points in his life—no horse—no money—and he couldn't remember the last day he'd eaten a meal. He'd been so sick of his life and so desperate for a second chance he'd been willing to work at almost anything. He still marveled at the odds of coming upon a man for whom he'd once done a good deed—a deed that prompted the man to return the favor. The way he looked at it, Eulis Potter had pretty much saved his life. He tried to convince himself his feelings for Letty were all mixed up with his appreciation of Eulis, but when he was being honest, he knew that was a lie. He coveted his friend's wife and had almost from the moment they'd met. And, everything she'd done since had only enforced the emotion. He admired her strength, her faith, and her spirit. He loved her face, her laughter, and her body—even the baby within. Still, he had no rights and no hopes beyond what already was. He'd told himself he could be happy just knowing Letty and her child would be happy and live a good long life. Most of the time, he believed it.

* * *

Carson Mylam rode up the mountain with ease. The weather was a little hot for the wool uniform, but he was convinced it would help make his case. Even though his hired horse was less than remarkable, unlike his fine, blooded gelding back home in Philadelphia, he knew he looked good.

He had a letter from Abraham Lincoln himself, as well as letters of reference from his immediate superiors, both of whom were generals. He had no doubt Mrs. Potter would be suitably impressed—Lord knew he was impressed with himself. The visions he had in his head of returning to Philadelphia with what amounted to "the fatted calf" were many and all awash in grandeur.

Only he had to get past Robert Lee Slade to make that happen—a situation of which he was yet unaware.

* * *

Robert Lee saw the man coming from a quarter of a mile away. That he was wearing a soldier's uniform was somewhat surprising, but Robert Lee held his opinions to himself. He didn't care if the man was sporting badges from every law enforcement agency in the nation, he wasn't getting to Letty until Robert Lee said so.

He glanced back toward the Potter house. Katie was playing with T-Bone in the front yard. Delia was digging in the flower bed beside the steps. From time to time, he caught glimpses of Mary, who was in the back of the house, hanging out laundry. Since it was nearing noon, he knew Alice would be in the kitchen preparing the meal. He looked up at the second floor, where he knew Letty's bedroom to be. He imagined her reclining, with her feet up and her body great with child, only his imagination was far from the truth.

Had he been able to see a little farther around the back of the house, he would have seen Letty standing beside an open fire and stirring a large iron pot. But he couldn't see, and the wind was taking the odor of soap making in the other direction.

Unaware and uncaring of the small drama being played out on the other side of her house, Letty was focused on the last part of what amounted to making lye soap. Among other things, it took animal fat and wood ash to make the concoction, which in itself, before mixed and cooked down, made a phenomenal mess. Although she could have ordered tons of fine, scented soap that wouldn't have put a dent in her finances, she favored her own over what Milton Feasley kept in his dry goods store.

"Need some help?" Mary asked, as she walked toward the house with an empty wash basket.

"Yes. I'm about ready to pour it up," Letty said. "Tell Alice to come help. It's going to take all of us to lift the pot."

Mary hurried into the house, returning moments later with Alice at her heels. Together, the three women emptied the pot into four long, shallow, wooden troughs. The liquid soap would cool in the troughs, and as it cooled, would solidify. At that point, the women would cut it into small bricks, to be used in washing everything from dishes, to bodies, to clothes. As they were filling the last wooden flat, Major Mylam was topping the hill upon which Letty's house had been built.

* * *

It was the sight of a magnificent elk bounding out of the trees and into his path that distracted Carson Mylam. There was a moment when man and animal looked into each other's eyes and knew, at another time, they would have been adversaries. Fortunately for both, today they were focused on other agendas. The elk whistled sharply, then cleared the road in one leap and bounded away.

Carson inhaled deeply. Still lost in admiration of the spectacle, he missed seeing Robert Lee appear. When he did return his attention to the road in front of him, he realized there was an armed man standing between him and the two-story house with its elegant columns and white-washed shutters.

"I say!" Carson exclaimed and automatically put his hand on his pistol.

"Don't do it," Robert Lee said softly. "State your business."

Wisely, Carson Mylam obeyed. Still, he hadn't expected this kind of reception and his good mood was broken. Defensively, he lifted his chin and put his hand on his coat, taking comfort in the crackle of paper from the inside pockets.

"I have an appointment with Mrs. Potter and letters of reference from the President himself."

"The president of what?" Robert Lee drawled.

Carson Mylam frowned. It wasn't the first time he'd encountered uneducated beings in this part of the country and feared it wouldn't be his last.

"Why...our country, of course," he said, then added with a smirk. "Surely, you're aware of your nation's leader."

"Out here, the name doesn't come up all that much. I'd say I'm about as aware of him as he is of me," Robert Lee said, then fixed Carson with a pointed stare. "You're wearing Union blue."

Carson lifted his chin.

"Surely, I am not in the presence of a southern sympathizer?"

"The only thing in sympathy out here is gold."

Carson fidgeted. The mere mention of the word was why he'd come.

"As I said before, I have an appointment with Mrs. Potter."

"Get down and give me your gun," Robert Lee said.

"Now see here! I am an officer in the United States Army and I—"

"I said it once. I won't say it again," Robert Lee said, then added. "And just for your own information, you might want to downplay the war and officer part. Mrs. Potter's husband was shot dead right in front of her in her own yard a few months back. At the moment, she's not too fond of men with guns."

Carson stifled a moan of dismay. Obviously, he hadn't thought the mission through from her point of view. He dismounted, handed Robert Lee his pistol, and then followed the man toward the house, leading his horse. It was not the arrival he'd planned.

"So, how long have you worked for Mrs. Potter?" Carson asked.

Robert Lee gave the man a quick glance but didn't bother to answer.

Being ignored by a man he viewed as lower class, aggravated Carson. He spoke out before he thought.

"Marvelous...ignorant...and hard of hearing. Where were you born...in a barn?"

Robert Lee stopped. For a few moments, he just stared at the ground without speaking. For Carson, the silence became uncomfortable, then threatening. When Robert Lee finally looked up, the glitter in his eyes was all the warning Carson knew he was going to get.

"Actually, I was born in Virginia," Robert Lee said. "When I left, which was several years ago, my father, Justin Slade, was governor. I learned to read at the age of four from the tutor Father hired for me and my four brothers and sisters. I speak Latin and French," Robert Lee paused briefly, "and nobody has been able to out draw me since the day I shot my first man. So, I suggest you get your sorry blue-ass up to the house, state your business, and then get on back to where you came from while the gettin' is good."

Carson felt an instant urge to pee. However, stating the need was not something he could say to a man like this. Not only did he feel out of place in this wild, socially inept country, but he was obviously in the presence of a southern sympathizer. He couldn't help wondering what he'd gotten himself into.

* * *

Katie was the first to see the men coming.

"Look, Miz Delia...Robert Lee's bringing a visitor."

Delia stopped and looked up. She knew from Letty one was expected and got up quickly, brushing the dirt from her hands as she waved Katie into the house.

"Go inside and tell Miz Letty that her company is here."

"No one's in the house. They're all out back making soap," Katie said.

"Oh, Lord," Delia muttered, thinking of what they would all be wearing. Whatever it was, it was bound to be dusty and smeared with ashes and animal renderings.

"It doesn't matter what they're doing. Letty still needs to know her company is here. You let her know. The rest of what happens is her affair."

"Yes, ma'am," Katie said and scampered around the back of the house with T-Bone at her heels.

Letty saw Katie and T-Bone running toward her and paused, absently rubbing her aching back and smiling at the sight.

"Hey there, honey...what's the rush?" she asked.

Katie pointed toward the front of the house.

"Robert Lee is bringing your company up the road."

Letty looked down at her hands, then her clothes, and shrugged. In the grand scheme of things, it mattered little.

"Thank you, Katie."

She patted T-Bone, then gave his ears a playful tug as she moved toward the back door. The least she could do was wash her hands and face before attending to the bothersome business of company. As far as she was concerned, the only good part of it was the fact she would get to visit with Robert Lee, no matter how brief the meeting.

The baby kicked as she moved into the house.

"I don't like this any more than you do," she muttered, as she poured some water up into a wash basin and scrubbed at her hands and face.

Quickly, she removed her work apron, then smoothed the tendrils of her hair away from her forehead. The bang of the front door signaled the arrival of her visitors. She smoothed her hands down the front of her gray, stained smock and lifted her chin.

The swell of her belly preceded her entrance into the parlor. She saw the man in Union blue, as well as the perturbed expression on Delia's face, but it was the tall, somber man with dark hair and black eyes standing by the fireplace who captured her attention. As always, Robert Lee's quiet presence intrigued her and, at the same time, filled her with a sense of peace.

"Good morning," Letty said, letting her gaze linger longest on Robert Lee. "Thank you, Robert Lee." Then she included everyone else in the greeting. "Please...have a seat."

"Mrs. Potter, my name is—"

"Robert Lee, I know you're terribly busy." He was already on his way out the door when Letty interrupted the soldier and called him back. "But, I would appreciate it if you would stay while this gentleman and I have our conversation."

Carson Mylam frowned.

Robert Lee pivoted on one heel, walked across the parlor to the chair nearest where Letty was sitting, and sat down with his hat in his lap.

"Letty, would you like for me to fetch some tea?" Delia asked.

Still hot from her soap making task, Letty was already fanning herself with a small, paper fan. She arched an eyebrow at Robert Lee, who stared at her for a moment, then looked away.

Letty saw a muscle jerking in his jaw and knew he was irked with her for asking him to stay.

"I think these gentlemen would most likely prefer something a bit stronger," Letty said and pointed toward a cupboard in the corner.

Delia was as familiar with men's likes and dislikes as Letty and headed for the whiskey decanter and the small shot glasses on a shelf above.

Once Delia was at her task, Letty eyed the officer again.

"I'm sorry. I interrupted you. As you were saying..."

Carson was out of his element. This woman was nothing like he'd expected. There was perspiration on her face, stains on her clothing, and her hands were obviously reddened from some sort of menial labor. He would have expected a woman of her wealth to have her every wish granted by servants. Instead, she appeared as a servant herself and showed no embarrassment in receiving company while being so great with child.

He cleared his throat.

"My name is Carson Mylam. I'm a major with the Union army." At this point, he pulled papers from his pocket. "I have letters of reference from President Lincoln, as well as two of my superiors, both of whom are generals. I've come on the behalf of the government of these United States to speak of a matter most urgent."

Letty frowned as she stared at the papers he was holding.

"You've come all the way from Philadelphia to talk to me?"

"Yes, ma'am."

"Why?"

The skin on Carson's neck turned bright pink.

"Why...because of your great wealth and power," he said and even as he was saying it, knew how foolish it sounded.

Letty stared at him for a moment, then laughed. Out loud. Without care for the unlady-like behavior.

"And what is it you think my wealth and power are going to do...stop your foolish war?"

Carson's neck flushed a darker shade of pink. He waved the letters he'd carried across hundreds of miles in the air.

"Just read these, madam." Then he added. "I'm assuming you *do* read."

Letty's smile departed about the same time as her patience.

"I read. I read just fine. However, you need to know, out here in the territories, reading is about the last skill you need to keep yourself alive. You also need to know I've been making lye soap all morning, and I'm not sure what hurts worse...my back or my feet. Pissing me off before you state your business isn't the smartest thing you could be doing."

Robert Lee smiled. He didn't mean to. But when Letty got her feathers in a fluff, he just couldn't help it. And, there was even a small part of him that felt sorry for the blue-ass officer in his hot, wool suit.

Carson, on the other hand, was stunned. He got up, laid the letters in Letty's lap without saying another word, and then sat back down.

Letty glared at him, then thanked Delia for the glass of water she brought and took a long drink as Delia handed whiskey to the men.

Robert Lee took a small sip of his, savoring the fire it put in his belly.

Carson Mylam downed his fast and neat. He figured he was going to need it and more before this meeting was over.

Letty chose the letter from the President to read first.

"Look, Delia. Abraham Lincoln wrote me a letter. He's wondering if I would be interested in helping fund his war. Isn't that something?"

Carson started to smile with a bit of relief until Letty finished what she'd been saying.

"I'd like to know where the hell he was when I was servicing drunks for fifty cents a poke to keep from starving to death."

Carson choked on his own spit.

Robert Lee toasted Letty with a smile and what was left in his shot glass, then downed it in one gulp.

Delia grinned.

Letty laid the letter aside and picked up the other two. She scanned them quickly, then folded them and laid them on top of the first.

"Okay. Let me see if I understand you right. You traveled all the way from Philadelphia to see me because I'm rich, and because you're thinking that, in my womanly wisdom, I might be swayed to donating a good sum of money so men can go kill each other? Is that about it?"

Carson's mouth opened but nothing came out.

"Delia, maybe you ought to pour the man another drink. He doesn't look as if he's feeling well."

Delia filled the shot glass.

Carson downed it, wheezing slightly as the liquor hit his belly.

"Mrs. Potter, I don't think you're getting the full picture here," Carson said. "There are people down in the south who—"

"I know all about slavery," Letty said. "I've been one, but it wasn't finding gold that set me free. It was the man who became my husband who did that for me. He's dead, and this has been the saddest year of my life because of it. If you think I'm going to donate money to something that is going to widow thousands of women and cause just as many mothers to weep over lost sons, then you're crazier than you look, sitting here in this hot house in your fancy wool uniform with gold buttons and gold braid."

Carson wondered if he was in as much danger as he felt and decided to toss out a small threat. He wasn't sure if it was the truth, but it sounded good.

"Mrs. Potter, you do know that the government could confiscate your gold mine for the good of the country."

At this point, any kind of threat to Letty lit a fire under Robert Lee. He leaned forward and fixed Carson Mylam with a cold, angry stare.

"Now that you've shared that bit of information with us, there's something you need to know, as well. I put the last man who messed with Letty Potter six feet under. Now, you can sit there and think it would be a small thing to remove me from the picture, and you'd be right. However, you might want to know before you start messing with the woman herself, that she rode down the man who killed her husband, shot him between the eyes with a rifle she didn't know how to reload, then burned the bastard down to his bones and brought them back to the sheriff to bury. Threats don't scare her, mister, but they do piss her off. And threatening her, pisses me off, too...a lot."

Carson didn't believe a word Robert Lee had said until Letty stood up and handed him the letters. She shoved them into his hands, then thumped his chest with her finger, tapping sharply on each gold button as she spoke.

"You take your sorry ass back to where you came from, and you tell your president and your generals I will not be donating to their war. As for trying to take the mine itself, tell them to come on down and give it a try. I'll blow it up and them with it before I'd see the gold spent that way. They can spend eternity in the belly of that mountain and see how important their damned war is then."

It was the lack of emotion in her voice that told Carson he'd made a monumental mistake. Not only was she serious, but he was beginning to believe she could make good on her threats.

"I'll see myself out," he said and started toward the door.

Robert Lee stood up.

"No. *I'll* be the one seeing you out." He followed the man all the way to the horse he'd tied up outside, then waited until Mylam was mounted before he added. "You were the first, and you had better be the last, who comes harassing this woman about her money and your war, or I'll be seeing them in hell." Then he gave Carson back his unloaded pistol.

Carson holstered his gun and rode away. He didn't breathe easy until he was out of sight of the house. At that point, he kicked the horse in the flanks and ran it all the way into town, got a ticket on the first stage out, and went back to fight a war. At least there, his enemies were recognizable by Rebel gray.

* * *

Letty viewed Carson Mylam's visit as she might have a disease—one she didn't want to repeat. It had been her experience that if something caused her concern or made her sick, the best thing to do was rid herself of the possibility that it could happen again. A couple of days after he'd gone, she walked down to Robert Lee's tent and asked him to drive her out to the mine.

"Why?" he'd asked.

"I'm rich. Getting richer isn't going to change my life."

He frowned, waiting for her to continue.

"And...despite what the newspapers are touting, I don't think that damned war is going to go away any time soon. I fear the longer it continues, the greater the possibility someone else will come for whatever it takes to win, and you and I both know money will make it happen. Whoever has the most guns, the most ammunition, the most food, and the most men is going to prevail. I don't know if my money will be safe in all those Yankee banks, but I can keep either side from coming after the mine."

"How?"

"By blowing it up."

Robert Lee blanched.

"You can't be serious. There must be tens of thousands of dollars worth of gold ore still in those shafts."

She shrugged.

"It won't be going anywhere."

"But you could destroy the whole thing by blasting wrong."

"So, we'll make sure to do it right."

"Jesus," Robert Lee muttered.

"So, are you going to help me, or am I going to do it by myself?"

"Hell no, you're not going to do it...by yourself or with me. I'll blow the damned thing, but you're not going to ride all the way out there."

"I won't be riding a horse. I will be sitting in a wagon."

"It's not safe."

"I will do it with or without you."

"Fine," he finally muttered. "Whatever happens is on your head, not mine."

"Fine," she echoed. "We'll do it tomorrow after breakfast."

"What if it damages the old cabin?"

She turned away, unable to think about losing the place where she and Eulis had been the happiest.

"It can't matter more than making sure the gold doesn't fall into the wrong hands."

Robert Lee shrugged and walked away.

Letty watched him go, then went back to the house.

She was ready and waiting for him just as the sun came up. He helped her into the wagon seat, took the reins, and flipped them across the backs of the mules. The mules took off with their passengers, a box of dynamite, and a sack of fuses and blasting caps.

Letty hadn't been to the mine since Eulis's death and thought she was prepared, but when they came down off the mountain and she saw the old cabin at the other side of the valley, she winced. Before she thought, she caught herself looking for Eulis, half-expecting him to step out of the entrance to the mine and wave her on, just as he'd done so many times before.

Robert Lee heard the change in her breathing and caught a brief glimpse of tears in her eyes.

"I'm sorry," he said softly.

Letty sighed.

"Oh, Robert Lee...so am I. So am I."

When they reached the cabin, he helped her down from the wagon.

"I think I'll just take a quick look inside," she said and hurried forward before he could follow.

Robert Lee knew she was saying goodbye to more than the mine and wisely kept his distance.

It was dark inside, and Letty left the door standing open as she entered. It wasn't the same as when she and Eulis had lived there. She soon realized Robert Lee had put his own stamp on the place. In a way, it made leaving it easier.

She glanced back out the door, making sure she was still alone, then moved to the far wall of the cabin where she'd first found the old entrance to the mine.

Only when she tried to find it, the door that had been hidden in the wall was no longer there. She didn't know, at Eulis's orders, Robert Lee had rebuilt it. Now, the only entrance into the mine was the newer one that had been dug outside the cabin to connect with the old shaft, which lay about a hundred yards away from the south wall.

She stood inside the darkened room, eyeing the bed where Eulis had nearly died from the smallpox that had swept through Denver City on their first winter, remembering the injured wolf she'd fought and killed outside their door. They'd had nothing to eat but deer and elk meat all winter. She still disliked the taste.

Wind whistled through the open door, and for a moment, she imagined she heard a soft, keening sigh, but when she turned, all she saw was Robert Lee unloading the dynamite from the wagon. Lifting her chin, she walked out of the cabin and closed the door behind her without looking back.

Within the hour, Robert Lee had the dynamite in place. He'd tied up the mules several hundred yards from the blast sight, then left Letty with them.

He didn't know if what she was doing was the right thing to do, but he didn't question her right to do it. She'd found the damned mine. It had made her rich, and in turn, the wealth she'd garnered from it had widowed her. He didn't blame her for wanting to put an end to what must seem like a vicious cycle.

He glanced back at her.

She nodded vigorously, then waved an okay.

He turned around, took a deep breath, lit the long fuses, and ran like hell.

The first blast rocked the ground beneath their feet.

The second one caused the outer layer of the mountain above the mine entrance to crumble.

When the third one went off, the entrance was already gone. By the time earth and rocks had stopped falling, tons of debris had settled between them and the gold.

Letty stared at the dust cloud and the rocks. The blast had laid waste to a large portion of the front of the mountain, leaving bare a wound where grass and trees had once been. In time, the grass would grow back, and unless someone knew what had been there before, it would be next to impossible to imagine the riches hidden deep within.

Robert Lee brushed at the dust on his clothes as he walked back to the wagon.

Letty was standing beside the seat, her eyes bright with unshed tears.

"Are you all right?" he asked.

She looked at him briefly, then shook her head.

The expression on her face broke his heart.

"I'm sorry it came to this," he said gently.

Before he knew what was happening, she lowered her head against his chest. A moment of shock swept through him, then he wrapped his arms around her and held her while she wept.

16

ROCK A BYE BABY

Shock reverberated throughout Denver City as news spread of an explosion at the Potter mine. Letty sent a telegram to Major Carson Mylam of Philadelphia, Pennsylvania containing four words.

Explosion destroys Potter Mine.
Stop. Leticia Murphy Potter.

Carson received it during a meeting with General Titus Morris, his commanding officer. He turned pale, handed the telegram to Morris, and then looked out the window toward the soldiers marching on the parade ground. The telegram was nothing more than written proof of his failure. His bags were already packed. He'd be accompanying the troops marching south tomorrow.

* * *

Back in Denver City, no one would ever, in their wildest dreams, have believed the explosion was anything but a tragic accident. But in a way, it signaled the beginning of the end to the gold fever that had rocked Denver City throughout the past two years. The dreams men had fostered of getting rich quick seem to have been prioritized by the intermittent news they received of the distant war. Many left their claims to return to their homelands, concerned for the families they'd left behind. Others opted to go farther West, vowing if they had to fight, they'd rather fight redskins than their own friends and families.

Letty remained neutral about the whole thing, more concerned with having a healthy baby than taking sides in a war destined to be a disaster, no matter which side won.

And, like every other woman in her condition, she began what Alice and Mary called nesting. Curtains were taken down and washed. Mattresses were hauled out of the house to be aired and fluffed. She cleaned floors already clean and washed windows that were already streak-free. She counted and sorted the baby clothes they'd all made, then counted and sorted them again.

Each night as she was going to bed, she would look for the lantern light at Robert Lee's tent. Then she would go upstairs to her bedroom window, squinting through the oncoming darkness until she located the cross on Eulis's grave.

Each night it seemed harder and harder to find, and she made a mental note to get the grass cut down between the grave and the house. There was an underlying panic in her need to be able to see it—as if losing sight of it would mean she was forgetting him. And, by the same token, she wouldn't let herself consider why it was so important for her to know that Robert Lee was close by.

* * *

By the time October arrived, there was already a strong hint of winter in the air. Mornings were always chilly, while most days it warmed up some by noon. When Letty's due date finally arrived, it was just ahead of a gathering thunderstorm.

Alice had taken the wagon and gone into town to pick up supplies, taking Katie and the other women with her. It was the first time Letty had been alone in the house since Eulis's death.

She walked through the rooms with a judgmental eye, making mental notes as to what would have to be moved once the baby began to walk. Even as she was planning the changes, she couldn't help looking back at the changes in her world.

A year ago, she and Eulis had been in the first throes of learning how to be rich. They'd spent money frugally until it became apparent they weren't going to run out any time during the next hundred or so years. After that, Letty had been generous with her choices of furnishings for the fine house they'd been building. She'd imagined growing old with Eulis in this house, not living a life without him, let alone raising their child alone.

The house seemed stuffy as she moved through the rooms. Although there was a small fire in the parlor fireplace, it wasn't quite cold enough for fires in all the rooms. And, though the weather outside was somewhat mild, it was too cold to open windows. She felt aimless —too awkward and too close to delivery to start a new project—but still anxiously awaiting what would be the biggest project of her life.

The women had been gone for almost an hour when she finally wandered out onto the front porch and sat down in the rocking chair. T-Bone jumped up from his spot in the flower bed and ran up the steps to plop down at her feet.

Letty eyed the dirt on the dog's side and the big bare spot in the flower bed and frowned.

"You do know that you're going to be in trouble with Delia. She's not going to appreciate you napping in her flowers."

T-Bone's tongue lolled from the side of his mouth as he gazed up at her in adoration. The scar from the knife wound he'd suffered at the robber's hands was still visible but slowly fading as hair continued to grow back over the old wound.

She patted his head, then leaned back in the rocker and cupped the girth of her belly, groaning slightly as the baby rolled beneath her palms.

"Lord have mercy, Little Bit, I'd appreciate it if you'd settle yourself down for a while."

When the baby finally stilled, she closed her eyes with a satisfied groan. A few minutes later when she happened to look up, she caught Robert Lee watching her from a distance.

She raised her hand in a quick hello.

He jerked, as if surprised she'd seen him, then nodded briefly before disappearing behind his tent.

Letty frowned. She'd already made up her mind he was not spending the winter in that damned tent—not when there was a spare room off the kitchen. She'd mentioned it to the women earlier, and they'd all agreed they were not only okay with him moving in, but they would welcome his presence in the house. Now, all she had to do was convince Robert Lee of the fact.

A rumble of distant thunder sounded across the mountains as the wind began to rise. It wasn't much, but enough to cut the sultry feel in the air. She knew how miserable a winter rain felt in the mountains and decided today was the day that Robert Lee succumbed to her will.

And, in typical Letty fashion, she hefted herself up from the rocking chair, walked off the porch, and headed for his tent.

* * *

Robert Lee hadn't intended to be caught watching Letty, and yet it had happened. He cursed the hopelessness of his situation and wished he was hard-hearted enough to just saddle up and ride away. During the past few weeks, he'd busied himself through the days by chopping wood for the coming winter months and had a wagon nearly full and ready to be hauled to the house to unload. It would be the fourth load he'd cut. He was already back at splitting some logs when Letty rounded the front of the tent.

"Robert Lee."

He spun abruptly. The rising wind was pushing the skirt of her smock against her belly and tangling the tendrils of her hair that had come loose from the pins. He glanced up at the gathering clouds, dropped the axe, and grabbed her by the arm.

"It's going to rain."

"Most likely," she said and pointed at the tent. "Gather up your things. You're coming to the house with me."

"Letty, you know—"

"Do shut up, Robert Lee. Winter is upon us and I won't have you sleeping out here in this pitiful tent when there's a perfectly good room off the kitchen. Mary and Delia made up a bed for you. Alice is raring to cook for a man. She claims none of us eat enough to warrant all her hard work."

"But what will people—"

Letty snorted.

"Surely, you know me well enough by now to know I don't give a damn about what people think. Don't make me ask you again. Get your stuff and be quick about it. I don't relish getting myself all wet."

Robert Lee moved like a man in a trance. Even as he was gathering up his things, he knew everything was going to change. Whether it would be for the better, or just make everything worse, remained to be seen. Still, from past events, he feared leaving these women alone on the mountain.

By the time he was through, the wind was rising even more. He started across the yard with Letty at his side. Alice was at the reins of the wagon, coming up the road from town at a hasty clip and trying to beat the storm, when she overtook them and beat them back to the house.

The women unloaded their supplies quickly, then Mary and Delia unhooked the team of horses and led them to the shed just as the first drops of rain were beginning to fall.

Katie had fallen asleep in the back of the wagon, and Robert Lee quickly dumped his belongings inside the kitchen and ran back to get her.

"See...this is working out already," Letty said, as he carried the little girl into the house.

"You don't know what you're talking about," he muttered, as he carried the little girl into the parlor and laid her down on the red settee.

Delia glanced around the room, then shivered as a blast of wind rattled the leafless lilac bush at the side of the house.

"I'll add some wood to the fire in the parlor," she said and hurried to the back porch to get firewood.

Only a short time ago, Letty had walked through these rooms, feeling the space and the loneliness, and now, with everyone back and noise being made, everything felt right and safe.

Watching Robert Lee as he followed Delia out, then as they both returned carrying firewood, she felt a great sense of satisfaction. Delia put down her load and left the room as Robert Lee set about stirring the embers in the fireplace before adding dry logs. She knew he was uncomfortable around her, and when she was honest with herself, admitted she was a little uncomfortable around him. His presence in the house was going to change everything. Whether it was for the good of her odd little family still remained to be seen. All she knew was, she didn't want to see him ride away.

Rain was coming down in earnest when she felt the first stirring of pain. It began in the low of her back, then rippled around her belly like a belt that was being pulled too tight.

"Oh," she grunted and clasped her hands against what had once been her waist.

Robert Lee stood up from the fire and turned around. "What's wrong?"

"I'm not sure. Maybe it was just a—"

The second wave of pain hit her in the same place, only harder.

"Oh, Lord," she said, then took a slow, deep breath. "I think it's the baby."

Robert Lee felt as if he'd been sucker punched. All the air went out of his lungs as his knees went weak.

"Don't move," he cried.

She grimaced. "I'm not accepting any dances in the near future if that's what you're worrying about."

He shot out of the room, calling Alice's name. Moments later, they came back running.

"Get her upstairs," Alice said.

Robert Lee picked Letty up in his arms.

"I can still walk," Letty said, but no one was listening. Moments later, as another pain tore through her, she was glad she'd been ignored.

He got her to her bedroom just ahead of the women. Once he laid her down, he was shooed out of the room. His last glimpse of Letty, was her waving a hand in Delia's direction, with a determined jut to her chin. Like everything else she did, she was already taking charge.

After that, time seemed to stand still. He carried his things into the extra room off the kitchen, trying not to think of what was going on upstairs.

There wasn't much to unpack. A straight razor and shaving cup—a couple of changes of clothes—and a mirror with a crack up the left side. He set a wooden box on the floor behind his bed, then toed it under. It contained extra ammunition and the equipment he used to clean his weapon. All in all, it was a poor accumulation of goods considering his age and the places he'd been. He couldn't help worrying about what hanging his hat under this roof would bring to the table. All he knew was that he had to be careful. The last thing he would ever do is hurt Letty—and yet he was here, where the opportunity to do so would constantly be presenting itself.

It took less than ten minutes to lay claim to the room. It wasn't nearly long enough to keep his mind off of Letty and the impending birth. As he paced the floor in front of the parlor fireplace, he couldn't help thinking of Eulis. He should be here—relishing the upcoming addition to his family—not rotting in a pine box in the backyard.

Thunder rumbled loudly overhead, followed by a sharp crack of lightning. He flinched as the momentary flash lit up the room. That one was close. Once it was over, it occurred to him how dark it had gotten outside. He lit an oil lamp and then a candle, set one on the table and the other on the mantel and poked at the brightly burning fire. The storm had hastened nightfall. If only it sped up the birth of the baby, as well.

One hour flowed into a second, and then a third. Once as he was passing the foot of the stairs, he heard a low, anguished moan. The sound ripped through him like a knife to the heart.

He stood there, listening—waiting—praying for a signal that her suffering would soon be over.

It didn't come.

Five hours, then six, came and went. Alice came downstairs. Her face was flushed, her hair hanging around her cheeks in tangled wisps.

"Go get Dr. Warren," she said.

Robert Lee froze.

"Is something wrong?"

Alice wrung her hands. "I don't know. It's just that she's not progressing as she should."

"Jesus," Robert Lee whispered.

"Pray to Him as you ride," she said and then hurried back up the stairs.

Robert Lee headed for the shed to saddle his horse, running as he went. He untied a poncho from the back of his saddle and pulled it over his head. It wasn't much protection from the downpour, but it was better than nothing.

The thunder and lightning had long since passed, leaving behind nothing but rain. As he rode, the wind blew it in his face. He pulled his hat down a little tighter on his head, tilting the brim just enough to keep it out of his eyes. Twice, his horse lost its footing and slipped, the last time going all the way to its knees. Robert Lee gritted his teeth, barely managing to stay seated. When he finally saw the lights of Denver City, he urged his horse forward.

The town had grown so much in the past years it took longer to ride through main street. Since he was going to the doctor's house, his destination was at the far end of town.

Unknowingly, he rode past it in the dark, then backtracked quickly with his heart in his throat. He dismounted, calling out the doctor's name, even before he knocked on the door.

After a round of frantic knocking, he saw the faint glow of lamp light through the curtains at the window. But when his call was answered, it was Mildred, the doctor's wife, who let him in.

"Robert Lee? Is that you?" she asked, as she held a lit candle above her head.

"Yes, ma'am, it's me. We need the doctor up at the Potter house. Letty is in labor."

"Oh, Lord," she cried. "Angus is out of town tending a family with typhoid. He won't be back for at least a day or more."

Robert Lee felt sick.

"Then you come," he said.

"Do you know what kind of trouble she's in?"

"No, ma'am. Alice just came downstairs and told me to go get the doctor."

"All right. I don't know how much help I'll be, but I'll come. Just let me get dressed."

"Oh...ma'am...I didn't bring the wagon."

Mildred Warren waved him toward a chair on the porch.

"Will your horse carry us both?"

"Yes, ma'am, but—"

"I can ride. I won't win any prizes, but I can ride."

"Yes, ma'am," Robert Lee said, as he sat down in the chair. "But if you don't mind me asking...please hurry."

The door closed between them. Robert Lee bowed his head, and for the first time in years, really prayed.

Within minutes she was back, wearing a pair of her husband's pants and a long overcoat.

"If Letty can dress like this, then I suppose I can, too," she said and took the help Robert Lee offered as she crawled up on the horse.

As she claimed, it wasn't pretty, but she was astride. Robert Lee climbed on behind her, and together, they rode out of town and back up the mountain to Letty.

* * *

Letty was tired—so tired she didn't think she'd ever be rested again. She wanted to quit and just close her eyes, but she didn't have the luxury. She was in the middle of a breath when the next wave of pain came, pulling and twisting at every muscle in her body until she felt as if she were coming apart.

She arched toward the pain, screaming aloud as it rolled down the length of her spine.

Delia was in tears.

Mary was tight-lipped and frightened.

Alice was almost as weary as Letty, determined that this birth would not be a disaster.

They'd put Katie to bed hours ago, but unknown to them, she was still up and sitting in a corner of the upstairs hall, afraid to close her eyes.

She was the first to hear the commotion downstairs and jumped up and hid. She saw Robert Lee dragging someone up the stairs and scooted to her room before she was discovered. They were dripping mud and water all over Miz Letty's clean floors. She thought about telling them they were going to be in trouble, but she decided against it and stayed put.

Mildred was shedding her coat and hat as she went, and it was all she could do to keep up with Robert Lee as he pulled her along. But his haste came to an abrupt stop when he heard Letty scream.

"God in heaven," he muttered.

"It doesn't mean anything except that it hurts," Mildred said and dumped the last of her weather gear in the hall by the door. She left the door ajar as she rushed inside, giving Robert Lee a clear view of Letty's face.

Her hair was stuck to her face from perspiration, and she was holding on to the headboard so hard her knuckles were white. Before he could move, someone shut the door. He felt as if someone had cut off his breath.

He didn't know how long he stood there without moving, but it was long enough for Letty's screams to be branded into his brain. When Alice came flying out of the room sometime later, he was still there.

"Sakes alive!" Alice muttered and had to side-step Robert Lee to keep from plowing into him. "I didn't know you were there."

"Why isn't the baby coming?" he asked.

Alice rolled her eyes.

"I don't know...but if I didn't know better, I'd swear Letty just doesn't want to give it up."

Robert Lee frowned. "What the hell are you saying?"

Alice swiped her hands up her face, pushing the hair from her eyes.

"As long as the baby was in her, she knew she could keep it safe, but once it's born, a mother can do her best and still lose it. I learned that the hard way."

Robert Lee remembered then that Alice had lost her baby.

"Oh...I'm sorry. I didn't think."

"It's all right. Now, go on with you. This is women's work."

Robert Lee frowned as she sped down the stairs. What if Alice was right? What if Letty was putting her and her baby in danger by her unwillingness to let go?

He ducked his head and started down the stairs, then stopped. By God, he hadn't come this far with that woman just to lose her this way.

He set his jaw and turned on his heel. Moments later, he was standing in the doorway, his gaze fixed directly on Letty's face.

"God damn it, Leticia! You can't control everything. Give up the fight and let that baby be born!"

Surprised by his presence, everyone froze.

Letty threw her head back, meeting his gaze with something akin to desperation. She was still staring when he slammed the door shut between them. They heard his steps receding, then heard him stomping down the stairs.

"What on earth?" Alice muttered.

"Pay him no mind," Mildred said, as she braced herself for Letty's next contraction.

The pain was subsiding, but Letty was already gathering herself for the next. She'd heard Robert Lee through a numbing fog, and only now, was absorbing what he'd actually said.

Was he right? Was she delaying this birth by refusing to give up the control?

Alice's hand was on her belly.

"Here comes another one," she said, as she felt the muscles contracting again.

Letty closed her eyes, took a deep, weary breath, and then this time, instead of holding her breath against the pain, rode all the way through it.

"That's it! That's it!" Mildred cried. "You can do this. You're a strong-willed woman, so make this happen."

When the next pains came, Letty pushed—and then she pushed—and then she pushed again. She was somewhere between exhaustion and unconsciousness when she heard a loud, angry cry.

"It's a boy!" someone cried.

Letty gritted her teeth, willing herself to stay focused, and held out her arms.

"Give him to me."

"Just a minute," Mildred said, as she quickly cut the cord and began cleaning up the baby.

The little fellow was wailing lustily as Mildred wiped him down. She wrapped him in a blanket and then laid him on Letty's chest.

Within seconds, Letty's arms closed around him, holding him close—holding him safe—as close to her heart as she could get him.

"Prop me up," she said.

Mildred frowned. "But the afterbirth—"

"Will tend to itself," Letty muttered. "I need to see my son."

And she did.

His little face was red and puckered—his mouth wide open in a loud, toothless wail. His hair was thick and dark, and as she unwrapped him to count fingers and toes, his complaints at being thrust into this world continued.

When she was satisfied that he was perfect, she rolled him back up in the blanket and held him close.

"Here...give him to me," Alice said.

"Not yet," Letty said. "It's only fair that, as his mother, I am forced to listen to his first complaint."

Having said that, she looked down at his angry, red face and grinned. The louder he wailed, the more she smiled. Finally, the baby's cries eased somewhat, leaving him with a squeak, not unlike that of a baby kitten.

At that point, Letty laughed aloud.

* * *

Robert Lee was sitting at the bottom of the stairs with his head in his hands, struggling to stay sane between Letty's moans and wails. The room was lit now by nothing but a single candle and the glow from the dying parlor fire in the other room. Sitting in the dark only added to the drama of the night. True panic hadn't come until one long, agonized scream.

He stood abruptly, ready to dash back up the stairs and beg Letty not to die when, moments later, he heard a baby cry. Every muscle in his body went weak. Even though the cries continued, he felt certain the crisis had passed.

He leaned against the stair rail and then swiped a shaky hand across his face as the wails continued. One long, angry yelp after another ricocheted through the rooms downstairs. Finally, the cries began to subside and there was a moment of blessed silence.

Then he heard Letty laugh.

After what she'd been through, it was the last thing he would have expected to hear.

He reached for the newel post as the echo of her laughter faded around him. He looked up—waiting for someone to give him the news.

Moments later, Alice appeared at the head of the stairs with an oil lamp in her hand.

"It's a boy," she said. "But if you ask me, I'm predicting here and now that he's just a male version of his mother. Never heard so much complaining from a newborn in my life."

Robert Lee grinned.

A boy.

Then his smile slipped.

Eulis would have been so proud.

"Reckon I can come up?" he asked.

"Oh. Yes...I almost forgot. Letty sent me to get you."

Robert Lee took the stairs two at a time, then smoothed his hands down the front of his shirt, wincing as he felt the dampness. He should have thought to change into dry clothes, then abandoned the notion. He'd had them on so long they were almost dry again.

He entered the room behind Alice, his gaze going immediately to Letty.

She was sitting up in the shadows, leaning against the headboard with the baby in her arms.

"Come say hello," she said.

Robert Lee could have easier faced a man with a gun.

If she'd asked him to strip naked in front of all these women, it wouldn't have been any harder than it was to walk to her bed.

Robert Lee looked at the baby. It was little and red and wrinkled. He wished he could say the same for Letty, then maybe he wouldn't be so damned tied to staring at her face, because she looked beautiful. He cleared his throat then nodded.

"He's a fine baby. Eulis would have been real proud."

Letty looked up.

"That's part of why I asked you to come in. It's because of Eulis and you that my child was born."

Robert Lee looked startled.

"No, ma'am, I didn't have—"

"Eulis gave me the baby, but you kept us both alive." Then she looked down at the sleeping baby and lightly ran her finger down the side of his cheek. "Eulis hated his name, but I got real fond of it and him." Then she looked up at Robert Lee, watching the expression on his face as she announced. "I'm naming the baby Eulis Slade Potter after the two men who made this night possible."

Robert Lee's mouth went slack. His vision blurred.

"I don't know what to say

"Well, for starters, sit down in that chair and hold out your arms. Alice...if you don't mind, would you hand Little Bit to Robert Lee? I think the two men on this place need to get acquainted."

"Little Bit?" he asked.

"He's going to have to do some growing to handle the name I just gave him. For now, Little Bit will do."

Alice grinned.

Robert Lee paled as the baby was laid in his arms.

At first, he couldn't feel anything but the thunder of his own heartbeat, pounding in his ears. Then the baby squirmed, and he felt the warmth and the weight and reality dawned. He blinked away tears only to find the baby's eyes were open, and he seemed to be looking right at Robert Lee.

"See there," Letty said. "He likes you."

"What do I do?" Robert Lee asked.

Letty leaned back against the pillows, watching the changing expressions on Robert Lee's face.

"Exactly what you're doing right now," she said softly, then closed her eyes. Within seconds, she was asleep.

"Let her be," Alice said when Delia would have scooted her back down in bed.

Together, the women gathered up the basins and bedclothes and carried them out the door.

Delia followed with an oil lamp to light the way.

Mildred glanced back at the sleeping woman and the man sitting beside her bed.

"Wait!" Robert Lee said. "What am I supposed to do?"

"We'll be back soon enough," Alice said. "For now, you're doing just fine."

Robert Lee started to shake. What if he did something wrong? What if he dropped the baby? What if—

The baby squeaked.

Robert Lee held his breath.

Letty hadn't moved.

The baby settled.

He exhaled slowly, then leaned back in the chair, shifted his hold on the baby, then looked up, and for the first time since he'd walked onto Potter land, gazed his fill of the woman who held his heart.

17

A ROOSTER IN THE HEN HOUSE

By mid-morning of the next day when Alice drove Mildred back home, the news began to spread. Letty Potter had given birth to her dead husband's child. That it was a boy baby was viewed by most as good fortune. At least Eulis Potter would have someone to carry on his name.

It was Milton Feasley who first coined the phrase, 'a little rooster in the hen house', but it soon took hold.

Letty basked in her new role as mother. Her manner was softer, her voice less strident. Everything in the Potter household was moving at a slower pace. But it wasn't slowing down winter. It came blasting through the Rockies within two weeks of Little Bit's birth, dumping six inches of snow and a drop in temperature that chilled a man all the way to the back of his teeth.

Robert Lee took on the role of tending to the animals and the wood cutting, as well as going into town now and then for supplies. Letty had ordered new coats for Katie and the women some time back, as well as a good long heavy coat made for riding for Robert Lee. She'd also ordered some knitting yarn, some school books for

Katie, and a large assortment of embroidery cotton. With a houseful of females likely to be snowed in until spring, they needed to be doing something through the long, cold days besides getting on each other's nerves.

She didn't know how Robert Lee felt about a houseful of women, but so far he wasn't complaining, and there was the draw of Little Bit to keep him satisfied. Every evening when he came in from doing chores, he made it his business to rock the baby while supper was being cooked.

Letty often watched the interplay of emotions between the only two males in the house—now and then feeling a tiny bit jealous. There had been a couple of times when Robert Lee had been the only one to calm the baby's fuss. At those times, a part of her resented the fact Eulis hadn't lived to see this. But then Robert Lee would look up at her with a laugh in his eyes, forcing her to remember she hadn't died when Eulis did.

Christmas neared. Down in the city, Letty Potter's son had taken on a persona not unlike that of a young prince. Women who'd shunned her for her wild ways now hinted at an invitation to visit.

Finally, it was Alice who came up with the idea to have an open house, similar to the ones her family had held during the holidays back in Boston. Letty was hesitant to expose Little Bit to so many people. Mary suggested they hold the party, and some time during the fete, Letty could introduce the child to everyone, then he'd be whisked away. Everyone's curiosity would be satisfied and maybe life would settle down for all of them.

And so the planning began.

Invitations were sent out, and Alice began baking. With Robert Lee's help, Delia and Mary were responsible for decorating the house with fresh pine and cedar boughs. Katie got the job of polishing the silver and spent hours working on everything from flatware to teapots.

Robert Lee secretly bought a new suit and boots for himself and had his hair trimmed to shoulder length. No one knew he'd grown up in a whirl of grand parties and soirees' his parents often held, and he wasn't about to admit it at this late date. Growing up, he'd taken wealth for granted, then learned the hard way how to live without it. The irony of how his life had come full circle was not lost on him.

And then there was Letty. If she was going to host this grand party, she needed a grand dress to mark the occasion. She had one she'd ordered right after they'd struck gold, but the occasion had never presented itself to be worn. Now, she wasn't sure if she could still fit in to it.

However, when she tried it on, she was surprised to see that it fit—even better than before. Where it had once been a little lose in the bosom, she filled it out nicely. The neckline dipped in all the right places and the skirt billowed out behind her as she walked. It would do.

The week passed in a flurry of excitement to which was added the arrival of Letty's order from back East. She was excited when Robert Lee came back from town with the crate.

* * *

The back door opened with a thump against the wall, letting in a cold blast of air, upon which Alice promptly complained.

"Mercy sakes, Robert Lee! Close the door! It's freezing outside."

"Yes, ma'am, that it is," he said, as he staggered toward the kitchen table with his load. "Milton Feasley down at the dry goods store sent this box along with the list he filled for you. Said it was Letty's order."

Letty came into the kitchen with her skirt flying out behind her and her hair coming down around her ears.

"Don't open it! It's surprises for Christmas!" she said.

Robert Lee eyed the box and sighed.

"I suppose you're not gonna let me leave it on the table."

"Well, of course not, Robert Lee. Would you please carry it up to the sewing room?"

"I'd be delighted," he muttered and hefted it up again, before settling it on his shoulder.

Letty led the way out of the kitchen.

On a normal day, Robert Lee would have enjoyed the view and the sway of her hips beneath her dress, but the damned box was too heavy to linger on lust.

"In here!" she said and stepped aside as he moved past her and set it down on the floor with a thump.

"You cut your hair," Letty said, eyeing the new length. "It looks nice."

Robert Lee looked up. Breath caught in the back of his throat. He wasn't comfortable being under her scrutiny—ever. He'd made it plain how he felt about her, although he'd never stepped over the line. But being alone with her—in any situation—made him ache to touch her—hold her—to taste those lips that had a constant penchant for spouting sarcasm and wisdom within the same breath.

Letty caught the glitter in his eyes and knew what he was feeling. The troubling part about it all was that she wasn't sure what she was feeling back. Before, it had come as a shock to even think about caring for another man. But she'd learned the hard way how short life could be. She wasn't the kind of woman to waste a moment of her own. Now, the notion of testing the waters with Robert Lee often crept into her dreams. She had apologized daily to Eulis for the betrayal, but Eulis hadn't bothered to voice any kind of disapproval, so she was stuck to deal with her own sense of what was right and what was not.

The fact that Eulis hadn't answered her was nothing new. He did a lot of that these days, and it was beginning to aggravate her to no end.

"I said...your hair looks nice."

She saw his chest expand as he drew a deep breath. Expecting him to turn away as he always did, she was shocked when he reached toward her instead, brushing the loose tendrils of her hair away from her face with both hands.

"Yours looks like Little Bit has been swinging in it."

Her eyes widened as she considered the familiarity of his touch.

Robert Lee meant to draw back, but he got caught in her gaze. He saw her nostrils flare. When she lifted her chin, he shuddered. Her mouth was too damn handy for his peace of mind.

"I suppose he has," she said, then reached up and pulled out what pins were still left.

Her hair fell down around her shoulders.

Robert Lee froze.

Letty's lips parted, as if she was about to speak. Nothing came out but a sigh.

"Letty...."

There was a warning in the way he said her name. She hesitated. Once this step was taken, there would be no going back.

And then the baby cried.

Robert Lee's eyes narrowed sharply as he took a step back.

"Don't tease, woman. I'm not a man to mess with."

"I didn't mean to—"

"Yes, you did," he said. "Don't do it again unless you mean it."

He left as abruptly as he'd come.

Letty's heart was pounding as she listened to the sound of his receding footsteps. She sighed as she ran to her child. Later, as she was letting Little Bit nurse, she couldn't help wondering if the pain in her chest was from the abundance of milk she had for the baby or from what was lacking in her life.

Was she ready to take another man in her life?

If she offered, he would take her in a heartbeat. But would it last? Even more important, was she ready to take a chance on love one more time? Losing it hurt so damned bad, she wasn't sure she had the guts to try it again.

* * *

The day of the party was finally here. The cooking was done. The house was decorated to the hilt with garlands of red ribbon and fragrant pine boughs. Katie and Alice had decorated a small cedar tree with bits of colored paper and ribbon. The sideboard was awash in dainty edibles, and Letty's silver was as bright as a new moon.

Alice's excitement was palpable as she flitted from room to room, making sure all was ready for the arrival of their guests. The final stitches on her plum-colored dress had gone in after midnight last night, as had the ones on the smock Katie was wearing. Technically, like Mary, she was a widow, but mourning a man like George seemed ridiculous, considering what he'd done to her and Letty's lives. She knew it was nothing less than a miracle that Letty Potter could forgive the misery Alice's presence had caused and thanked God every night for delivering her unto the Hen House on the hill above Denver City.

Mary's choice of black taffeta was befitting the widow she was, although she had yet to admit how pissed off she was at her Robert for the cowardly act of suicide. He'd thought nothing of what would befall her by leaving her alone, and she wondered if she was being a hypocrite to present herself to the public in this light. Still, she wouldn't let it bother her. Not today.

Delia had chosen a cream-colored taffeta to make her gown, and the demureness of the color was almost lost in the low neckline and tight fit. Tonight, she was going to be an elegant woman and to hell with those who judged her past.

Letty had left the color of her dress a secret, although all she'd admitted to was that it was Eulis's favorite color on her.

She'd fussed with her hair between tending to the baby, and finally chosen to pin it all up on top of her head and let the curls cascade down the back of her neck. She was leaving her throat and chest bare, except for a narrow, black velvet ribbon tied around her neck. Dangling from the ribbon was a single gold nugget, held within a cameo-like setting—a reminder of what had changed her life.

Downstairs, Robert Lee was carrying in extra wood for the fires and making sure the front porch had been swept free of snow and pine needles, so the guests wouldn't be tracking up Letty's floors.

Katie's pale, yellow smock dress with matching ribbons in her hair made her look like the angel atop the Christmas tree. Alice had set her on a little chair near the parlor fireplace with orders not to mess herself up. It was an unnecessary warning. Katie didn't want to miss a minute of the upcoming event.

When it was almost time for the guests to arrive, Robert Lee disappeared. It didn't occur to Letty until she saw the first buggy coming up the road from town he was missing, but by then it was too late to figure out why.

The second set of guests were stomping snow from their shoes as the first were being shown into the parlor. Letty stood at the door, calmly welcoming Denver City's finest into her home—well aware that as they talked and smiled, they were mentally taking her apart. The funny thing was, she no longer cared what others thought.

Milton Feasley and his wife arrived in a flurry of awkward excitement, followed by Dr. Warren and Mildred. Amos Trueblood, her banker, preened as if he were responsible for all of this himself. Barbers, lawyers, and a couple of dentists who'd set up shop down in town followed in on his heels. There were three new preachers who'd set up business in town, as well as a few bachelors who didn't want to miss the opportunity to check out the women who'd taken shelter in this place.

Letty couldn't help noting, while she had been busy burying a husband and birthing his child, Denver City had been undergoing a change, too. She didn't know half of these people, but they all sure knew her.

"Please, you must try some of Alice's fruitcake," she said, as she waved toward a table laden with food displayed on crystal and silver.

Within the hour, the whole downstairs of the Potter mansion was full of people talking and eating and making merry. It was at this point, Letty disappeared upstairs. She reappeared twenty minutes later with her baby in her arms.

She was halfway down the stairs when her guests realized an introduction was imminent. The oohs and aahs were followed by someone tapping their cane upon the floor to signal the coming speech.

"Ladies and gentlemen...my friends and I are honored to have you in our house tonight. Some of you I've known since the early days...some of you I'm meeting for the first time tonight. But I'm inviting all of you to meet my son, Eulis Slade Potter. We call him Little Bit...a name he will probably grow to hate."

There was a round of easy laughter as she unfolded the blanket from around him and then lifted the crook of her arm so they might easier see his face.

At three months and twenty-plus pounds, he was a sight to behold. Little round face, turned up nose, and a thatch of dark, mahogany-colored hair, not unlike his mother's.

He stared at the crowd with as much curiosity as they all stared at him, then delighted the gathering with a sudden flailing of his arms and a loud, piercing squeal.

Letty laughed.

"That means he likes you, and while he's still making a good impression, he's also going to make his exit before he shames himself and me, by revealing how much I've already spoiled him."

"A toast...to the little rooster in the Hen House!" someone called.

"Here, here," they all shouted and raised glasses to the baby in her arms.

"Give him to me," Alice said and waved Katie up with her. "Katie here is almost asleep on her feet, too. I'll put them both to bed, and then come down later. You stay with your guests."

"He's already nursed," Letty whispered.

Alice nodded, took the baby from her arms and herded Katie along with her.

The blacksmith had brought his fiddle and was seated in a corner near the parlor fireplace, tuning up his bow.

The sounds of chairs being scooted back against the wall signaled the start of a dance.

Letty had moved to a spot near the punch table and was holding a cookie in one hand and a napkin in the other, listening to two women who'd once shunned her gushing about her son, when she heard a low, familiar voice at her ear.

"Letty."

Robert Lee!

She turned, then forgot what she'd been going to say. She'd never seen him like this—handsome beyond words and so at ease in his elegance. His frock coat was black, as were the matching pants of his suit. The shirt under his silver-gray vest was white, with a black string tie at the neck.

His hair was as black as his eyes, and when he held out his hand, she took it without thought. He was as far removed from the half-starved gunfighter she'd first met as she was from the fifty-cent whore she'd been.

"If I may be so bold, I believe it's the hostess's duty to start the dancing. May I?"

She handed one of the women her cookie and then walked away with her hand on Robert Lee's arm.

The room fell silent.

The blacksmith ran the bow lightly across the fiddle strings, testing the tone.

Robert Lee couldn't quit staring at her. She stood out in the room, like a wild rose in a bed of plain daisies. The dress was satin, and a deep shade of garnet, making her skin appear as white as the snow outside. Her hair was magnificent, like a crown on the queen she'd become, and he wanted nothing more than the pleasure of taking it down and thrusting his fingers through the depths.

Just as the first notes of the waltz began, she looked up at him and smiled.

He put one hand lightly at her waist as he held the other level with his shoulder. When he swung her into the first steps, he felt like he was flying. The lights of the room spun around them as they dipped and swayed. Within a few moments, they were joined by more than a dozen other couples, until most of the room was awash in rhythm. When the music was as loud in his ears as the thunder of his heart, he leaned forward.

Letty felt his cheek against the side of her face near her ear. She could smell the witch hazel from his shave, as well as the scent of the man, himself.

She shivered.

He felt it.

"You are so beautiful," he said softly.

Letty surprised him when she leaned back in his arms enough to meet his gaze.

"So are you."

A sharp glint came and went in his eyes.

"Are you teasing me again?"

"No."

He tightened his grip at her waist. His voice was shaking as he whispered again.

"You know what's in my heart."

He felt her sigh, then saw the corner of her mouth tilt slightly upward.

"I know," she said.

He swung her around again, then danced them in a circle as the people around them seemed to dance out of sight.

"You don't have to love me," he said. "I love you and your son and your crazy family enough for the both of us."

"Is that so?"

He ventured a look. She was smiling.

"Jesus, Leticia...say what's on your mind and put me out of my misery before I die at your feet."

"You're what's on my mind," she said softly. "Have

been for some months now. I guess what I'm needing to know now is...if you're as good in person as you are in my dreams."

He stumbled, stepped on both of her feet and then cursed.

Letty laughed.

Out loud.

The echo of it rocked him all the way to his toes, just as it had the night her son had been born.

He didn't know what it was going to be like to be married to a woman who could laugh at giving birth as readily as she could at making love, but he was damn sure going to enjoy finding out.

The End

Epilogue

The war had been over for six years. Letty had been married to Robert Lee for eight.

On his seventh birthday, Little Bit had announced he was going to black the eye of the next person who called him by that name, except of course if it was Mama. Although, he would certainly appreciate it if she would stop using it and call him Slade.

He was tall for his age, and in Robert Lee's opinion, the spitting image of his mother in all the ways that counted.

He had her dark hair and blue eyes, and most times, her disposition, which meant he was mule-headed but smart enough to keep himself out of most troubles.

Robert Lee went to sleep every night knowing if he died before morning, his life thus far would be enough.

Letty had bloomed under Robert Lee's love in a way she would never have believed possible. The home she and Eulis had built had become the center of Denver society. The grounds that had once been awash with wild flowers and knee-high grasses were kept clipped and landscaped with the help of three gardeners.

They had a stable of horses and a six foot high rock wall around the perimeter of the mansion, with only one way in and one way out.

Robert Lee had never gotten over the sight of seeing Letty held captive under a stranger's gun. The protectiveness he'd felt toward her then had multiplied a thousand times since their marriage. He didn't have words to explain what she and Slade meant to him.

Three years ago, they'd built Alice a home of her own down in Denver. Katie had gone back East to a finishing school, and had come home last Christmas with a fiancé. Alice had wept copious tears, then set about planning a grand wedding, which was to take place within the next six months.

Mary had taken ill and died in the spring right after Letty and Robert Lee married. She was buried two spaces over from Eulis, and next to Alice's baby girl.

The spring after Little Bit turned three, Delia was introduced to a new lawyer who'd come to town. Within months, they were married.

Except for Letty, there was nothing but roosters in the Hen House these days, and few left down in the growing city who even remembered what that meant.

There was a steadfastness in Robert Lee that Letty treasured above all else. She loved him in a way far removed from the love she'd had for Eulis. She and Eulis had been bound by tragedy and a comedy of errors, and separated as harshly as they'd lived.

Robert Lee had offered a stronger, more peaceful kind of love that had proven to grow with time.

Each night when the weather was good, Letty would walk out onto the back porch and sit down on the top steps.

Wherever he was, Little Bit would come running. He would sit down beside her, and then, weary from the long day at play, would lay his head in his mother's lap and wait for the weight of her hand to cup his head.

Together, they would sit in silence, watching the sun going down behind the tall, stately pines, while waiting for the moon to appear.

And as night came to the land, the first fireflies would come out, darting about in somewhat of a frenzy that never made much sense. Usually, the owl who lived in the barn would be the first to venture out, swooping past them on silent wings as they sat in growing darkness.

"Mama...do you hear it?" Little Bit would ask.

"Not yet," Letty would say.

The screen door to the back porch would squeak, signaling the arrival of Robert Lee.

Without word, he would take a seat on the step beside Letty and put his arm around her as he patted the little boy's head. At this point, Little Bit would look up and whisper....

"Daddy...we're still a listenin'."

"Okay," Robert Lee would say and then smile, his heart full to bursting with love for the pair.

Then, with her hand on her son and her head on her husband's shoulder, Letty would let go of the day's frustrations.

Dark settled around them like a comfortable blanket, and from somewhere in the distance, the first call would come—a plaintive, but persistent trill piercing the silence of the night.

Crickets always honored the call with a momentary hush. Tree frogs suspended their chorus, like Letty, awaiting the answer to the night bird's plea.

A second trill would sound, and Little Bit would tense. Letty often caught herself holding her breath—waiting—always waiting.

And then the answering call would come, as it always did each night when the lone whippoorwill got an answer from its mate.

"There!" Letty would always say, with quiet satisfaction. "He's found her."

"Just like I found you," Robert Lee would say and then kiss the smile his words put on her lips.

"And me!" Little Bit would cry. "Just like you found me."

At that point, they moved from the porch steps to the house, shutting themselves in, and the night out—right where it belonged.